THE
MIND VIRUS

Also by Donna Freitas

Unplugged

The Body Market

THE
MIND VIRUS

Donna Freitas

An Imprint of HarperCollinsPublishers

HarperTeen is an imprint of HarperCollins Publishers.

The Mind Virus

Copyright © 2017 by Donna Freitas

www.epicreads.com

ISBN 978-0-06-211866-0

17 18 19 20 21 PC/LSCH 10 9 8 7 6 5 4 3 2 1

❖

First Edition

Let us pass, then, to the attributes of the soul . . . if it be true that I have no body, it is true likewise that I am capable neither of walking nor of being nourished . . . Thinking is another attribute of the soul; and here I discover what properly belongs to myself. This alone is inseparable from me. I am—I exist: this is certain; but how often? As often as I think; for perhaps it would even happen, if I should wholly cease to think, that I should at the same time altogether cease to be . . .

—René Descartes,
"Of the Nature of the Human Mind;
and That It Is More Easily Known Than the Body,"
Meditations on First Philosophy (1641)

THE
MIND VIRUS

PART ONE

1

Ree

virtual mortality

"A LIFE ON the Apps is the only life for me."

That's what Char kept saying, over and over, ever since that chick Skylar had given her emergency broadcast. Char was lying on her back in the grass of Main Park, staring up at the Night Sky 3.0. This one featured the Southern Cross, and it sparkled above us like a shining sword. Honestly, I preferred Night Sky 5.0, because Orion is more my thing.

It was a beautiful evening, regardless, like all evenings here.

Same as usual, in other words. Blah, blah, blah.

The only difference: this evening was the day after

half the City had unplugged. Half the people we knew in this world were—*poof!*—gone.

"Like, who cares about a clunky chunk of flesh when I have the entire virtual world at my fingertips?" Char was laughing, her voice alternately a shriek and a cackle, sounding like she'd downloaded one of those Wicked Witch Apps when on the outside she was all Betty Boop and Pinup Girl, her plump, red, heart-shaped lips all pouty and pursed. "Can you believe that Harry left? I mean, how dare he! I was totally going to Kiss App him at some point."

I closed my eyes, brain-blocking her. I didn't want her to know my thoughts at the moment, which weren't pretty. I let them flow freely now, in the newly locked safety of my virtual head.

Yeah, that's easy to say when your daddy got rich on Pharmaceutical Apps and you have an endless source of capital.

Why am I friends with you again?

Has anyone ever told you how annoying you are sometimes?

I opened my eyes and let Char back in. If I kept her from poking around in my head much longer, she'd guess I was having nasty thoughts.

Char swiped a finger across the atmosphere and her App Store gathered around her like a cozy bowl of candy. Char's icons always came in shades of bright pink and yellow and green and purple and blue. They squeaked and giggled and played with her hair and tickled her ears. One of them even settled happily into her cleavage, and she smiled down at it like it was a dear friend.

She turned to me, head lolling to the side, her shiny black locks sultry and smooth. "What next, Ree? How shall I celebrate my continued virtual existence? Hmmm?" She put out a hand and a crowd of Apps settled into her palm like pastel-colored insects, looking at her adoringly, hoping to be chosen. "Ree? Ree! Are you listening to me?"

I crossed my legs, the grass tickling my thighs. They were bland and pale next to Char's rosy, flushed virtual skin. "I'm listening," I droned. "Why don't you try something new for a change?"

Char's pout grew even more pronounced. "What do you mean, *for a change*?"

I sighed. "I mean, why don't you pick Personality over Appearance?"

She glared. "I care about more than Appearance Apps."

"All right. So prove it," I dared.

Her long-lashed, dark-lined eyes narrowed. "You could use a Personality App today."

"You first." I crossed my arms to match my legs. "Then me."

Char turned her attention back to her Apps, trying to choose. She sat there pondering, lying back on her elbows, legs crossed, one red-heeled foot bouncing in the atmosphere in a classic pinup pose, like she had all the time in the world, when a single, beguiling App rose up out of the swarm. "Oooh! What's that?" she cooed.

The two of us stared at it.

It took the shape of a present and glittered with every color in existence. It didn't flirt or cajole, it just hovered in the air like a queen bee who knew all she needed to do was stand there and wait to be adored by admirers.

"I've never seen anything like it," I admitted.

"I don't care what it is, Ree, Personality or Appearance or whatever else, I'm picking it."

"I thought we had a deal," I said, but only halfheartedly. In truth, I wanted Char to download this App. I wanted to see what would happen when she did.

She didn't even bother to reply.

Char just reached out a long, red-lacquered nail and touched it.

The second her fingertip met the icon, she gasped. Her pinup features began to transform, fading away. Char's wide dark eyes lolled back into her head with pleasure.

Or, at least, that's what I thought at first.

Quickly, far more so than was normal, Char changed back into her basic virtual self. I waited, impatient to see what new and exciting traits would appear. Her arms and legs began to twitch, just a little. But then they began to jerk. Char's elbows slipped out from under her and her head crashed to the ground.

I scurried over and lifted it, cradling it in my hands. "Are you okay?"

"Let me go," she moaned.

I laid her head back on the grass and moved away, watching as Char's virtual skin turned from Caucasian 4.0 to a dark shade of gray. Something was wrong. Her mouth opened and closed, opened and closed. "Wait a minute," she choked out.

It sounded like someone was strangling her. "Char?"

"Ree," she coughed.

Her skin was an ugly purple now, like a bluish bruise covering her virtual self. Then, right before my eyes, her skin began to slip from her body like one of those Real World animals I downloaded once that shed their skin every so often, emerging renewed. But Char wasn't looking renewed. She was looking like . . . she was looking like . . .

Death.

But that was impossible.

Death was impossible. Death had been overcome.

The light in her eyes kept going in and out, like someone suffering a brain stall.

I leaned over her. "Char, what do I do?"

A scream lodged in Char's throat. She gasped, working her lips, trying to speak, her breathing hoarse and hiccupping. Finally, she managed a single word.

"Poison," she wheezed.

"Poison?" I said desperately, reaching for her, but afraid to touch her, too. "The App was poisoned?"

By now a crowd had gathered around us. People stopped to watch the scene Char was making as she twitched and jerked and choked in the grass. Parents out with their children for a nighttime stroll, Lullaby Apps tinkling softly above their carriages. Businessmen on their way home through the park. A crowd of young women heading to the bars for the evening, decked out in pricey Model Apps. A gang of fifteens, covered in tattoos and chains, trying to look badass but tittering and giggling underneath their downloads, were standing off to the left. As they watched, their laughter disappeared, their hands going to their mouths in horror.

I looked from one group to the other, willing one of them to do something.

No one stepped forward.

In fact, most of them began stepping away.

"Can't anybody help us?" I cried.

Not a single person answered. Everyone seemed frozen.

As I sat there next to my friend, I watched the virtual Char I'd known my entire life slip away, until she was nothing more than a giant string of tiny numbers, tightly wound, weaving in and out of themselves again and again.

All that was left of Char was code. Raw, naked code.

The numbers began to break apart. Disintegrate like virtual ash.

And then, suddenly, the dust that was left disappeared altogether.

Char was gone.

Vanished from the atmosphere, as though she was never there.

At first, everyone around me remained silent. A collective shock fell across the park, across those of us who'd witnessed Char's quick and ugly demise.

I scrambled to my feet, unsure what to do. Who to call. What came next.

Then, one of the models, a tall, bone-thin girl in a too-short dress, teetering on spiky heels made out of lightning bolts that flashed as she moved, began screaming.

"Virus! Virus!"

That was when everyone turned and ran.

2

Skylar

the king and queen

WE OPENED A door between worlds.

Correction: I opened it. And now everything was a mess. Zeera kept telling me it wasn't us, that the mess wasn't *my* fault, but I wasn't sure if I believed her. The people who'd crossed the border that day at the Body Market, fleeing for their lives, had suffered a rude awakening, to put it mildly. I'd thought my unplugging was bad, waking up on that dais with half the Real World staring at me. But at least I'd had the help of my Keeper afterward to ease my way into the real body again, to totter on my colt-like legs in the safety of her apartment, while she kept me nourished and helped me learn to speak again.

But that day, all those poor people.

I shook my head, picking at the loose threads of the comforter on my bed.

They woke like I did, to chaos and confusion. To the need to run on legs they hadn't used for decades, and for the younger ones, legs they'd never used at all since they were practically born on the plugs. Worse still, when things calmed down and Rain and everyone else helped get them to safety, it wasn't as though there were Keepers waiting to help people adjust. We hadn't had time to anticipate all that need, and with such a mass and sudden exodus from the App World, we didn't have nearly enough Keepers to go around. So all those people . . . they just . . . had to fumble through adapting to the body and the Real World on their own. To say that most of them were traumatized was the understatement of the App Millennium.

"Skylar?"

Parvda raised her head from the pillow, her big eyes heavy with sleep, the skin around them red and puffy. The covers stretched all the way up to her neck even though the September air was warm and still smelled like summer. The briny tang of the ocean wafted into the room through the open sliding doors.

"I'm right here," I told her and set my book down. "I told you I wasn't going anywhere." A single tear ran down Parvda's cheek. "You should try to sleep more if you can. Get some rest."

Parvda opened her mouth to answer but a sob choked from her throat instead. She breathed deep, trying to hold back the next one. "I'm so sorry," she said, her voice raspy. Then she began to weep.

I pulled her closer and ran my hand over her long black hair. "You don't have to be sorry, I told you it's okay. I know how you feel," I added in a whisper, as a tear leaked from my eyes. Parvda continued to cry and I held her, looking out at the dunes and just beyond, at the sliver of sea I could see from my bedroom at Briarwood. A wave would crash and drown out the sounds of Parvda's sadness, only to calm and reveal them again in all her pain.

It was true, the App World citizens were struggling, trying to make a life here and failing, despite our attempts to help. So many of them wanted to plug back in. They were homesick, they had App withdrawal, they'd returned to a Real World they'd long ago rejected. Little did they know that here in the cavernous underground of Briarwood sat tens of thousands of empty plugs, plugs that we could control and protect so they could go home in peace, knowing their bodies were safe. Though it was also true that before any of that could happen, before anyone could have the choice of staying or going back to virtual living, we would have to convince the powers in the App World to grant them asylum. If they returned without this, they would be considered illegal immigrants and might even be hunted down. The second everyone took advantage of our offer to repossess their bodies, they became personae non gratae in the City. There were rumors about border patrols and monitoring plugging-in activity, Big Brother types searching for surges in the fabric of the App World, signaling an illegal plug-in. There were even threats of jail if someone dared try to return home.

It was more dangerous than ever to move between worlds.

I tore my eyes from the sea and they settled onto my friend once again.

Her sobs had subsided a little.

It might be more dangerous than ever to move between worlds, but it wasn't as though it couldn't be done. It's just that no one had dared to try—no one but Adam. He'd used the Shifting App to plug back in months ago. He and Parvda had a terrible fight, she still wouldn't tell me about what, refused to talk about it. Afterward he'd stormed off and disappeared. An entire day passed before Parvda realized he'd gone down to the plugs and crossed the border.

Lacy, of all people, had helped him do it.

Parvda was staring into space, quiet now, eyes empty.

"Sweetie, maybe today is the day that we pull him out? Make sure he's okay?"

"No," she croaked. "He needs to come back on his own." She glanced at me, eyes ablaze. "And before you suggest it again, *no*, you are not going to find him. Nobody is. If Adam wants to waltz his way into danger, then he can decide to waltz his way back by himself."

I tucked the sheet more tightly around her. As much as I wanted Parvda and Adam to fix whatever had happened, a part of me was relieved by her refusal. If I never had to go to the App World again I'd be a happy person. I had about a million reasons to avoid the City. Jude was rumored to be living there now and I wasn't ready to fix that relationship. Then there was my power-mongering father, Emory Specter, who I didn't know if I'd ever be ready to deal with. This, and the fact that I was public enemy number one, didn't make crossing the border to find Adam very appealing.

I wiped a tear from Parvda's face. "You can be really stubborn, you know," I said, but with affection. This—Parvda's stubborn refusal to go find Adam or let anyone else do it—I understood, too.

It had been months since I'd last seen Kit, since our one night together. The very next morning he'd betrayed me to my sister. I didn't know if I would ever see him again. Sometimes the pain of losing him was so great I felt like a zombie walking through the Real World, unable to see or breathe, less human than before. In the App World, I hadn't known that heartbreak could literally make the body feel pain, make the chest constrict, the lungs ache. Even though I didn't want to go back to the City, I envied the possibility of sending endless downloads into my code, App after App after App racing through me until I couldn't even remember Kit's name. Sometimes I wished Zeera could dig through my brain like she'd done to create the Shifting App until she found the piece of it that contained Kit, erasing it somehow. I'd actually asked her if this was possible, but she shook her head. *Real brains don't work like that, Skylar*, she'd said.

There was a knock on the door. "Come in," I called out.

Rain entered a step, eyebrows raised.

I did my best not to look away. It was as though Rain could read my mind and knew each time I had thoughts of Kit. "Parvda's awake," I told him.

"Good morning." He revealed a tray with steaming coffee and two plates of cake from behind his back. "Your mother sent me to check on you both, with some breakfast."

The mention of my mother made me smile. It was so good to see her, to have her in my life, to have her take care of me and do the things that mothers do, like make their daughters breakfasts on occasion. Morning treats like coffee and cake. She'd outdone herself with the mothering ever since we'd been reunited. It was as if she was trying to make up for all those years apart.

Rain set the tray onto the bed and sat down next to it. Then he leaned toward me and planted a kiss on my lips.

I closed my eyes until he pulled away.

"I missed you last night," he said.

"Me, too," I told him, and busied myself by reaching for a cup of coffee. As I did, I saw Parvda staring, trying to catch my attention.

Only she knew how I still felt about Kit. Only with Parvda could I let my guard down and show my true feelings, the total despair in my heart that Kit had been willing to sell me back to my sister after all, too cowardly to show his face afterward. And while Kit was gone, Rain had worked his way into my life again, finding my mother for me, an act for which I would be eternally grateful, no question about it. I wasn't really sure what else was going on between us, but as far as Rain was concerned, we were together. Or we were sort of together. Or maybe even he didn't know either. People were treating us as a couple, there was no question about *that*, my mother included. And Lacy—Lacy, too, which was a total nightmare. But in private, things with Rain and me were not so simple.

Though I was doing my best to wrap my head around being with him.

I smiled at Rain now. "Thank you for this." I gestured with the coffee cup before I took a sip. I'd grown pretty addicted to my jolt of caffeine. Lately, I needed a jolt to get myself moving for the day. Now I understood why so many of the Over Eighteens, especially the parents, would download the various Caffeine Apps—the Espresso, the Latte, the Extra-Dark Diesel Fuel—throughout the morning. These last months it felt as though there was some sort of permanent glitch in my code. Zeera worried there might have been permanent damage done to me, to my brain, from all that business with the Shifting App. I pushed this uncomfortable thought away.

Rain was watching me.

"What?" I asked him.

His eyes shifted to Parvda, who'd burrowed deeper under the covers. "Nothing. I was just thinking. We really should talk. You know, about what's going on in New Port City."

Everything in me tensed. "I know. I know, I know."

He opened his mouth to say something else but I got there first.

"Rain?"

He smiled a little. "Skylar?"

"Would you stay with Parvda for a bit? I want to go for a walk. Maybe a swim."

Rain's smile faltered. "Sure. Go ahead."

"I'll see you later," I said, without looking at him. I got up from the bed and slipped outside through the screen door. It was only then that I felt like I could breathe again.

There was laughter. Words and talk that floated along the breeze and across the sand to the place where I stood, staring at the ocean, water streaming off me from my swim.

I turned.

They didn't see me at first.

Trader and Inara were stumbling along, hugging each other, smiling rapturously, oblivious to the rest of the world. They were about to crash into me before they noticed I was there. At least one couple I knew was happy.

"Hey, Sis," Trader said, and they halted. His cheeks bloomed bright against the pale color of his complexion.

Inara's face was lit up with joy. "Skylar!" She gave me a quick hug.

"Hi, guys." Things had thawed quickly between us after I found Inara's hiding place in the App World and facilitated a Real World reunion between her and my brother. They weren't quite back to how they used to be before I unplugged, but they were getting there. She turned her attention to her feet as she scraped them across the sand, writing her name with her toes. I joined her and wrote mine next to it.

Trader rolled his eyes, but he was beaming. "Cute." His black hair shone in the sunlight, and his dark eyes were alive. Inara's return to the Real World, her sheer presence, transformed him. Trader's mood had always been dark, as dark as his features, yet lately, with Inara, he'd become a different person.

I liked this new Trader.

He was turning out to be a nice brother. Nicer than I could have predicted.

"You went swimming," he said. "Isn't the water freezing?"

I shrugged. "It is, but I don't care. I bet I could even swim in winter."

Trader laughed. "I'd pay good capital to see you do that."

I squinted into the sun. "Watch out or I'll hold you to it." I nudged Inara. "Remember when you made me download the Arctic Explorer App and the Teeny Tiny Bikini App at the same time and dared me to go swimming in one of those little ice-cap fishing holes? I nearly became a virtual popsicle."

Inara looked up from the sand, where she'd been drawing a gigantic flower around our names. She chuckled. "I remember." She wandered off a bit, bent down to pick up a coin of mother-of-pearl, and used it to decorate the inside of the first *a* in *Inara*.

Trader leaned close and started to whisper. "Skylar, I've been hearing rumors, and they aren't good."

The warmth of the brief moment shared with my old best friend left and the breeze felt cold against my skin. "About what, this time?" I shivered. "How I ruined so many people's lives? How unbearable it is to be in the real body?"

Trader glanced at Inara, who'd wandered a few steps farther down the beach. She was crouched low, searching the sand for more shells. "No," he said. "These rumors are about the App World—about the people still living there."

I didn't flinch at this. The borders might be more dangerous than ever to cross, but Trader always found a way to get information from the other side. "What about them?"

"There's talk of a virus."

My stomach clenched. "A virus in the City?"

Trader's head bobbed slightly, his eyes going to Inara once more. Her parents were still there.

"But I thought viruses were impossible. I thought the code for the App World was virus-proof." Mrs. Worthington, all of our teachers when we were growing up, everyone in the government, had bragged about this, though they'd always carefully avoided using the word *virus* when discussing it. App World living was eternally safe from such threats, they'd always claimed.

Inara stood and started back toward us.

Trader bent closer. "It might just be a rumor. And if it's not a rumor, it's probably just a tiny bug. Nothing really bad."

"Yeah, probably," I agreed, even while my heart did flips at the center of my chest. "Those are pretty," I said to Inara as she returned, her palm full of pearly shells.

Trader held my gaze. "Where are you off to?"

I tried to read his expression. There was worry in his

eyes, more than his words let on. "I want to check on the App World refugees."

Trader and Inara turned, their eyes following the curve of beach toward the camp. Tents flapped in the wind, the canvas a blinding white in the light. "Those refugees need a real place to live," Inara said. "They can't stay in tents forever. At least the others have moved into the abandoned buildings in New Port City."

"Yes, though they aren't doing much better than the ones who are here." I closed my eyes against the glare, against the weight of being responsible for the well-being of so many people. It made me exhausted to think about it. "There isn't nearly enough housing for all of them." I sighed. "One thing at a time, I guess."

The two of them nodded, but stayed silent.

We all knew the refugee crisis was growing and expanding by the day. And it wasn't just the coming cold we had to worry about.

"It will get figured out," Inara said eventually. "Some-how."

Trader opened his mouth to speak, but Inara got up on her toes and whispered to him. He closed his mouth again. After another moment of silence, he spoke. "We're headed down the beach, Skylar," he said. His dark eyebrows arched. "See you later?"

"Definitely," I said, already on the move. "Bye, guys," I called over my shoulder. I could barely hear their responses over the sound of the waves and the wind. Gray clouds hung heavy above. Maybe it was going to storm.

The camp was enormous. Sprawling.

It reached all the way down the beach as far as the eye could see and kept going around the curve and went on from there. On and on and on. Enough refugees had crossed the border to repopulate several Real World cities, and this was only one of the camps. Refugees had taken over entire mansions in New Port City, abandoned buildings, apartments, whatever they could find. They were everywhere and they'd maxed out the available housing. These refugees were the ones who hadn't been so lucky.

Soon I could see the tent that had grown the most familiar over the last few months. Scarves bright with greens and reds and purples hung down over the openings, some patterned with polka dots and others with paisley swirls and flowers.

"Rasha? Andleeb?" I called when I was close.

Andleeb poked her head through the dripping fabric. "Hi, Skylar," she said, smiling.

"Welcome back to our humble abode," Rasha's voice greeted me.

These two sisters, with their big dark eyes and deep olive skin that turned golden in the sun, had been a bright spot in my life ever since the three of us met. They wore head scarves that covered their thick black hair when they left their tents, but not because they were in hiding as I once was. It was a custom of the women in their family, they'd explained, before they'd plugged in, one that they'd restored since they'd returned to the Real World. The App World had prohibited the practice of such old traditions because they got in the way of the ideal of sameness, broken up only by the Apps. Andleeb and Rasha had resented this prohibition. Their parents were still living virtually in the City. They hadn't wanted to leave, so the two sisters were here on their own.

"And where is your . . . *friend* today?" Andleeb asked, with a grin. "I was hoping you'd come by with him again."

"My sister's been in love with Rain Holt *forever*," Rasha said.

Andleeb elbowed her. "I have not. I just like looking at him."

My smile grew tight. "You'll have to be satisfied with just me. Sorry to disappoint."

"We're not *really* disappointed, don't worry," Rasha said.

I looked around their cramped tent. Their sleeping bags were laid out over a sheet of plastic along the canvas that made up the floor. We'd distributed these sheets as an added precaution against the rain. I knew they did their best to keep things neat, but after months of living like this, everything was damp and dirty. I pushed away the thought that it might storm again soon. "I wanted to check in and see how you were doing."

The sisters' smiles faltered.

The lashes framing Rasha's eyes fluttered. "Have you made any progress in figuring out where to put the rest of us?"

"We're working on it," I said, thinking we really needed to work faster. It was unacceptable to allow people to live in these conditions.

Andleeb smoothed the edges of her quilt with her fingers. "We're all right for now," she started. "But a lot of people regret their decision to cross the border. There's tension brewing." She stared at me hard. "Everyone is grateful, Skylar, that you told us the truth about the Body Market. But some people want to go back to virtual life. For good."

My cheeks grew hot. We'd given people a choice and the refugees had unplugged of their own volition, but the fact that so many of them were suffering, that so many were unhappy, that so many were considering plugging back in, was my fault. They felt that we'd misled them or worse, that they'd followed me willingly from a virtual life they'd wanted into a real life they didn't.

Now all they felt was regret.

And what else could I really expect? They'd made a snap decision. In a matter of minutes, they'd chosen to leave the life they'd always known. In truth, they should be able to plug back in if that was their choice. At least they would still have control over their bodies. But what if it was no longer safe to plug in?

"Thank you for being honest with me," I said finally. "But I have one more question. How much longer do you think the refugees in this camp will give the Real World a chance?"

Andleeb and Rasha looked at each other.

Then Rasha spoke. "Maybe a couple of weeks? It's going to get colder and the weather more . . . difficult, so if our living conditions don't improve, maybe less?"

I nodded. "Then I guess we'll need to change things sooner."

As I made my way out of the camp, I saw a group of App World children gathered at the water's edge. They stared at the ocean, the way it swept in and out, the water rolling tiny pebbles up the sand and washing over their feet. Seeing the awe on their faces, the way they shrieked with delight as the cold surf splashed along their ankles, put a small smile back on my face. It helped me forget that it would probably rain again this evening.

One of them, a tiny girl, maybe six years old, saw me there and whispered to the others. The rest of them turned and watched me approach.

I waved.

They waved back.

"Hello," I called to them.

"Hi, Skylar," they chorused over the wind.

A couple of other children ran down the beach, their skinny legs a blur, as though they hadn't plugged in as babies and instead had grown up using their legs like Real World kids did. The youngest of the refugee children had taken to the Real World like an App to someone's virtual code. They'd adapted quickly—they'd done everything quickly, really. Walked. Talked. They were eating and running around like they'd always lived here.

Anyone who was an eight on up to an adult was another story.

They were having a lot of trouble adjusting to life in their real bodies. Many of them couldn't walk yet and some of them refused to get out of bed, as though their limbs were too heavy to move. We'd done our best to help them in groups—there were simply too many to do much one-on-one physical therapy.

Then, almost all of them were going through major App withdrawal, their brains accustomed to the near-constant downloads rushing through their codes like a drug. It was well-known that the more years a person lived virtually in the City, the more difficult it was for their body to adjust to being unplugged. This was why Service had always happened before a person became an eighteen. Even though I'd known this—even though *everyone* who unplugged knew this—it was startling to see the suffering people endured. Many of the parents of these children were nearly catatonic, their brains refusing to adjust to life without an App fix. It was only recently that some of the older adults were coming out of their stupors, opening their eyes to the Real World and starting to live on a more normal schedule of day and night, of waking and sleeping.

Their suffering is my fault.

I shook my head, wishing I could shake off thoughts like this that plagued me. "Maybe you guys should go for a swim," I said to the children cheerfully.

"We don't know how," said the biggest of the boys, who was maybe seven or even eight.

"We're not allowed to," said another. "My parents say that swimming in the real body is dangerous. When you swim in the real body, water fills up your mouth and your lungs and then you die a horrible death."

I tried to laugh this off. I'd grown used to listening to people's recitations of all they'd learned about the body in the App World. I'd learned the very same warnings and could recite them by heart, myself. "Well, only if you try to *breathe* underwater," I explained. "But I promise you that swimming is fun and you're going to love it once you learn. I'll teach you next summer if you want. The water is going to be too cold for it very soon anyway."

The boys seemed disappointed.

One of them frowned. "Are we really going to be here for that long? A whole year without Apps?"

His question made me feel tired again. Everyone talked to me, looked to me, as if I somehow had all the answers to people's lives and their futures. The rumor of a virus, however small, seemed to echo over the breeze and I wilted even more. I opened my mouth to respond, but the tiniest girl in the group seemed like she might burst if she didn't speak soon enough.

"I can't swim but look what *I* can do!" Her words spilled over one another, her wide blue eyes blinking.

"Show me," I said, encouraged by her enthusiasm.

Without another word she began turning cartwheels, perfect cartwheels, all the way down the beach. I shook my head. App World kids might be afraid of the water, but some of them could do . . . this. The girl must have turned twenty cartwheels before she stopped and ran back to us.

"You must have downloaded a lot of Gymnastics Apps," I said. "That was impressive."

Her chin tilted slightly upward. "The Nadia App was my favorite," she said proudly.

"So you're old-school, huh?"

She smiled. "I learned about her in Beginners' Real World History, the Sporting Update. She was the best a long, long time ago, back before there were Apps and they had this event called the Olympics."

"I remember that update," I said. "I downloaded it too, when I was your age."

The girl's face fell. "But now that I'm here, I won't be

able to learn anything else. I'll be doing cartwheels forever. And then I'll die and turn into dirt."

My brow furrowed. "That's not true—at least not about the cartwheels, not if you work hard at learning other things. And you're not going to die for a long, long time. Why would you say that?"

"Because the real body is a clumsy prison," she recited. "And it gets broken"—she paused to snap her fingers, an impressive skill for someone who'd only been in her real body for a few months—"like that!"

The other boys in the group nodded.

I glanced up at the sky above us, all that vast blue from earlier replaced by gray. "I know you all learned this in App World School 2.0—"

"—2.5," one of them chimed.

"Sorry, 2.5," I continued. "But the body can do amazing things. And it's true, the body can get hurt, but you'll learn to take care of it. It's not so bad. Really."

One of the boys whispered to another.

The girl scowled. "Skylar isn't lying to us. She wouldn't! She's the queen."

I started at this. "What did you say?"

The tallest among the boys shrugged. "She called you queen. Some of the people here say it."

"You're Queen Skylar," said another boy.

Now I laughed a real laugh. "Well, that is sweet, but I'm not a queen."

The tall boy snickered. "They don't always say it in a nice way."

"Yes they do," said the girl. She pointed behind me. "And he's the king. He was a prince at home but here he's a king. That's what my mother told me."

I turned and saw Rain walking up the beach.

"King Rain and Queen Skylar of New Port City," the girl affirmed.

The boys laughed, but their laughter was uncertain.

I frowned. I didn't want to be queen. I didn't want to be anyone. Not anyone important.

But Rain—Rain would make a good king.

I walked away before he could reach us.

3

Ree

stuck here

I GLARED AT my mother. "You should've let me unplug while I still had the chance."

She couldn't hear me, or was refusing to. My mother was three Cocktail Apps in as she sat on our terrace, which overlooked Main Park. She'd been Cocktail Apping a lot, ever since what happened to Char, and doing it by herself, which we were always getting warnings against on Reel Time. Apparently Cocktail Apping by yourself is a sign of antisociality, which was a no-no around these parts. Plugging in was supposed to reconcile the divide between real and virtual by making everything all virtual, all the time, and alleviating the anger and frustration people felt when they were still in their real bodies and always staring into virtual space, ignoring everyone else around them.

Well. Liars.

The virtual government was full of them.

I should know.

It was a government official who whisked me home the day that Char disintegrated, and who offered my mother and me a lifetime of unlimited downloads if we complied with two little directives—to which my mother agreed because all she cares about are App fixes. The two minor compliances that government wanted from us?

1. That we stay quiet about Char.
2. That we don't leave our apartment until the government gives us the okay.

What's more, the "staying quiet" included mind-chatting.

As in, *no* mind-chatting.

We were informed of this teensy detail as though it was no big deal, as if it was totally normal and utterly ordinary for the government to turn off our mind-chats. Right.

"No way are we agreeing to this!" I shouted that day, as I watched my mother's head bobbing like she'd down-loaded a Bobblehead App for children. But she barely even heard me. She was too busy taking in the virtual riches the government official was promising us if we stayed mum about what I'd witnessed in the park. "I am not letting us be bought! Mom!"

"Shhhhh! Ree! I did not raise you to be rude."

"Yeah, you raised me to drown my mind in only the priciest of Liquor Apps," I yelled, angry and helpless, since there was nothing I could say to my mother that would convince her that she was not doing the right thing. I was defeated the second this government lady—"just call me Mrs. Farley," she'd said, complete with a disturbing fake smile—started filling my mother's account with more capital than she'd ever dreamed of having, and we were well-off already. My mother's eyes literally had capital signs floating in them, and they began dancing around her head, too, having a party, *chinging* and *changing* like an old-fashioned cash register.

"Ree," my mother had protested, but weakly. She was too busy focusing on the capital dance-athon going on in front of her face.

I turned to the government lady. "Are you paying everyone at the park off like this? Because plenty of people saw what happened to Char! It wasn't just me!"

The government lady turned to me. "That's not for me to discuss," she said simply.

As though Char turning to ash before my eyes was simple.

As though this happened all the time.

Then again, what if it *did*?

The thought that it could, that maybe this wasn't the first time, that maybe this was the government's MO around—what was it the lady called it when my mother answered the door? Char's "unfortunate disappearance"? As though Char had wandered off somewhere and not practically suffocated and screamed her way into virtual oblivion. Maybe I wasn't the first person whose family they offered a lifetime supply of free downloads.

A shiver rolled through my code.

My skin flashed blue with it before returning to its normal Caucasian 4.5.

I stepped between my mother and Just-Call-Me-Mrs.-Farley. "You may be able to buy my mother with Apps, but you can't buy me!"

My mother was still sufficiently lucid at that point to snap, "My daughter can be bought, I promise you. Now have a nice day and thank you for bringing Ree home." She shoved Mrs. Farley out the door before she could take back the lifetime supply of downloads.

That was nearly six months ago.

I'd been trapped here with Mrs. Lush, aka Mom, ever since, totally unable to mind-chat, totally unable to communicate with anyone I know.

Maybe my friends at High School 4.0 thought I was dead.

I went to the edge of the terrace and leaned over the

side, so far that my legs lifted off the ground and I teetered precariously. My feet were in the air and my torso was angling toward all the guys and girls strutting around the park, showing off their fancy downloads, like normal people my age who'd just gotten out of High School 4.0 for the day.

Was I worried about falling and crashing to the ground on my head?

Oh no.

There was an electric fence around our apartment courtesy of the government.

Aka, the government lady was just being polite when she asked for our compliance. What she really meant was, "You and your mother are now prisoners of the state because you know too much information. Here, have some free Apps for your troubles!"

Thanks a lot, government lady!

Thanks a lot, Emory freakin' Specter!

At first, I didn't believe it. Could they *really* imprison us like that? *Would* they?

But then I started testing the boundaries of the apartment, pushing at them. I could go into the hallway outside the front door, but only by about two yards, just to the edge of our neighbor's place, before a tingling would start in my code. The farther I tried to go, the more it became electric.

Electric like it would electrocute me.

You know, like zap me to virtual death.

Like I was some dog inside a fence surrounding a yard.

In the beginning I'd assumed I could just push through that painful buzzing somehow, that it wouldn't be pleasant, but that it wouldn't kill me either.

Wrong!

It didn't kill me, obviously, but there came a point where the world just stopped. I couldn't go any farther into the hallway, any farther into the City outside our apartment, because the electricity racing through my code began to burn like lightning and I wondered if I really would die some terrible death like Char. I kept pressing my hand into the edges of it, like there might be a hidden hole or a way through, but eventually, if I pressed far enough it would propel me backward.

Once I figured out my mother and I were trapped, that we weren't just being nice staying home a la the government's request, I went a little crazy. It didn't even matter that I'd spent so much time lighting up my code with electricity that I'd come away with my virtual skin blackened like I'd downloaded a Barbecue App to my face. It didn't matter that I was gasping, nearly unable to breathe in the Atmosphere 6.0.

I had to get out, whatever the cost.

So I ran onto the terrace and stretched my hand over the railing.

At first there was nothing, and the breath seemed to

return to my virtual body.

I stretched my hand farther.

And there it was—that tingling again.

I leaned over the side and felt the tingling intensify. Farther and farther I went, and the tingling became a burning like before. Steam poured off my skin. In a moment of desperation and delirium, I climbed up onto the railing, balancing there, feet curled like a bird's around it, arms wide, fingers stretched into the atmosphere.

I closed my eyes.

Then I stepped off the edge.

There was some sort of electrically charged net around the terrace and I fell right into it, a fly caught by the government spiders' invisible web, suspended there until it zapped me unconscious. At some point, I guess my mother came out of her stupor and pulled me back onto the terrace. When I woke I was staring up at the moon and the stars, lying on the ground. The App World had just switched seasons to the Spring Night Sky, and the Big Dipper was winking straight overhead. My virtual skin was gray and still smoldering orange in places.

Right now, at this very moment, my mother had moved on to her fourth Cocktail App of the day, drinking her lunch like always. Palm trees shaded her lounge chair and the fake blue of pool water splashed her legs. She must have downloaded a Piña Colada, one of those special enhanced cocktails that came with the atmosphere included, a vacation and a drink all packed into one pricey App.

"Might as well enjoy it, Mom," I said, echoing what she kept telling me over the last few months, even though I knew she couldn't hear me or would ignore me if she did.

Ever since the throwing-myself-from-the-terrace incident, I'd stopped trying to escape.

Well. That's not *exactly* true.

I was biding my time, testing alternative ways out of this prison, ways out via the Gaming Apps, seeing if any of them led me to another place in the City. It was known to happen. It was one of the glitches in the fabric of our world.

The palm trees rooted around my mother's chair began to fade, along with the splashing of pool water. I watched as she called up her personal App Store.

She must have been imagining a European vacation.

Cocktail Apps in the shape of the Eiffel Tower, Big Ben, and even the Colosseum swirled around. Her head lolled left and right. She laughed happily, her finger hovering between some sort of fancy cathedral and what looked to be one of those crazy houses in Barcelona, by that nutty architect—what was his name? Gawdi? Gaudí? I was almost impressed that my mother had moved beyond palm trees and fake blue pool water to something with a little cultural value, when her attention and mine was caught on a new App that appeared, hovering right between her eyes, steady and confident and irresistible. It glittered and sparkled, an icon in the shape of a present that beguiled like no other App I'd seen before.

Except one.

That day that Char . . .

"Mom, don't!" I yelled, and ran to her. I yanked her virtual hand away before she could touch it.

She shrieked and finally came out of her drunken stupor to look at me, to really see me standing there, my fingers curled around her thin bangled wrist.

"Insolent girl," she shouted. "Get your hands off me!"

I let her go and jumped back. I stood there, gaping at her.

My mother opened her mouth to say something else. I could see her white pearly teeth, nearly glowing from the Dental Whitening App she downloaded each morning. But then her lips closed tight and her face went slack. She passed out in the lounge chair, the liquor finally sending her code into automatic shutdown.

The Apps from her App Store popped out of the atmosphere.

The poison one, the one that had ended Char, disappeared along with the rest.

For now, my mother was safe. We were safe.

But for how long?

4

Skylar

body snatchers

I STARED UPWARD.

My stomach churned.

A wide banner was draped across the library entrance. *REFUGEES GO HOME,* it said, in big block letters.

The place was bustling, full of Keepers moving in and out of the grand building, running up and down the marble steps. Children played on and around the sea monster statues on either side of the entrance, laughing and shouting. People sat on the stairs, their chins tilted toward the sun, taking in the warmth and the light of the morning, now that the rain from the night before had stopped. It reminded me of my first day out in the Real World, when I'd snuck out of the Keeper's mansion and come here to find Rain and ended up seeing the New Capitalists marching down the street with their big black boots, looking for some girl, looking for me. Things had changed since then. New Port City was full of activity lately, the dark sense of dread and division that Jude's people had hung over everything and everyone finally gone.

Replaced by a new kind of dread and division. For the refugees.

The banner flapped in the breeze.

I rode my bicycle here as often as I could to check on people camped out in the parks and vacant houses. Each time I visited, there was more graffiti in the street, on the sidewalks, everywhere I turned.

YOU ABANDONED US. DON'T EXPECT FORGIVENESS.
GO BACK TO YOUR APPING LIFE.
DOWN WITH APP WORLD CITIZENS.
THE REAL WORLD DOESN'T WANT YOU HERE.

Then, the worst of them, or, the worst in my opinion:

THIEVES! BODY SNATCHERS! YOUR BODIES ARE OUR
BODIES TO SELL!

After Jonathan Holt first announced the borders were closing in the App World, there had been virtual slogans that people chanted in the streets, full of celebration and the accompanying relief about not having to support Singles like me anymore. Wards of the state, dependent on charity. That day seemed like a million years ago. Now the App World refugees were dependent on us to take care of them, to find them homes, to help them assimilate back into real life, to learn to do the most basic things so they could care for themselves. It's amazing what people forget. And it's amazing how difficult it can be to reteach the body the simplest of simple tasks. Or to learn to walk and talk and read when you've been plugged in since birth.

I took a deep breath.

Right below my feet, scrawled on the sidewalk in the chalk that the children used to play, was the simple phrase *YOU'RE NOT WELCOME HERE* in a bright, angry red.

Facilitating peace between the refugees and the long-time citizens of New Port City was proving incredibly difficult. We'd all known it wouldn't be seamless. But it was shaping up to be far more problematic than anyone had predicted.

A gust of wind whipped at the banner and it snapped loudly.

It was true, the refugees were packing this city, nearly tripling the population and well outnumbering the port's original residents. But for now, the refugees were keeping to themselves, staying away from the city center where the Keepers socialized and worked. Maybe everyone had grown to like the emptiness of their city, the quiet and manageable size of the population before the recent exodus from the App World. They certainly didn't seem to feel obliged to help people reintegrate into a new and productive life in the Real World.

"Whose side are you on?" said a man who was sitting on the stairs.

At first, I didn't realize he was talking to me, or that he'd been watching as I stared up at the banner. "What?"

The man was older, with gray hair and kind eyes. The skin on his hands was wrinkled and brown and run through with thick veins. "Are you prorefugee or anti–body-snatcher?"

He asked this like it was the most normal question in the world, like he might be wondering what I'd eaten for lunch or if I thought it might rain later on this afternoon. At least he didn't seem to know who I was. "I'm prorefugee." I tried to keep my voice even. "What about you?"

The man tilted his head a little, thinking. "I haven't decided. I'm not sure I like . . . *foreigners* in our city."

I made sure my tone was steady when I responded. "But the refugees aren't foreigners. They're people who were born here and will always belong to this world."

He shook his head, the silver of his hair shining in the sunlight. "I've lived in New Port all my life, and you won't convince me they belong here as much as I do. These people abandoned this place for a virtual life." He chuckled. "And left all of us to care for them like servants."

"Janitors of bodies," I said quietly, more to myself than to him, that phrase Jude had used the first night I saw her echoing from my mouth.

"Exactly, just like that," he said. The man began to pull himself off the ground, slowly, until he was standing. His movements were tired but fluid, like someone who'd lived in a real body his entire life. He smiled, the lines around his mouth crinkling across his face. "Well, you have a nice day."

"You too," I said, watching as he shuffled away.

I pressed heavily onto the bicycle pedals and rode off toward my Keeper's mansion, putting my conversation with the old man behind me. My hair flew out behind me as I went, a feeling I liked now that I no longer was a wanted person and could move freely about the city, head uncovered. I still got looks from people who recognized me, but I no longer felt afraid. And some of the refugees who recognized me smiled and waved. The ones who were glad to keep their bodies, I supposed. The rest just stared.

I stopped at a corner. Snatches of speech rang in my ears. *Queen Skylar. King Rain. Refugees go home. Body snatchers.* I stared up at the beautiful tree rooted into the cobblestones. A weeping beech. They were everywhere in New Port City and I loved them. The glossy green leaves cascaded toward the ground like a waterfall. I knew I should keep going straight to see my Keeper, who was busy these days helping the refugees who were staying with her. Straight would take me down the old boulevard peppered with mansions once stately and majestic and jaw-droppingly beautiful, abandoned for decades until recently. Now they were full of App World refugees seeking a new and real life.

Right would take me down the hill to the Body Market.

My hands tightened around the handlebars of the bicycle. The sunlight pressed into me, burning my skin, making my face hot. I squinted up at the sky and took a deep breath. Then, once again I put my foot to the pedal and pressed down hard.

I went right.

There it was, just ahead.

The hotel, once bustling, rose up alongside the Body Market. A grand archway beckoned passersby to enter its stalls, open to the air, modeled after the famous markets of Europe, the ones that used to sell fruits and vegetables and meats in the cities of old, back before technology forever changed the ways of the world and all the people in it. Back before markets like these began hawking bodies and body parts. The first time I visited it was freezing cold, everyone bundled in winter coats, crowded into the aisles, waiting in long lines, well-heeled shoes sinking into the lush red carpet. But today it was empty, the canvas tarp stretching out over the entrance to provide shade for the crowds tattered with holes and dark in places, dirt-stained from weather and neglect, the red carpet lush no longer, and not even red. It had faded to more of a dull rust color.

The Body Market was still in operation as far as I knew, though I'd heard it was severely diminished.

Today it seemed closed altogether.

The metal garage doors were pulled down, locked tight to the ground.

The chaos we'd created on its opening day had ruined its reputation. Word got out among the Body Tourists that the market of New Port City wasn't reliable, that maybe it wasn't even legal, that the bodies available for sale might be bodies that their owners did not bequeath to the state and were instead being snatched right out from under their plugged-in minds. The New Capitalists never saw it this way. The New Capitalists argued that the bodies in the market were legally obtained, regardless of their owners' knowledge of the plan to sell their bodies.

There were two kinds of body snatchers, in other words.

The kind that my sister and the New Capitalists were, and the kind the New Capitalists were accusing the App World refugees of being—people who'd relinquished their bodies to the Keepers in exchange for eternal virtual life, who'd broken this contract and taken their bodies back unlawfully with the help of our Shifting App. The New

Capitalists' defense didn't matter much, though. They could plead with the Body Tourists all they wanted, argue that what they did was legal, but it wouldn't change things. Not anytime soon. The damage was done.

I stopped pedaling and took a deep breath, inhaling the fresh, salty air.

The wharf and the ocean were visible farther down the hill, beyond the Water Tower that shone a bright clear blue to match the sky and the peaceful September weather.

My heart pounded in my chest.

It did this every time I came back here. A part of me always wondered if I'd run into Jude, even though she was probably in the App World. I wasn't sure what I'd do if I did see her, if I'd run the other way or try to talk. Now that she'd fallen from grace, she wasn't really a threat. But I didn't know if we could ever repair our relationship, or if I even wanted to try.

I hopped down from the bicycle and propped it against the wall behind a patch of sunny yellow flowers that grew through the sidewalk, and headed along the street and around the corner, my heart pounding even harder. I nearly expected Jude's familiar face to appear in a window or out of thin air. Unlike the happy bustling movement around the library, the streets were empty near the Body Market. People were staying clear. The place had an air of foreboding that the warm breeze and bright sun couldn't mask. Even the abandoned neighborhoods and mansions of New Port City before the refugees occupied them hadn't felt like this. They at least had cheerful and wild gardens that sprung up in the weeds throughout their grounds and birds that chirped in the tree branches outside their windows, the sound of the waves rolling in and out on the nearby beaches that made a person think of lazy afternoons and swimming.

But this part of the city just felt . . . wrong.

Plus, I hadn't seen another soul since I'd turned down this street.

I walked a few more steps and halted. Hissed in a breath and clutched at my racing heart.

The sounds of a motor, loud, obnoxiously loud, approached from down the hill.

I was standing in the very same spot where last winter I'd left the Body Market after scouting it for the first time. Snowflakes had started to fall and I'd marveled at them, right at the same moment I'd heard a similar roar of an engine and around the corner came Kit. He'd parked his bike and said my name as though we'd been introduced at a party, as though we'd known each other our entire lives.

I pressed my hand harder against my chest, the fabric of my top warm from the sun beating down onto it.

The roar got closer.

I watched as the motorcycle raced up the hill to the place where I waited, rooted to the spot, and came to an abrupt halt. The motor was cut and the world fell silent. I saw a flash of stars inked on skin and wished the eyes of the rider who was right now dismounting his bike weren't hidden behind dark sunglasses.

He hesitated, then walked straight up to me.

"Hello, Skylar," Kit said.

Just like that. As though six months and a terrible betrayal hadn't passed between us. One part of me wanted to throw my arms around him, to kiss him like I'd dreamed of ever since that night we'd spent together and all those days during the blizzard at his cottage. But the other part of me was far stronger, so instead I turned my back on him and walked away.

5

Skylar

wildflowers

"SKYLAR, WAIT! PLEASE talk to me!"

I kept walking, faster and faster up the hill, in the opposite direction of my bicycle. It's not like I could make it to my Keeper's on foot, but maybe I could get far enough that Kit would give up and leave so I could go back for it. I grabbed at a railing along the front steps of an old townhouse, then propelled myself forward again.

Did I really want Kit to give up? Or did I want him to catch me? To finally explain what happened after all of this time apart and so much terrible, painful silence?

"Skylar!"

Kit was close. I didn't need to turn to know this. His voice was so clear to my ears and I could sense his nearness, imagine him, the curve of his shoulders, his torso, my body and mind having memorized everything about him whether I wanted to or not. His footsteps sounded behind me and then . . . and then . . .

His hand reaching for my arm, his fingers on my skin, urgent.

I yanked my arm away. But I stopped walking. My back was still to him, my breathing fast and heavy. We were in front of a beautiful gray-blue house covered in wooden slats, and I stared at it, trying to pull myself together. A plaque next to the shiny red door said that it was built in 1827. For a second I wondered who might live there, who had kept it so nicely painted, the lawn trimmed and flowers brimming from the boxes outside the windows, when so many of the other houses on this block were nearly falling down.

"Skylar, we need to talk," Kit pleaded.

I crossed my arms. I didn't trust them not to reach out to him. I almost couldn't bear to turn around and see his face, the face that appeared in my dreams, the memory of him when I was awake making my chest ache, my heart in so much pain. No matter how hard I tried to get over everything, to forget it, to forget him, to focus on Rain— someone who'd worked so hard to regain my trust—I couldn't. I stared at the base of the house in front of me, at the daisies shooting up from the ground, like little stars bursting with joy.

I hadn't felt joy in so long.

My eyelids shut to block out the flowers, my hands balled into fists. There were refugees that needed help, children and families, people without homes for the winter, and there was anger in New Port City, and here I was, totally undone by Kit's unexpected appearance. "There's nothing to discuss," I said, finally finding a few words for him.

He laughed bitterly. "You know that's a lie."

My nails dug into my palms. "Who's calling who a liar?"

Kit's breath grew ragged. "Are you going to look at me at some point?"

"Are you going to keep hiding behind those sunglasses?"

"I'm not trying to hide anything from you."

"Are you serious?" I spun around and nearly toppled over, my balance off, the sight of Kit's eyes, the way he was looking at me, the same way he used to look at me, so startling after so much time had passed. "You've been hiding for months. You've been gone for *months*. Sometimes I wondered if I might've dreamed you."

A pained expression appeared on his face. "I thought you'd be better off without me. I'm not good for you, Skylar. I'm not good for anyone."

I bit my lip so hard I tasted blood. "If you're so bad for

me then what changed your mind? Why are you talking to me now?"

Kit stared at the sunglasses he held in his hands and polished the lenses with the hem of his shirt. "I've missed you. I think about you every day. And every day I've ridden here, to the spot where we first met, because I can't get you out of my mind."

"You mean the spot where you first kidnapped me?"

"Yes, there," he said heavily. "I didn't really believe I would run into you, though. Then today, there you were, and I almost wondered if I was seeing things."

"If you'd really wanted to see me, you knew exactly where to find me. You knew I was at Briarwood. Which means that you chose *not* to find me. All this time you *chose* not to see me." I forced myself to keep my eyes steady on Kit's face. Maybe if I could just not look away, if I could just master the feelings bashing around inside my rib cage, then I'd stop being so powerless where Kit was concerned. "And I didn't expect to see you here. If I had, I wouldn't have come."

"Is that really true, Skylar?" Kit shifted from one foot to the other, his thick boots scraping along the sidewalk. He ran his hands through his hair, and inky stars appeared from under one sleeve, birds in flight from under the other. "You haven't wished to see me even a little?"

Any resolve I had left crumbled. I wanted to trace the arc of those birds and stars on his skin, one by one. "Of course I've wished to see you. I've wished it every single day. Just as I've wished every single day that you hadn't betrayed me. You told me I could trust you. You promised not to hurt me." I breathed in, gasping for air. "You betrayed me. Worse than Rain ever did. How can I forgive you?"

Kit looked up from his glasses and met my eyes. "I don't know. But maybe we could find a way? Maybe if you wanted to forgive me, eventually you would. Do you want to forgive me?"

Tears stung my eyes and blurred my vision. "Yes," I whispered, because it was true. "But I don't know if I can. Or if I should. I probably shouldn't."

Kit was shaking his head. "No, probably not. And I probably should be a better person and not want you to. But I do want you to forgive me. I'm sorry. I've never been so sorry in my entire life."

My arms twitched at my sides, my fingers stretching toward the ground. But instead of reaching out to Kit, instead of telling him I wanted to start trying to forgive him this very minute, to ask him the questions that had been plaguing me ever since that night at his house and everything that came afterward, to try and begin to understand how he could have betrayed me so terribly to my sister, to tell him that I was worried about rumors in the App World and the refugees here and how I could use his help, his company, his reassurance, instead of all of these things, I said, "I'm with Rain now."

Kit took a sharp step back. The water far off down the hill framed the upper part of his body, deep blue with angry whitecaps. "What?"

I nodded, slowly, even though I already regretted telling Kit this thing, regretted speaking Rain's name aloud between us. "We're together, Rain and I. We have been, ever since . . ."

Kit opened his mouth. Then he closed it, his eyes dropping once again to the ground. He dug the toe of his black motorcycle boot into the place where a cobblestone was missing from the street. "I don't believe it. I don't believe *you.*"

"It doesn't matter what you believe," I said, my voice rising. "What you believe stopped mattering a long time ago."

He looked up at me. "I guess that's true."

"Yes."

He shrugged. "All right, Skylar."

"All right, Kit."

"I guess . . . I guess I'll see you around."

"I know where to find you if I want to talk," I said, the familiar ache in my chest growing as I realized that this was it, we were about to part ways, and the moment I'd thought about, of our meeting finally after so much time, was already over.

Kit put his sunglasses back on. He stared off into the distance. "If you say so, Skylar," he said, then turned around and started down the hill to where he'd left his bike, leaving me standing there, alone again.

All I could do was watch him go.

When I arrived at my Keeper's, I was sweating and she was nowhere to be found. I'd pedaled hard all the way here. Maybe she was somewhere in the mansion, talking to the refugees occupying the upper floors. I went inside the entrance that led to her rooms, a bouquet of daisies in my hand, relieved I was alone for a while. I searched the cabinets until I found a vase and filled it with water. I considered leaving the flowers on the counter to die in the last heat of summer, dry and wilting. I don't know why I picked them. It's not like I wanted another memory of something to do with Kit that made me feel pain. But after he walked away I went to that wild patch of flowers in front of the pretty blue-gray house and yanked at one of them, hard, until the stem of it snapped. Then I yanked at another and another until I held a thick bunch of them in my fist. The sunny flowers stared up at me happily and my heart began to slow, little by little. I dropped them into the vase and set it onto the table. Every time I looked at the daisies my heart sped in painful, sharp bursts. Kit made me lose my control, my judgment, my sense. From the moment we met it had been like that. Then again, meeting Kit brought me back to life all those months ago during that blizzard, and right when I'd lost the will to care about anything.

The sound of a car engine brought me to the window.

Rain got out and started toward the door.

I opened it, surprised to realize I was happy to see him. Rain was steady and dependable and was always there for me. A quality that Kit could not boast, no matter what else he made me feel. "Hi," I said, and smiled. "What are you doing here?"

He smiled back. Rain was beautiful—of this, there was no doubt. This, I could never forget. "I thought you might need a ride back to Briarwood," he said.

"I thought I might stay here tonight."

His smile slipped. "I could stay with you."

I shook my head. Then I decided to give in. "No. We can both go to Briarwood," I said, and his smile steadied. "I probably shouldn't be away from Parvda."

Rain's eyes clouded. "I know."

I headed back into the kitchen and Rain followed. "I don't even know what she and Adam fought about."

Rain pulled out a chair and sat down at the table. "I don't either." He reached out and tapped the vase. "Did you pick these in the garden? They're pretty."

"Yes," I lied. Then I changed the subject. "Have you seen the banner outside the library?"

"No. Why?"

I sat down in the other empty chair. "It says, 'Refugees go home.'"

Rain grimaced. "Wow. The graffiti is one thing, but a banner outside the library takes such . . . such . . ."

"Effort?" I supplied.

"Yes. Exactly."

"Things seem to keep getting worse, by the day." I looked at Rain, my eyebrows arching. "And did you hear what they're calling us at the camp on the beach?"

Rain chuckled. "The king and queen of New Port City?"

The happiness I felt for him moments ago turned to annoyance. I dug my finger into a knot in the rough wood of the table. "You knew? And you let them think something so ridiculous?"

"Skylar." Rain's tone was playful. "You know they called me a prince in the App World, so it wasn't that far of a leap from prince to king. To the refugees, I'm still royalty. And now, here, they see me with you. Do the math."

"Fine," I said, remembering so clearly that Rain was— had always been—royalty and treated accordingly. "You can be king, but I don't want to be queen."

"But you saved those people. You deserve the title more than me."

"I didn't. Not really. Everyone worked together to get the refugees across the border. And it's not like all of them are happy with the decision." I huffed. "I'm sure a lot of them are calling me plenty of other names, none of them as kind as Queen Skylar."

"I think what they're calling us is kind of sweet."

"I bet Lacy doesn't," I said, before I could think better of it.

Rain sighed. "Lacy is Lacy."

"Lacy is angry and she has a right to be."

"Lacy will get over things."

"But will she?" I closed my eyes a moment, and an image of Kit immediately appeared, so I opened them again. "Should she even try?"

"Yes," Rain said, sounding hurt. "What do you mean, even asking me that?"

I laid my cheek on the cool surface of the tabletop. "I don't know. Forget I said it. I'm just tired." I lifted my head. "Let's talk about the refugees on the beach. They need places to live for the winter, and the available housing here in New Port City is maxed out. And we need to figure out what to do about all the resistance to them."

Rain stared at me, blinking. I worried he might refuse to drop the subject of Lacy, but after some more hesitation he spoke. "I think the resistance will die down eventually." His eyes drifted to the ceiling, to the elaborate crown molding surrounding the chandelier above us, with its dusty teardrop crystals signaling the glory of another age. "People will get used to the presence of the refugees and begin to integrate them. It's just that they weren't prepared for such an influx and they're struggling to adjust."

I nodded, hoping that he was right. "In the meantime, maybe we could get everyone to help with scrubbing that graffiti. It's not exactly . . . inviting to the refugees. Or helpful toward their integration."

"If we scrub it, someone else will just graffiti over it," Rain said.

I stared at the cheerful daisies and nearly winced. "Probably."

"We'll figure it out," Rain said. "It will be fine."

"There's something else we need to consider," I began, hoping that this was a good moment to raise a topic I'd been pondering. "A lot of the refugees want to go back to the App World. And we have those plugs in Briarwood. . . ." I trailed off. I'd been mulling this idea over for weeks, but the word *virus* whispered itself inside my head, adding to all the other things that made this idea seem not merely difficult, but possibly terrible.

Rain was staring at me like I might be crazy. "You're kidding, right? Do you know how complicated that would be? It's *illegal*, first of all, never mind incredibly dangerous with the border patrols."

I sat up straighter in my chair, banishing thoughts of viruses and bugs for the moment. "But what if we could negotiate a truce? Get your father to help us? You and I could plug back in, and negotiate permission." Rain's eyes grew suddenly interested at this mention of the two of us working together, so I barreled on forward. "A kind of passport system for people to go back and forth? Yes, setting everything up would be complicated, maybe even impossible. But it could be worth a try since once we did it, after all these years, people would have real choices about how much time they'd like to spend in each world." I pulled out the tablet that lay dormant in my jeans pocket and swiped my finger across the surface. Then I pushed it across the table toward Rain. I'd scribbled all sorts of notes about the possibilities and I wanted him to read them. "They could exercise their right to be citizens of both worlds—and wasn't that the whole point? To reconcile real life with the virtual one? To give people options?"

"Yes and no," Rain said, getting up from the table and walking toward the door without even glancing at what I'd written. He looked out through the windowpane. "Let me think about it. It's not as though my father is the person running things anymore. I don't know how much he could help us." I waited for him to mention Emory Specter, but he didn't, and once again I was relieved to avoid talking about the various members of my family. "And as much as I'd like for you to go back to the App World with me," Rain went on, "it would be *extremely* dangerous for you to cross the border. So if anyone goes, it will be me alone."

I got up and took a couple of steps toward him. "But

what if we didn't cross the border by plugging in? What if we—what if *I*—crossed it by shifting instead? Maybe if we circumvent the traditional methods we'd get through undetected."

Rain was shaking his head. "We don't know that it would work. Besides, shifting nearly killed you."

"That was a long time ago, now. I'm feeling so much better—"

"—Skylar, *no.*"

"But—"

"—no buts." Rain's eyes flashed. "You're not going to the App World by any means. End of story."

"You don't need to protect me. I can take care of—"

"—it's getting late," Rain cut in. "We should head back to Briarwood."

I shook my head. I hated when Rain got like this, when he thought he could control me or decide what I would and wouldn't do. "Fine," I snapped. "Let's just go."

He was turning the knob on the door and heading outside before I could say another word. But just before I joined him and before I could think better of it, I went to the table and lifted the bunch of daisies out of the vase and took them with me.

6

Ree

watery grave

THE APPS SWIRLED around me.

I took them in, one by one, contemplating all the things they promised to reveal to me, show me, make me. The tennis racket and its bouncing ball, entreating me to a game. The chocolate bonbons tempting me on a binge. The car inviting me to a race. There were the usual Fantasy Apps that would allow me to fly, to change my appearance in a million ways, both beautiful and strange, the Apps that would make me smarter, that would allow me to kiss the boy or girl of my dreams and a thousand other people I'd yet to meet and never would.

The Bedroom Redecorator App kept coming at me, jumping up and down in front of my right eye and then my left, probably because it knew I'd downloaded it or one of its cousins about a thousand times since being imprisoned in this apartment. I mean, what else was I going to do, cooped up in this place, my mind closed to everyone I'd ever known? My bedroom lately had resembled that of a medieval princess, an Arabian palace, and a Parisian bohemian in the 1920s. When I'd gotten bored of these styles, I'd transformed my room to copy Tonna Tomson's beach house. She was the celebrity Over Eighteen Char and I had been obsessed with since we were twelves. She became famous for never having downloaded an Appearance App in her life, making herself into a symbol of "natural virtual beauty" for an entire generation. I'd even made my bedroom look like something out of Loner Town for a change, shutting down each night on a bed tilted at an angle because it was missing a leg, and staring at my face in a shattered mirror each morning. I'd only changed things back to normal after my mother yelled at me about tripping every time she entered my room on the broken floorboard.

I swiped my hand across the atmosphere and the App Store disappeared.

I'd called it up at least a hundred times since yesterday, but no matter how many times I did, I couldn't get that ominous glittering icon to appear for me like it had for my mother. I'd watched footage on Reel Time over and over again, but there was nothing to suggest that this App had appeared to anyone else—and no evidence that it had happened to Char either. No warnings about viruses and untimely virtual deaths, no talk of unlawful imprisonments of citizens of the City by the government. The only blip among the gossipy celebrity news was occasional discussion of the terrible plight of the App World refugees who'd listened to Skylar Cruz and gone and unplugged themselves and now probably regretted going back to that horribly clunky real body.

And I should've gone with them, despite the tragedy of our floppy, fragile, original forms. Except that, for some unbelievable reason, the day of Skylar's emergency broadcast I chose to listen to my mother and stayed put as a virtual girl. Speaking of . . .

"Mom?" I called out.

There was shuffling in the hall. My door opened.

My mother's face was a horrible shade of pea green, a visible sign she'd overdone it again with the Cocktail Apps. I supposed this was part of the punishment for having an unlimited supply of any App you could ever want.

"What, Ree?" My mother's virtual voice was clipped and angry.

"Can you please not be perpetually annoyed with me?" I was so tired of her being nasty to me on a constant basis.

"I'm not annoyed," she replied, sounding absolutely annoyed and unwilling to hide this.

I took a deep breath. "Listen, I need you to, I don't know, like, find some lucidity for a minute, because we need to talk about something important. Okay?"

The pea-green color in her virtual cheeks only deepened as she pondered this proposition. But then, to my surprise, she was shuffling again, this time entering my room, stumbling only once on her way. She join me on the bed, which sent the two of us rocking and swaying like we were on a little boat floating across a stormy sea.

"What in the—" she cried, clutching her virtual stomach, her cheeks turning a shocking shade of gray-green this time.

"Sorry!" I placed a hand gently on her shoulder. "Try not to spill your code, Mom."

The bed eventually began to steady and she managed to hold things down.

"What did you do?" She glanced around the rest of my room.

I smiled a bit sheepishly. "I've reverted back to being a seven."

The bed was still bobbing, my mother's fists closed around the fabric covering the duvet, hanging on for dear life. Everything was a different shade of Mediterranean blue, except for the colorful fish that darted across the walls now and again and the sea grass that grew up from the floor, all of it coordinated to make a girl feel like she was living underneath the surface of the ocean. The Under the Sea App I'd downloaded promised to make my child-hood underwater dreams come true, and the bed itself was modeled after those old-timey ones they used to have in the Real World that made you feel like you were sleeping on water. Or, I don't know, sleeping on a boat, maybe? Back when I was a six and a seven, it was a super-popular App and everyone I knew was downloading it, except for me. I'd been really obsessed with Arabian horses and my bedroom was always decked out in a horse-related theme, and I was often sleeping on a mattress stuffed with hay, which meant I missed out on the water-bed craze. So I figured, why not now? Who cares if I'm a seventeen?

Also, I've been really bored.

"Remember how unhappy you were about the Loner Town theme? I redecorated my room, Mom, because you asked me to." I gestured at the walls right as a shark chased a smiling goldfish from one end of the wall to the other.

Given the sick grimace on my mother's face, she wasn't really appreciating the cuteness of my altered environ-ment. "Why was it you wanted to talk to me? What's the matter now?" From her tone, she clearly regretted giving me the time of day. This and she sounded exhausted.

"Well," I started, knowing that the sands in the hourglass were already running low. She was probably anxious to download her usual eleven a.m. Bloody Mary App, the extra-spicy version she preferred, and get going on her big day of liquoring herself up on the terrace and then passing out into shutdown. "I want to talk to you about something that happened yesterday." I hesitated. "Do you remember yesterday?"

"Of course I remember," she snapped.

"Of course," I agreed, though I wasn't convinced that she did. "Yesterday, when you called up your App Store, there was this App in it—it's quite beautiful, really, all glittery and so compelling. It was in the shape of a present? I was wondering if you did something to call it up. Like, where did you find it or how did you get it to appear for you?"

My mother's virtual brow furrowed. "I don't remember any glittery Apps."

I sighed. She didn't remember a thing from yesterday. "You were about to download it," I tried. "Your finger was nearly touching it when, um, suddenly you went into shutdown."

The color in my mother's cheeks became a horrible mottled red mixed with dark green, like one of those clunky-looking heirloom tomatoes Tonna Tomson was always downloading into her vegetable garden. My mother was blushing. She must be embarrassed about Apping until she was unconscious. "Ree, I really don't remember."

The bed bobbed us as gently as the sea on a calm summer's day. "Okay. But if you do see an App like that? I want you to call me right away. And most important of all"—I looked at her hard, so she could see I was serious—"you *cannot* touch—"

"—wait a minute!" The red began to fade from her cheeks and her eyes grew wide and clear for the first time since she'd entered my room. "I do remember. . . ."

"Mom, what? Think hard. It's important."

She began nodding, so forcefully the bed began to sway. "I remember . . . I remember a *beautiful* App, like nothing I'd ever seen before!" Her voice grew wistful, the look in her eyes far away and dreamy. "I remember wanting it so badly, I was thirsty for it. . . ." The look in her eyes turned dark and cold as she turned them on me. Two giant sharks hovered on the wall behind her. "And then you took it from me! You stole my most beautiful App!"

"Mom, I did not—"

"—what did you do with it? Where is it? Is it in *your* App Store now?"

"I swear, I didn't—"

"—I knew you were selfish, but really, Ree? We have an unlimited supply of downloads and you had to take what was mine for yourself?"

"But Mom," I pleaded. "That App, I think it's dangerous and I—"

"—stop lying to me," she seethed.

I shut my mouth. When she got like this, there was no use arguing.

My mother got up from the bed and a great wave

of blue-green duvet rolled toward me from the shift in weight. "If I ever catch you stealing from my App Store again we are going to have some serious problems. Do you understand me?"

I nodded.

"Are you *sure* you understand me?" she shouted.

"Yes," I barked.

She turned on her heel and stumbled, caught herself by poking her fingers into an unsuspecting sea anemone, and stomped out of my room. It was only after she'd slammed the door so hard that even the sharks fled that I finally managed to speak what I'd wanted her to understand so badly amid all her ranting.

"But I saved you."

I stayed in my room practically all day, floating listlessly on my bed with only the fish and the sharks and an occasional lobster crawling across the ocean floor to entertain me. I waited until I couldn't take it anymore, the confinement, the boredom, the frustration with my mother, before I decided to go out onto the terrace to try and talk to her again. To explain why I'd come between her and her precious App Store. I opened the sliding door and enjoyed the feel of the fresh atmosphere on my virtual skin. It was nice after being cooped up all day. At least the government didn't take our terrace away from us, too.

There was my mother, as usual, all the way in the

corner where one of the tallest trees from Main Park stretched its branches overhead, creating a nice shady place to relax. She was in her lounge chair, which had transformed itself into some sort of luxurious raft. The sound of water splashing rippled across everything. I guess she'd grown to like the water bed and was trying to duplicate the swaying of it. I didn't know you could download a lounge-chair version, though. Maybe they made them for adults?

Her App Store encircled her.

"There you are," she was cooing. "Finally!"

It took me a moment—one moment too long—to realize what was happening. The horrible, irreversible error my mother was about to commit out of stubbornness or rage or some combination of suspicion and insolence that I hope didn't get passed down into my virtual code.

"Mom, no!" I screamed.

It didn't matter what I did or what I said or why my mother chose to insist on doing what came next. And I was too far to knock her hand away, too late to stop her, and she was too angry to listen to any warning from me regardless. She heard my words—of that much I was absolutely certain, because she turned my way, a satisfied look in her eyes, a cold triumphant glare, really, and watched me straight on as she reached a long, crooked, heavily ringed finger out like some wicked witch.

Our eyes met right as she touched the poisoned App.

7

Skylar

emptiness

"I'M NOT ARGUING any more about this, Skylar!" Rain shouted.

"Stop yelling at me," I said, keeping my voice even. Rain and I had been up all night, sitting in my room, arguing. I'd decided that someone should go check on Adam in the App World. And privately, I was worried about what Trader had said about the virus. Rain was adamantly against anyone crossing the border, though. Especially me. To put it mildly.

"I wasn't yelling." He lowered his voice. "But there isn't anything you can say that will convince me this is a good idea. Not for you to go, or me either. Not yet, at least.

We need to gather a lot more information before we do anything that stupid."

"It's not stupid!" I was the one shouting now.

Rain stood up from the edge of my bed. His eyes blazed. "Skylar, yes it is. We have no idea what could be waiting for us on the other side."

"Adam is there and I'm worried about him!"

"It's too dangerous." Rain was shaking his head, looking at me like I was some child who didn't know anything. "Adam could be in virtual prison for all we know."

I huffed and glared. "Well, if you've been worried that Adam is in prison, then you're not a very good friend. We should have gone to find out if he's okay a long time ago."

Rain sighed. "If anyone is going to do *anything* in the App World, it's going to be me, not you, and it's only going to be after we get more information about the situation we'd be crossing into. Let me talk to Zeera and see what she can find out. We need to know where your sister is, exactly, and we need to make sure that Emory Specter hasn't laid a trap for any of us—me included. But you especially. I'm sure it's you he's after most."

"Don't talk about them," I whispered.

Rain threw up his hands. "Why not? We need to talk about Jude and Specter at some point. They're not exactly your biggest fans! You decimated their plans, and regardless of your sister, Emory Specter is the most powerful person in the App World right now. The exodus of those refugees made him even more powerful in the City. And I'm not telling you anything you don't know. The people who stayed behind were against us and grateful to him for the Cure. They could care less about the Real World and their bodies."

I got up from the bed and stood before Rain. "I don't care how powerful he is. I have to go to the App World and I have to do it soon."

He stared down at me. "You're being reckless and unreasonable."

"No. You're the one who's being unreasonable."

Rain's eyes narrowed. "What else is in the App World that you need to see so badly?" he asked. He was quiet a moment. "Does this have something to do with Kit?"

"No." Frustration and anger welled up again. Tears pricked the corner of my eyes. "And if you'd stop being so overly protective, then maybe I'd actually want to answer your question."

"You're impossible sometimes!"

"Well, I guess we have that in common then!" I stormed out the door, slamming it behind me before Rain and I could say anything else we might regret.

I went straight to see my mother. It didn't matter that it was early.

I knocked on her door.

I wanted her on my side about going back to the App World. If I got her on my side, then maybe she'd help me go on my own.

I waited and waited. There was no answer.

"Hi, Skylar."

I turned. Brandy, a fellow seventeen—well, now an Over Eighteen—was passing by in the hallway. "Hey, Brandy," I said, and tried to smile, despite the anger still churning in me from my fight with Rain.

Brandy was tall with beautiful skin, the same color as my Keeper's. She wore dreadlocks that came all the way to the middle of her back. She'd gathered them into a ponytail today. "I thought I saw your mother headed down to the plugs earlier."

"The plugs? Really?"

Brandy shrugged. "It seemed like that's where she was going. See you later," she added, before rounding the corner.

What would my mother be doing down there?

I knocked once more, just to be sure, and when there was still no answer I changed direction and headed downstairs. Soon I was entering the caverns, the sounds of the ocean tunneling into the rocks nearly constant. The plugs were powered by the water and the wind howling behind everything. The glow of glass coffins met my eyes, row after row. By now I was used to it, but still this place always sent a shiver over my skin.

"Mom," I called out, my voice echoing. "Hello?"

When there was no answer, I began walking through the rows, searching, but I couldn't find her, not even near Adam, who still seemed peaceful as he lay there, plugged in—something I was relieved to see. But then when I got to the far side of the caverns I saw her at the end of the row, so lost in thought she didn't realize someone was there.

"Mom?"

She jumped at the sound of my voice. She'd been stooped over one of the shiny glass boxes. Which was supposed to be empty.

But I could see that it wasn't.

Her eyes grew wide. "Skylar!" The surprise on her face was quickly erased, replaced by a smile. She hurried toward me, carefully placing her own body between the coffin and my line of sight. "How are you today, my darling?"

"I'm fine. Mom," I said, pronouncing each word slowly. "What's going on? What are you doing here?"

We stood there looking at each other. She was a few inches shorter than me, her real skin glowing the same golden color as mine even in the odd lighting of this place.

"It's good to see you." Her voice faltered. "You look upset," she said. Then she moved, just enough that I could see the coffin she'd been blocking, I could see *into* it, and even from here I could tell there was a body inside—a body I'd never seen before.

And something was wrong with it.

It was . . . off.

Off, as in, not quite settled into the cradle that was the plug.

My eyes flickered to my mother's. I pointed behind her. "What's wrong with that body you were looking at? Who is that?"

My mother moved a step, again placing herself between me and that one glass box. "It's nothing for you to worry about, Skylar. Why don't you go out for a swim? It's still nice weather for this time of year and you may not have too many more days like this before it gets colder!" There was false cheer in her voice, a fake casual tone that clearly required effort.

"What are you hiding?" I stepped aside to move past her but she stepped to match me and planted herself in front of me.

"Skylar, don't," she warned.

"Don't what? Do you really expect me not to go see what's going on?"

"Please," she begged, and pressed her hands into my shoulders.

"Mom," I began, "I've had enough lies and secrets to last me forever. I can't stand any more of them, especially if they're between us. And I'm tired of people trying to protect me." Gently, I lifted her hands off me and moved around her, but not before I visibly saw her posture slump, her glossy black ponytail falling forward along her cheek.

I went to the glass box.

Her footsteps trailed softly after me.

Inside the coffin was a teenage girl, maybe a fifteen or even younger, a fourteen or a thirteen. But she was no one I knew—no one from Briarwood, that was for certain. Freckles dotted her cheeks, her eyelashes were blond and long, and everything about her was normal for someone her age, perfect, really. Except . . .

Goose bumps covered my arms and legs.

The color of her skin . . . it was . . . I don't even know how to adequately describe it. There was a gray-green tinge to it, like the color of the Real World sky before a terrible thunderstorm. This, and she wasn't moving. Not at all.

Her chest was still.

"Mom, what's wrong with her? She's not breathing! We have to do something!"

"Skylar—"

I turned to her, my heart pounding wildly. "Do you know . . . CPR?" For that string of letters I had to reach all the way back to Mrs. Worthington's class, and the time she'd taught us of the "pathetic" and "sad" methods Real World citizens developed for fixing real bodies, whereas our virtual ones could be restored to perfection instantly, with the help of a quick download. "I don't know CPR, Mom—"

"—Sweetheart—"

"—I never learned it. . . ." My voice trailed off and a dreadful silence filled the space around us. My mother's face was stricken. "Is she . . ." I couldn't bring myself to say the word.

My mother said it for me. "Dead? Yes, Skylar. She's dead."

My mouth gaped. "She's too young! She's not even—"

"—a fourteen," my mother supplied.

"But why? Who is she? How did she even get here?" I dropped down to my knees and studied the girl's lifeless body. I knew, we *all* knew, the dangers of the real body, its weaknesses, its eternal fragility, its propensity for sickness and broken bones. It was one thing for someone elderly to die on the plugs, someone whose body had aged as long as a person can and whose organs, whose heart and lungs, simply gave out. Yet it was something else for a body this young to die. "She couldn't have been sick, because the glass seals out viruses and bacteria, purifying everything."

My mother remained silent. Even her breaths were quiet. Then she held out her hand. "Come with me, darling," she said as I let my fingers slide into hers. "Let's talk."

"About what?" I asked in a whisper. I let her pull me along until we came to a door in the farthest reaches of the cavern, a sliver of light shining out from underneath it. It was nearly obscured because of its placement behind one of the rows of boxes. I hadn't even known that it existed until now.

Beyond the door were more bodies.

Maybe twenty of them. Too many to count with a single glance. They were laid out in the glass coffins that held the plugs. Different ages, genders, skin colors, hair colors, facial features, so much beauty in the many forms a real body could take, forms and differences that would be erased by virtual reality, a feature of the App World I hadn't even understood until I'd unplugged, and one I'd grown to despise now that I had. The App World was a world of sameness, where people could only distinguish themselves via a download and one they must pay for. It was not a world I wanted to be a part of anymore, that much I knew.

But the bodies before me did have at least one thing in common.

They were dead. Clearly dead.

Not a single chest rose with the intake of breath.

Not a limb twitched with evidence of life.

Could this be because of the virus?

I took a step back, seeking the comfort of my mother's presence. "What is this room? Where did all these people come from?"

My mother hesitated before speaking. "It's a morgue."

"A morgue? That's a place where the dead are kept."

"Yes."

I turned to her, my brow furrowed tight, as a horrible thought took hold of me. "Was it the Shifting App that killed them?" I whispered. "Was it because of the trauma of it? Or trying to shift and then not making it? Is that it? You didn't want me to know that this little girl died because of me—because of what I downloaded into her brain. Is that what's going on here? You've been hiding the bodies that died all this time?"

My mother went to one of them. She peered down at a lifeless man, who was maybe her own age. His hair was graying at the temples. "No. It wasn't the Shifting App."

I studied her. "How can you be so sure?"

"I was a Keeper all my life and I just know things," she said, as if this was a real explanation. She glanced toward the far back wall and sighed. "This place is a morgue, Skylar, but it's also a lab."

I followed her gaze to a series of tall, long black tables, notebooks stacked high on one of them, and all sorts of instruments and metal things I didn't recognize. "What kind of lab?"

"My lab," she said simply.

"Your lab?" My voice went up an octave. "What are you talking about?"

She inhaled, a sharp hiss. "I was a special kind of Keeper. Before the worlds split, people would have called me a scientist—a scientist and a doctor. While you were plugged in, I studied medicine for many years." She beckoned me toward the table stacked with notebooks, patting her hand on one of the two stools that stood next to it and taking the other one for herself.

I climbed onto it. "You're a doctor. You have a lab. And you're just telling me this now?"

Guilt entered her eyes. Her arm stretched along the black top of the table, her hand placed firmly on one of the notebooks. "With everyone leaving for the App World, New Port City had an overabundance of bodies that needed care and a shortage of trained doctors who could diagnose and treat problems and illnesses, when they occurred. You can live virtually and happily as though all is well, while your body might be suffering in this world with, I don't know, cancer for example. It was probably about a year after you plugged in that there was a call for volunteers to attend medical school."

I stared at my mother. "And you volunteered."

"I did," she said. "As it turns out, I was good at the profession, and I loved it. It's one thing to care for the basic needs of a plugged-in body, but it was something else to care for the sick. To save someone's life."

My mind was stuck on one of my mother's words. "You're using the past tense. Why?"

My mother's eyes clouded over and shifted to the stack of notebooks where she'd placed her hand. "Everything changed because of Jude, and so much of it is my fault. I got so wrapped up in my work. That's how I missed seeing how obsessed she'd become with you, with the App World. When she founded the New Capitalist movement, I didn't realize where she meant to go with it, or maybe I just refused to see. I thought it was a phase, and then . . . it wasn't. By the time I realized what she was planning, things were beyond saving." She picked up one of the bound journals and opened it, its paper wavy with use. Then she turned to me, eyes unblinking. "This is something I've wanted to tell you for a long time, Skylar, but I've been ashamed. That's why I avoided telling you I was a doctor and about this lab. I've been coming here at night when you're asleep. But I suppose I couldn't keep it from you forever."

I bit my lip, afraid to hear what came next. Yet another terrible truth about my family, the terrible truths stacking up like layers of cake laced with poison. "What else aren't you telling me? Just say it. *All* of it."

"As you already know, your sister was—*is*—very good at threats. And she threatened you. Your life. At the beginning, I didn't know that the threats to you would never end." My mother took a deep breath. "But a few years ago, your sister made me come work for her on the project that would help her live up to the promises she made to Emory Specter."

I winced at the mention of his name.

"The promise," my mother went on, the words seeming to choke her, "was to figure out how to allow for virtual eternal life. To find a way App World citizens could be liberated from their bodies."

"That was *you*?" I asked. "*You* found the Cure?"

My mother shook her head. "Not just me, but me and a small team of scientists and doctors working together. But yes, we discovered what the App World refers to as the Cure. Please don't hate me," she added quickly. "You have to understand, your life was threatened, it was *always* under threat with your sister in charge, and I didn't feel like I had any other choice. I never dreamed you'd find out about her or me. I always thought you were living a happy virtual life, and that you'd forgotten all about the little family you left behind when you were small."

"I never forgot." I stared at my mother. "I wish you'd finally trust me enough to be honest. No one ever thinks I can handle anything." I shook my head. "I can't believe that all this time you've been keeping secrets and sneaking around behind my back." I slid off the stool. Pulled at the neck of my shirt. It felt difficult to breathe in here, like I might suffocate.

My mother gripped my arm to stop me from leaving. A tear ran down her face. "Skylar, it's not that I've thought you couldn't handle things. But *this* thing I have to carry myself. It's my legacy, and much of what's happened between our worlds is my fault, or at least partly."

I shook my head. "No it's not. It's Jude's fault. Jude's and Emory Specter's. You just got caught up in it."

"But I also went along with it," she said. "I didn't do anything to stop it. Not in a way that made a difference." My mother tilted her head and studied me. "You really had no idea about any of this?" she asked, sounding honestly surprised. "This place?"

"No," I said. "How could I have known if you didn't tell me?" I narrowed my eyes. "Unless someone else knew . . . *Mom*." This one syllable fell heavily. "Who else knows?" I yanked my arm from her grasp. She didn't even have to say his name. "Rain. Rain knew. He always knows everything and then he keeps it from me. Right?"

Two circles of red appeared on my mother's cheeks. "I asked him to keep it from you"—when I opened my mouth to protest, she got there first—"I made him promise. He wanted to tell you but I pleaded with him not to. He was only following my wishes. You were so wrapped up in what was happening with the Body Market, and I didn't want to become yet another one of your worries."

I took this in, trying to do the math. "Wait—he's known since before *February*? But that would mean . . ."

A look of horror came over my mother's face.

"He knew where you were." Anger flooded through me. "All that time we were preparing the Shifting App and he knew!" I thought back to the night when I caught Rain coming out of a room in that deserted part of the mansion—or I'd *thought* it was deserted—and how strange he'd been acting. That same night Lacy had cornered me and claimed she had something to tell me, something to show me that I'd definitely want to see, but as we were on our way out the door we'd run into Rain and she decided not to follow through. "It was you that Lacy wanted to show me that night," I whispered, more to myself than my mother.

"I don't know," my mother admitted. "Rain was protecting me. I've known about the deaths on the plugs for a long time, nearly a year—that's how I know that it wasn't the Shifting App that killed them—and I was worried I might be in danger from Jude because of this knowledge. But I still think you should be understanding with Rain. I put him in a terrible position."

"How I feel about Rain's decisions is between me and him."

"Skylar—"

"Mom, please!" My voice was rising again. "I don't want to talk anymore about Rain!"

She closed her mouth.

I'd wanted to find an ally in my mother after my fight

with Rain, but instead I'd found more lies and secrets and more fighting. And our conversation wasn't even over yet. I turned away from her to take in the scene of so many dead bodies again. "This has been happening for a year and you're just dealing with it now?"

"At first, it was just one death, and it seemed like a freak occurrence. Then it was one more, and eventually another. But it wasn't until the last few weeks that the deaths have begun to multiply more quickly."

I took this in. "How did these people even get in here?"

"They came in through friends I have connected to the Body Market," she said quietly.

I gaped at her. Sometimes it struck me hard how little I knew about my mother. *You have friends at the Body Market?* I wanted to ask. *Are you in touch with Jude, too?* was the next thing that popped into my head, but I held all of this back.

"These bodies were tossed into the trash once they were no longer saleable," she went on. "They died on the plugs, and dead bodies can't be used for parts, at least not for long. That's why they were dumped. A Keeper I know brought them to me so I could try and find out what happened."

There was a time when such statements would have knocked the wind out of me—bodies thrown out, used for parts, dumped in the trash—but I'd grown used to hearing ugly ideas thrown around like nothing. I did my best to stay focused on the matter at hand. "And . . . so? What do you know?"

"Not much yet, unfortunately." My mother slid off the stool where she'd been sitting. She led me to the glass boxes, each one set out in its own place on the floor. "You can see that whatever killed them has done so regardless of age and gender." She stopped before a little boy. He couldn't be more than a five.

I stared down at him, at his tender, perfect skin the color of milky coffee, his eyes closed as though he were sleeping peacefully.

My mother began to walk again among the bodies, pausing before an old woman, her hair completely gray yet her skin still smooth for someone her age, the same golden color as mine and my mother's. "What I do know is that the deaths aren't from natural causes. It's not the body that's failing, or it doesn't seem to be. I have some theories, but they're still very unformed. I need to do more tests before I'll know anything even close to concrete."

I tried to take this in. "Are you worried, I don't know, that *all* the plugged-in bodies might die?"

My mother's gaze moved on to a woman with red hair. Her eyes were closed, her head tilted toward the ceiling, chest unmoving like all the others. "Not yet," she said. "As of now, we're still dealing with a tiny percentage of plugged-in bodies. Not enough that I would advise we pull everyone off the plugs. That would create such chaos . . .

I can't even imagine the repercussion of such a statement to the public." She shook her head. "What we need first is more information."

My skin grew cold. I shivered as another possibility began to take shape in my mind. "Mom," I began, bracing myself for the words I was about to speak. "Could it be . . . do you think . . . is it possible that a *virus* might have caused these deaths?"

She looked at me, startled. "I'm not sure. I hadn't even thought of that." She went on to say something else that sent more chills across my skin. "But whatever it is, Skylar, it's coming from the App World."

8

Skylar

breaking and entering

I TOOK THE car without telling Rain, but driving wasn't
enough to distract me from everything going through my
mind. This morning was becoming more and more demor-
alizing by the minute. It was even clearer now that we
needed to go back to the App World to find out what was
happening there, and whether it would ever be safe for
the refugees who wanted to plug back in. The blood raced
in my veins as urgently as the situation, my foot pressing harder on the gas. My mother and Rain kept claiming
they did what they did to protect me, yet all that so-called
protection only made me feel more alone.

But maybe I didn't have to be alone in this.

I turned the wheel on the long, winding road that

circled the remotest parts of the island, then headed over the bridge. The breeze from the open window washed over my face. The waves were rough on my left, sending spray high into the air when they crashed onto the rocks. My skin was salty with it. Clouds covered the sun by the time I was close to my destination.

The cottage appeared on the horizon.

I saw the familiar tree on the hill in front of it. The roof, weathered from the salt in the air. The shingles, faded and graying. The last time I was here, snow covered every surface and it was winter. Today the grass was lush and tall and speckled with flowers, that single tree bursting with bright-green leaves. A wall of cattails swayed in the wind as it got stronger. My eyes scanned everything but didn't find what they were seeking.

Kit's bike wasn't anywhere.

My heart sank.

I drove up the hill regardless, parked the car, and got out, searching for the spare key. Kit kept it in a tiny tin, hidden against the house at the base of the staircase. For a moment I worried it was gone, but eventually my fingers hit the thin metal side of the container in the dirt. I pulled it out and found the jagged key wedged inside. I fitted it into the lock and turned it. The bolt clicked. My hand grasped the knob, ready, but then stopped.

A sharp pain sliced through my chest.

Maybe this was a terrible idea. Kit wanted me to

forgive him. But could I ever really trust him again? I closed my eyes. I wouldn't know until I tried. I took a deep breath and opened the door.

There came a surprised yelp. A startled girl sat on the battered old couch where I'd spent so much of my time. The two of us stared at each other. I took in her long blond hair and pretty face.

"Maggie?" I said, right at the same time she spoke.

"Skylar?"

Finding Maggie was not what I was expecting, but for some reason it made me feel encouraged. I had questions about her brother. Maybe she could answer some of them. "You know who I am."

She got up from the couch. We were nearly the same height. Aside from her eyes, she looked nothing like Kit. "Of course I know who you are. I've known about you for ages. I was kidnapped by your horrible witch of a sister, for one, and then my brother is in love with you and won't forgive me for coming between you—his words, not mine," she added, blinking quickly.

My heart tumbled against the inside of my rib cage. "Kit will forgive you eventually. He loves you too much not to."

Maggie laughed. "So here we are, each informing the other about my brother's love?" She opened the door wider. "He's not here, obviously. But why don't you stop standing on the steps and come inside. I'll make us something to eat." She turned on her heel and crossed the room into the kitchen.

And I allowed myself to enter the familiar space.

The faucet ran with water and a pot thumped onto the counter as Maggie began to cook. I kept my back to Kit's room. It was odd to be in this place without him, to see someone else moving around the kitchen. My eyes landed on the wood stove, the spot that drew Kit and me together, that sparked the conversations and all the drinking and huddling together for warmth that changed everything about our relationship, that allowed us to somehow move beyond what began as a kidnapping and turned into something very, very different. Flashes of memory lit up my mind, one after the other. The wound on Kit's shoulder. Kit filling my glass with whiskey. Refilling it and then refilling his own. Inked stars on skin and birds in flight. A shared blanket. A promise. More talk and then more talk. The stove was empty and cold now. It sat there heavy and silent and neglected. I was grateful I'd chosen a time to visit when the weather was still warm. I don't think I could have handled staying in this cottage a single minute had that stove been burning hot when I walked through the door.

"Skylar, come eat." Maggie waved me toward the table where lunch had magically appeared.

I pulled out a chair, the same one where I'd sat dozens of times, and joined her. She piled pasta into a bowl and slid it toward me, then grated cheese over everything. "My brother taught me to make this dish."

"He made it for me, too," I said quietly.

"He's so predictable."

My eyebrows arched. "Is he?"

She banged the hunk of cheese against the grater until the last of it fell into the dish, then went to work grating some over her own bowl. "Yes. A creature of habit. Except lately."

"What sorts of habits?" I asked.

"What he eats. What he drinks." Maggie popped up from her chair and darted into Kit's room, coming back with one of the bottles from under his bed. She set it onto the table and grinned. "Want some?"

I shook my head slowly. "No, thank you. Too early."

Too many memories.

She shrugged and poured some for herself. "Let's see," she went on. "My brother's habits include riding that god-forsaken bike, even in winter. I already mentioned what he drinks." She paused a moment, to take a sip from her own glass, her face twisting as she swallowed it. "But I didn't yet mention his propensity to drink too much."

I picked up my fork and dug around in the bowl, listening as she continued down the list of ways Kit was predictable.

"My brother is a loner, he's a neat freak, and he always gets his work done so he can earn his money." Maggie let this last statement hang in the air.

I shoveled some pasta in my mouth and focused on chewing.

Maggie stared at her lunch. "The one thing that I never would have guessed he'd do"—her eyes flickered upward then and settled on me—"is fall for someone he met on the job. My brother has made it a habit to never fall in love. Until you." Her eyes returned to the contents of her bowl. She began to eat in huge gulps of pasta.

I put my fork down. "That's the second time you've mentioned your brother's love for me."

She kept on eating. "You don't believe that it's true," she said between bites.

I kept my gaze steady. "He betrayed me."

Maggie shook her head. "He never meant to, or at least, never wanted to. He was in an impossible position and knew I was the more vulnerable person. He couldn't allow me to die and he had faith that you'd be able to take care of yourself." She paused a moment. "My brother thinks the world of you. It's nice to finally meet you in person. You're going to have to forgive him eventually. He's a rather morose character in general, but lately he's worse. You can't allow him to mope forever. And if you forgive him maybe he'll finally get over my part in everything."

I swallowed a bite of pasta. It felt thick going down my throat. "Did Kit tell you he was in love with me? Did he just come out and say it?" The hope I heard in my own voice made my cheeks flush red.

"No," she replied slowly.

"Then why are you so sure?"

"Because of the tattoo."

This didn't make any sense to me. "Which tattoo? The stars or the birds?"

Maggie leaned forward in her chair. "Skylar, not those tattoos. Kit got a *new* tattoo. I inked it for him, just like the others. The new tattoo is about you. The moment he described what he wanted I knew my brother loved you."

"So what was it then?" I asked.

Maggie shook her head. "That's not for me to say. It's for Kit to show you."

My fork clattered against the bowl. "You're really not going to tell me?"

"No," she said.

My lips pressed together in a tight line. Then I sighed. "All right. I'll wait for Kit to show me."

She smiled with satisfaction.

I pushed the pasta around in my bowl, any hunger I'd felt evaporating. "But I have a question for you. About your captivity with . . . my sister," I added, a bit hesitant. I took Maggie's silence as permission to continue. "Did she . . . do anything to you? I mean, did she hurt you?"

Maggie shook her head, her mouth still full. She swallowed. "Luckily no, but she told me plenty."

"About me?"

She cocked her head. "A little. But mainly she had opinions about *me*. How I'd betrayed my brother just like she'd betrayed you. And you'd betrayed her." Her eyes widened.

I laughed hard, nearly spitting food from my mouth. "I betrayed *her*?"

"Well, you did poke out her eye. With a knife." Maggie's tone was almost admiring. "I'm not judging. She deserved it." Her stare became imploring. "But even the worst things a sibling can do deserve forgiveness, don't they? We all can't hate each other forever."

"We're talking about Kit again," I said.

She nodded. "I didn't take out one of his eyes, but what I did was far worse."

"What did you do, exactly?" I asked.

"I broke his heart by plugging in and leaving him here. Alone."

"Oh, *that*," I said, since I'd already known this.

Her cheeks flushed red, so red the color nearly blended with her freckles. "You don't sound surprised. He told you?"

"He told me something like it, yes," I admitted.

"And then you came along and fixed up his heart. Until he went and screwed everything up because of me again." She sounded anguished.

"Don't be so hard on yourself," I said. "The divide in our worlds hurts families and breaks hearts. It's a cruel situation and we're all caught in the middle of it."

"Then why is it so difficult for us to forgive each other's mistakes?" Maggie's earnest eyes blinked wide.

I played with my fork. Pressed my fingers against the edges of the tines. "That's a good question."

"I've been trying to convince my brother that he should forgive me, pleading with him. But he never will. Not until *you* forgive him," she added in a whisper.

Thunder rumbled outside. The more we talked about Kit, the more I wanted to see him. "Do you know when he'll be back?"

"No," she said. "He hasn't been here in days."

This information was like a punch in my gut. "Where is he then?"

Maggie gave her shoulders one long shrug. "Honestly, Skylar, I have no idea."

My entire body slumped. Maybe I would have to face everything ahead of me alone after all. Even without Kit. "You mean, you haven't seen him?"

She got up and took her empty bowl to the sink. With her back still toward me, she spoke. "He doesn't like staying in this house anymore. He said the memories are too painful."

Tears sprung to my eyes. I blinked them back. "Okay. I guess I should go then," I said, my voice hoarse. "I'm glad we met," I added.

"Me, too." She turned around. Leaned against the counter behind her. "You don't have to go yet, you know. And you're welcome anytime. Regardless of where Kit is."

I looked away. Got up and crossed the room quickly, unable to get out of the cottage fast enough. She followed me to the door. "Thank you for lunch," I told her, opening it.

Lightning flashed over the ocean, bright and jagged.

"You should stay longer, Skylar," Maggie urged.

I looked left, my eyes landing on that lone majestic tree in the yard. "It's going to storm." The sky rumbled again right then, long and low. A fat drop of rain splatted against the ground.

Maggie took a few more steps toward me, ignoring that it was about to pour. "If I see him, should I tell him you stopped by?"

My heart pounded so hard it made me dizzy. "Yes. Tell him . . . tell him I really need him right now," I said, then I crossed the rest of the distance to the car and got inside right as the skies opened up.

The rain running down the windshield blurred the figure of Maggie, standing in the yard, still waiting for me to change my mind and decide to stay.

By the time I arrived at Briarwood it was pouring.

And Rain was looking for me.

Everyone I met in the hall told me this as I passed, but I had no desire to see him after this morning. Instead, I went straight to Zeera's. She shared a small apartment with Sylvia, and it looked out onto the beach like mine. She didn't spend much time in the weapons room anymore because she hadn't needed to. She joked lately about how she was on vacation.

And I was about to ask her if she'd consider going back to work.

My knocks on their door were loud in the quiet.

Sylvia opened it. "Hi, Skylar," she said and smiled.

I still hadn't gotten used to having her at the mansion, safe and real. "Hi," I said, and the two of us hugged. Sylvia was tiny, spritely, even, as though she'd permanently downloaded the Tinkerbell App and was only missing the transparent fluttering wings and a sparkly wand. She was small but strong, her muscles compact to fit her body. Her hair was black and thick with tight curls. "Where's Zeera? Is she here?"

Sylvia rolled her eyes. "Yes, but of course she's playing on her tablet. She's out on the terrace under the awning. She likes the sound of the rain. Let's go disrupt whatever she's doing." She grinned. "Maybe she'll actually look up from that thing now that we have a guest."

I followed Sylvia through their room. It was strewn with clothes on every surface. The bed was unmade, one of the sheets tugged to one side and two pillows sitting on the floor.

Sylvia glanced at me before opening the screen door. "You know Rain—"

"—is looking for me, yes."

She studied me. "Okay, I won't ask what that's about."

"And I appreciate that," I said.

We went outside on the deck. The rain came down hard, but the awning from the house protected us. Sylvia and I went and stood next to Zeera, but she didn't seem to realize we were there. A tablet the size of a razor-thin notebook was in her lap and she cupped her hands around the screen to block the light, even though the sky was dark from the storm. Zeera wasn't the only person at Briarwood who'd become obsessed with her tablet. Plenty of others were glued to theirs constantly. I tried not to let it bother me, or let it remind me that this sort of behavior was one of the main reasons our worlds split in the first place.

Sylvia nudged Zeera with her foot.

She still didn't look up.

Sylvia pulled her own tiny tablet from her pocket and looked at me. "Maybe if I message her she'll respond?" Then she seemed to change her mind and put the tablet away. Bent down and took Zeera's face into her hands to give her a kiss.

Zeera smiled up at her, as though she'd just awoken from a trance. "Hi," she said. She looked at me. "Skylar," she said with surprise. She really hadn't noticed the two of us had been standing there.

I went to the small wicker couch next to Zeera's chair and sat, and Sylvia plopped down next to me. Zeera's eyes had already wandered back to her tablet.

"Don't be rude," Sylvia said.

She didn't even look up. "Skylar knows me and she knows I'm not being rude."

Sylvia gestured at Zeera. "Well, *I* think you're being rude."

Zeera set the tablet on a small table next to her chair and crossed her arms. "Fine. I am now giving you my full attention." Zeera looked at me expectantly. "What's up?"

Lightning flashed, lighting up everything on the terrace. "I need your help." I hesitated. "The kind that requires you to go back into the weapons room."

But Zeera was nodding. "I'm already aware of the situation."

"What?" I said, startled.

She leaned forward in her chair. "Rain was here earlier. He told me everything. I'm going to see what information I can get about who's watching the border, if there's a safe place to cross over into the App World. What's going on with Jude. All of it. I know you don't want Rain stepping into danger unprepared."

"It won't only be Rain," I said forcefully. "I'm planning on plugging in, too."

She shook her head. "Rain says you're absolutely not to do that."

I stood. "Rain's not in charge of me."

Sylvia reached up to put her hand on my arm. "Skylar—"

I stepped away, no longer protected by the awning, still staring Zeera. Water began to slide across my skin. "Do you agree with him?" I asked her.

Zeera pursed her lips. Thunder rumbled overhead and lightning flashed in the sky. The pounding of the rain picked up and it slapped the deck hard and loud and incessantly. Little droplets leapt into the air, wetting our feet. The left side of my body was getting soaked.

I looked from Zeera to Sylvia to Zeera again. The answer was plain in their eyes, and I hated it. "I thought you were *my* friends, too."

"We are!" Sylvia urged.

I zeroed in on Zeera. "I thought you would help me."

"I plan on it. I'm going to. But I think Rain's right. The App World is too dangerous."

I shook my head. I really was alone. More than ever. I made my way around the setup of chairs on the terrace, my skin slick with water. I couldn't get out fast enough.

"Skylar, don't leave," Sylvia was saying.

But I didn't respond. I didn't want to speak. I was

afraid I'd say something I'd later regret. Instead, I opened the screen door and disappeared inside the mansion again, leaving them with only their tablets and the thunder and lightning and the incessant sound of the rain for company.

9

Ree

hello?

I DIDN'T KNOW how much time had passed since my mother, well . . .

The sound of her screams still pierced my ears. It was worse than with Char. I wished I could erase the memory. Go back to the days of being one among the many popular girls at High School 4.0, my social success due to my sarcastic wit and not how my basic self took to various Appearance Apps. I had more important things to do than waste time exaggerating my looks.

Char never understood that about me.

Neither had my mother.

My code skidded with guilt. Even though we didn't get along, I've felt sad, tragic, even, about her absence. I've missed her more than I ever thought I would. Virtual tears kept running down my face. It frightened me, being without her, alone and trapped in this apartment.

A lion blinked at me from my wall. Its mouth yawned wide and a great roar filled my room. The safari theme I'd downloaded last night turned out to be loud and not at all soothing like the sounds of the ocean or the breeze running through the trees of the other Interior Decorator Apps. Besides, how long could a girl really tolerate sleeping in a flimsy tent? The App totally promised a "High-End Glamping Experience," but the simulation of mosquitos buzzing during the night went a bit too far for my taste.

I went out onto the terrace.

Perfect virtual weather again today. How shocking.

I rolled my eyes.

At nobody.

My mother's lounge chair sat empty, taunting me. It had deflated, the App she'd used to turn it into a bobbing raft-like bed long drained away.

I cupped my hands over my mouth. "Hello," I called out to the App World. I looked up at the terrace above ours, where I could see our neighbor. He was leaning over the railing and staring straight at me. I wished I'd bothered to go upstairs to introduce myself back when I could, but it's not like people ever cared to do that around here. He was actually a very good-looking Over Eighteen. More than once I'd fantasized about him rescuing me from this hellhole, leaping over the edge of his terrace onto mine, riding a gleaming white Arabian stallion, dressed as a medieval knight like in that game I used to play based on that story, you know, the one with the rock and a sword stuck in it?

"Hello!" I shouted at him again. "Hello?" I screamed.

His eyes were certainly on me, but he obviously couldn't see me. He blankly watched the floor of the terrace like I wasn't standing there at all.

So much for my knight-in-shiny-armor fantasy.

Or was it *shining* armor?

"Gahhhh!!!!" I yelled. Even the right words failed me. "You can't hear anything I say, right? Right? Right!" I shouted at the boy. "Because by the way, I think you're, like, really, really, *really* hot even without any downloads! If you could hear me right now, I'd actually introduce myself and invite you over to be my Boyfriend 12.5! And do you know how many people at my High School 4.0 would have wished for an invitation like that? You should feel impressed with yourself, honestly!"

Eventually, he went back inside his family's apartment, totally unaware that he had an exceptional girl admirer one floor down.

I sighed. Looked around some more.

In the next terrace over, our other neighbors, a couple, were outside downloading decorative plants. I'd never met them either. It's not like my mother and I ever needed anything from them, like in the olden Real World days when people supposedly would go to each other's houses to ask for, I don't know, a vat of sugar. Apps provided for everyone's needs, so there was no point in getting to know the people around you. "Yoo-hoo," I called out to them. "You both should know that your basic selves are, like, way better looking than those weird Alien Apps you think make you look more interesting!"

For the rest of the morning I kept shouting things at people I could see on the nearby terraces. When that got boring, I lay down on the floor, staring up at the Sunlight 8.0, which was a pretty pale yellow. And when I eventually got sick of lying there sky-gazing, I practiced walking on the terrace railing, which I was getting pretty good at, since being a prisoner in your own home can make you get good at lots of things. When *that* got boring, I hopped down and actually sat on my mother's deflated and sad lounge chair, studying my toes.

Which totally needed a Manicure App.

The last one I downloaded had nearly faded and my nails had only these sad little turquoise chips of polish left.

But then, why would I even care about my appearance?

Not only couldn't I leave, not only was my mind-chat permanently out of order, but absolutely no one could hear or see me. I could cover myself in dirt and leaves! I could yammer on all day, telling people what I really thought of them, confessing my most embarrassing secrets to everyone in the vicinity, to no avail! The government seriously thought of everything when they shut my mother and me away in our luxury apartment.

Well . . . except . . . maybe . . .

Last night, the buzzing of the mosquitos around my tent and the pitter-patter of elephant feet tramping around outside got so loud they'd pulled me out of shutdown. I'd been groggy, listening to the incessant scream of various flying bugs. Hearing them was frightening, but I was still too sleepy to put an early end to the safari download and call up a more peaceful scenario. For some reason I'd started to think about how I hadn't gamed in a while and how much I used to love my Atari Old School Adventurer App and the way it made my arms and legs look like boxy squares that jerked awkwardly.

That's when an idea had occurred to me!

I'd nearly forgotten it until now.

With a quick double-clap of my virtual hands I called up my App Store.

At first it swarmed with Interior Decorator Apps, since I'd been in a redecorating phase. I chased those away with a few angry swipes, until the ones I was looking for began to emerge from the dark, forgotten recesses of my Store. They were skittish. The way they played hard to get, hovering just out of reach, their icons giving me sad faces, almost made me feel guilty for ignoring them for so long.

I studied the Apps, trying to decide which one to try first.

The icon for Safari Adventure eyed me shyly, but I shook my head and it darted away. I'd heard enough lions roaring and animals stampeding through the jungle to keep me for a few lifetimes. If I didn't find a way out of this apartment soon I was going to go crazy and end up like some sort of weird virtual Miss Havisham, like in that novel I'd had to download to my brain once for Retro American Literature.

Hmmmm.

What about Moon Jumper?

Or Space Racer?

The Game of Facebook: The Beat-All-Your-Friends Popularity Contest?

Queen Bee or Queen Bitch: High School Popularity Contest?

The Bachelor, Under Eighteen, 49.0 Edition?

Real World Perils 75: Dystopian Terror?

All of these were Social Games, with multiplayer platforms. There were so many to choose from—Worldpocalypse 99.0, and Pandemic: The End of America, and Queen of the App World. The list went on and on. There were games for playing house, games for racing, games of Olympic competition, games of virtual world domination, and tons of games to compete to see who was the most successful, the most beautiful, the most amazing among all the people you know.

How had I not thought of these games before?

I couldn't get beyond the hall outside my apartment, leap from the terrace, or get anyone in my vicinity to hear or notice me. But would the same restrictions be applied *within* the parameters of a download? What if I entered a game and saw someone else? Would they be able to see me and interact like they should if the game was working properly? And if so, could I finally find a way out of this endless era of domestic discontent?

I reached for the Gaming App I'd settled on, the icon shivering and shaking way, way out in the farthest reaches of my Store. As though it didn't want me near it. As though it wasn't supposed to be there at all.

"Hello," I said sweetly as it leapt even farther afield. "You're going to help me break a few government rules, aren't you now?" I tried to coax it closer. Was it actually avoiding me or was I imagining this? "Did somebody tell you not to let me download you, hmm?"

Or maybe the problem was simpler. Maybe its feelings were hurt. Apps were known to be emotionally unpredictable and prone to pouting. They were coded to provoke guilt in their users and to toy with our emotions so we'd put more and more capital into them.

"Here, kitty, kitty! Don't be scared," I said, my spirit

fingers waving at it like I'd downloaded one of those annoying Cheerleading Apps that Char and I used to be obsessed with when we were tens. "Come to Ree!"

The icon with its mug, bubbling over with beer, crept a little closer.

"That's it!" I coaxed. "Come here! I won't bite!"

The second it was within reach my arms shot out, hands closing over it, trapping it like a bug in a jar. Or a virtual girl in a virtual City at the center of a virtual world.

"Gotcha," I said, and for the first time in a long, long while, I smiled.

10

Skylar

unlikely allies

"I NEED YOUR help," I said.

Lacy's back was to me, her fiery copper hair grown so long it reached the middle of her back. She was getting food in the cafeteria. "You've got to be kidding me." She didn't turn around. She gripped the sides of the tray, nails glittering green like always, clicking against the plastic. "You have *not* come to me asking for help. I am *certain* I just misheard you."

I walked around to her other side so she had to look at me. Lacy might seem like the last person I should go to for anything, but I had a feeling she would come around. I'd thought about going to Trader, but he'd grown protective of me too, lately, and I worried he would say no and tell

Rain about my plan. Besides, I knew what would interest Lacy about what I wanted to do. "Lacy, no, you didn't misunderstand. I know that you and I aren't friends—"

"—have *never been* friends nor *ever will be* friends," she spat, her eyes as fiery as her hair. "You stole my boyfriend."

I breathed slowly. I didn't want to fight. "Whatever happened between you and Rain is about Rain, not me."

Her eyes narrowed to slits. "That's a lie and you know it. The least you can do is be honest about the facts. You owe me that much. And the facts are this: with Rain, it's *always* about you. It's been about you for over a year, and if you haven't figured this out then you are stupider than even *I* ever realized."

I considered her words. "I don't know why Rain is so focused on me."

She laughed, short and loud. "Well, there's something we agree on." She took off toward the tables, all of them empty at this late hour of the afternoon. "Why are you here?" she called back. "Just tell me."

I joined Lacy at her table. "There's something going on in the App World and I'm going to—" I stopped, my next word hovering there, right on the tip of my tongue, and yet I hesitated to say it. Why I was here, what I was planning to do, why I needed Lacy's help to do it.

Shift.

I wanted to shift. I hadn't done it, not once, since the

Body Market. I hadn't wanted to, *didn't* want to, really ever again. Because there was so much in the App World I never wanted to deal with. Because of the dangers in crossing the border and the toll it had taken on my body and my brain. But there were things I needed to know— that *someone* needed to find out. And if I had to go alone, I'd go alone. Shifting wasn't the ideal option, but it seemed like the best one to avoid detection.

Besides, *Adam* was in the App World.

What if something had happened to him? What if he was in trouble?

I'd never forgive myself. And Parvda would never recover if she lost him. She'd never get over not plugging in to go and find him.

Lacy picked at the food on her tray. "What, Skylar," Lacy said, growing impatient. "What are you going to do? Spit it out, please. I haven't got all day."

"I've decided to shift. To the App World," I blurted, as if there was any other place where I might shift.

"Of course you have." Lacy rolled her pale-green eyes. She pushed her tray away, then crossed her arms and studied me. "But why would you need *my* help? You can shift all by your unattractive, lonesome self. That's how you got to act all heroic before, remember? Why everybody was so impressed with you." She sounded honestly unable to wrap her red head around this.

"I need someone to monitor my vitals when I shift.

And . . . I need you to run interference if anyone comes looking for me," I added.

"Like who—Rain?" The words dropped from her like acid.

I remembered to breathe. "I figured you would be glad to have the chance to talk to him while I'm not around. You know you're dying for it," I said, before I could think better of it.

Lacy's face flashed. "You're such a—"

I put up my hands to signal for peace. "I'm sorry," I said, before she could start name-calling. Lacy closed her mouth tightly. "I shouldn't have said that. I came here for your help, not to fight or go over old grievances."

"What's an old grievance to you is still a new grievance to me," she whispered. I could hear the hurt in it.

"You're right," I agreed. "And I'm sorry for that, too."

Maybe this was a bad idea—no, a *terrible* idea, to come to Lacy for help. The anger between us was so raw, our history fraught from the beginning. Lacy once had all the power while I had none, and then, after we got here, that power shifted from her to me. Sometimes I wondered why she was still here, why she hadn't risked returning to her lavish life with her richer-than-rich family in the App World. But of course I knew why. It was because of Rain. Everything she did was always because of him.

As I looked at her now I saw something else in her eyes—something other than anger. The pain in them was real and it was deep. I'd seen glimpses of this same Lacy here and there, even in the App World, when I'd watched clips of her childhood that revealed the many ways that her parents had failed her, abandoned her, really. When I saw evidence of *this* Lacy, the Lacy that Rain and Zeera were always trying to convince me was there, I sometimes wished we could be friends. Or had hope that someday maybe we'd find our way there.

So, despite everything, I decided to trust her. "Listen, is there any way the two of us can start over?"

Lacy laughed. She pulled her tray closer again and began to eat the chips next to her sandwich. "No. Way," she said, as they crunched in her mouth. "Not gonna happen. Like, *ever.*"

"Okay." It was time to admit defeat. "This was a bad idea. Forget I came here at all," I got up from the table. I was already heading toward the door of the cafeteria when Lacy spoke.

"Wait," she called out to me. "Skylar, wait! Please."

I halted.

"I'm willing to help you," she went on, "to monitor your vitals while you shift, run interference with whoever comes looking for you. . . ." She trailed off.

"If?" I supplied, turning to face her.

"I'll help you if . . ." She closed her eyes, wincing a bit. "If while you're plugged in, you really wouldn't mind if I talked to Rain. For real."

Lacy's eyes stayed closed. Her cheeks flamed as red as her other features. She was embarrassed to say all of this.

I tried to consider what Lacy wanted. There was a part of me that already knew she might be willing to help me shift for exactly the reason I'd spat out earlier—to get me out of the way for a while so she could corner Rain when I wasn't around. It wasn't as though she had to babysit me the entire time I was in the App World—just check on me now and then. But it was one thing for Lacy to take advantage of me being gone, and another for me to expressly agree to her doing just this.

Could I do something like that?

There was no doubt in my mind that I'd been uncertain about Rain ever since we'd gotten together in February. But did I *really* want to risk whatever it was that we had by allowing Lacy to step in like that? Because while I knew my feelings for him were complicated, I also had little doubt that his feelings for Lacy were complicated as well—complicated enough that he might end up choosing her in the end.

Lacy's lashes fluttered open. Her eyes had pooled with tears.

"Okay," I found myself agreeing. "In exchange for helping me, you can go . . . be with Rain. Talk to him about whatever you want, without me in the way."

She breathed in and out, in and out, and eventually the fire in her skin paled. "You need to realize that my intentions aren't just friendly. I love Rain. And I think he loves me back. Sometimes. Or at least, he used to. I need to know if things are over forever and I should move on . . . or if there's something still between us. If I should have hope." Lacy wilted, right before my eyes, all the venom and fight going out of her. "And I don't want to do this behind your back. I'm tired of us fighting over him. I'm tired of him choosing you over me. If he and I are going to be together again one day, I want it to be because *I'm* the girl he wants. Not because I stole him back from you with lies." She rolled her eyes, but more at herself than at me. "I can't believe I'm telling you these things. Or even that I'm saying them out loud."

"I appreciate your honesty," I said quickly, before she could feel worse for making herself so vulnerable, to me of all people. I had to give Lacy credit. "It took a lot of . . . courage to tell me all that."

She was staring at the ceiling, unwilling to look at me. "But?" she prompted.

"No buts," I replied. "I told you. The answer is yes."

"Yes?"

"Yes," I confirmed.

"Just yes? No conditions? No, 'Yes, but Lacy, you aren't allowed to kiss my boyfriend while I'm virtually cavorting around the App World'?"

I nodded. "Yes. No conditions."

Lacy stopped staring at the ceiling and returned her

eyes to me. "You wouldn't care if I tried to kiss Rain?"

I thought about this. I wanted to answer as honestly as I could since Lacy had been so honest with me. I owed her that much. "I *would* care. Of course I'd care. It would make me jealous," I told her, which was true. Despite our fighting and despite how controlling Rain could be and the way he was always trying to protect me when I didn't want him to. "But you're right. Rain has gone back and forth between the two of us long enough. If he still has feelings for you and wants to be with you, then he should. And you should kiss him. I won't get in the way. Not now, not during my shift, and not afterward when I wake up again."

She blinked at me, like she couldn't believe what I'd just told her. "Okay, then. We have a deal."

I put out my hand. "Good," I said, hoping with all my might that I wouldn't live to regret this.

Lacy placed her fingers into my palm, everything about them thin and delicate. Her lips parted. "Thank you," she said, with a sincerity I'd never detected in all the time we'd known each other.

Maybe this would truly be the beginning of a new chapter in our relationship.

A good chapter.

I could only hope.

11

Ree

nice to meet you

THE HOUSE WAS shaking with music.

Seriously shaking. Like there was an earthquake underneath us, rumbling through the ground. People were screaming downstairs, followed by the sound of something smashing against the wall, then more shouting and a lot of laughter. People were whooping it up.

I was in someone's bedroom, luckily a someone who wasn't here right now sleeping or doing something else unseemly. Then again, I didn't come here to hide. I came here to see and be seen, emphasis on the *be seen* part. This place could use a download of one of my Interior Decorator Apps, though. The bed was so narrow a person could barely shutdown comfortably in it, not to mention the mustard-yellow color of the duvet cover. Mustard yellow? *Really?* Vomit would be more attractive. Never mind the posters of Old Edition, the retro boy band that was popular in the City when I was, like, a nine. There was a mirror on the wall and I went to take a look.

Yup. There I was, my avatar like always whenever I played this game. Long, lush eyelashes. Silky black hair pulled into a perfectly perky ponytail, high up on my head. Pouty lips. Perfect boobs to go with my oh-so-amazing body.

The knob of the door rattled.

Was this it? Would someone finally find me? See me?

It stopped. Perhaps whoever it was sensed the bad taste of the decor from the other side of the door and realized it would be a mistake to submit to the sight of pea-green walls to go with mustard-yellow sheets. Did I not yet mention that the walls were pea green? Which truly is the color of vomit. I primped my hair, while at the same time trying not to internalize the severe lack of style in my vicinity.

Then I headed out into the hallway.

It was long, miles long, it seemed. It went on forever, doorway after doorway. But where were all the people? Was there seriously no one up here? It sounded like there might be thousands of people drinking and dancing one floor below. I made my way to the staircase and as I started down the steps the smell of stale beer assaulted my virtual senses. I covered my nose. The stench might be worse than the assault on my eyes from that bedroom. Well. That's life at a freshman college party, I supposed.

The game I chose was called Greek Life, College Edition.

And the tagline was: How fast can you make it to the top?

It sounded ridiculous as far as games go, but it was really hard to advance to the different levels. I know this because it took me forever to get to the level where my avatar had this many enhancements. Everyone starts out at a party full of drunken first-years, and must try and get the students higher up on the social food chain to give them the time of day. Ultimately you have to convince these vapid sorority chicks to let you into their houses or whatever, and eventually you have to try to become head sorority girl by acting really mean and nasty to other people. At least, that's how the game was played. The last time I played I nearly, *nearly* won by becoming VP of the most prestigious sorority around. Translation: in this game, I *am* one of those vapid sorority chicks, and an important one at that. There are different houses, all of them ranked from most to least popular, and the least popular ones are always where you find the nice people. The less popular, the nicer people became. The same went for the guys and fraternities and convincing them to let you . . . what was it? . . . *pledge*, I think it was called.

Along the way you could pick up extra points by doing stupid little things.

Convincing some guy to let you to the front of the beer line to fill your red Solo cup.

Doing a successful keg stand.

Winning at a drinking game.

Breaking a pricey vase.

Making out with some guy or girl, whichever person you fancy, on a whim.

Blah, blah, blah.

I'd tried them all and then some.

Not exactly the most respectable recreation I could have chosen. Char was the person who always wanted to play it and she'd drag me along with her. Eventually I learned how to make it through all the levels and keep Char from making an idiot of herself. Mostly.

Best of all, though, given my current predicament: everyone was always checking everyone else out to see who might up their status next.

It was time for my big debut! And subsequent salvation!

I uncovered my nose, gave my ponytail a little shake, and started down the stairs again, wading farther into the stench, giant smile pasted onto my adorable face. I could already see dozens of pairs of feet jumping up and down to the beat of the music.

Lower and lower I went.

Soon everyone would turn my way like always and I'd be flooded with admirers. Then all I'd need to do was find the right person to corner and explain my teensy weensy little situation back in the City with this whole government lockdown business and convince that person to help get me out of prison life.

My eyes were on my feet, taking care not to fall when I reached the bottom, since I couldn't afford to lose any status points. Plus, the heels on my sorority-girl avatar's feet were insane. Six inches tall and glittery enough to blind someone, at least temporarily.

One more step . . .

I reached the floor, my sparkly toe nearly catching on the ragged old disgustingly stained rug. Then, with a flourish, I looked up.

The party was crazy packed, people crowded into every available space and corner and chair and couch. The dance floor was bouncing and beer was spilling everywhere as people jumped up and down. There were keg stands happening everywhere and people making out all over the place. It was difficult to move, there were so many excited newbies.

I looked left, I looked right.

I waited for the adoration to flood my way.

I batted my eyelashes. Smiled prettily. Led with my boobs.

And . . . absolutely . . .

Nothing.

Nothing, nothing, *nothing*.

People pushed past me, seemed to look straight at me, screamed at each other over the music in their attempt at small talk, but it was like I wasn't even there. Nobody offered me a beer. Nobody tried to kiss me. Nobody complimented me on my amazingly toned legs on full view in this ridiculously short skirt I was wearing.

No, no, no, no, no!

This idea *had* to work.

Disappointment pranced through me to the beat, mocking me.

Was I totally wrong in thinking that entering a game would provide me a loophole in my government-aided disappearance? That in the City people may not be able to see or hear me, but in a multiplayer game they might? Did I seriously come to this stupid college party in this overdone bitchy queen-bee getup for nothing?

"Gaahhhhhhhh," I screamed.

It was loud in here, but I yelled right into the ear of some gangly freshman boy and he didn't even turn my way. I was so demoralized about my continued invisibility that I actually allowed myself to sit on one of the sticky, liquor-stained stairs. I put my head between my knees and did my best to breathe through the anguish, but after a minute or two, the stench became too much. I lifted my head, ponytail flopping to the side of my face in a way that was surely not very becoming, but then, what did I care?

As usual, nobody knew I existed.

But it was right then that someone caught my eye.

One of these things is not like the other! went the childhood song in my head. *One of these things just doesn't belong!*

A boy was slumped against the wall like he really did not want to be here, either, his face all broody and like he maybe just lost his best friend or his favorite App drained away too soon. My virtual skin tingled all over with static as bright and electric as the sparkle of my shoes.

Because he was looking at me.

He was looking at me like I was actually *there*.

I got up from the step, did my best to brush the beer scum from my mini, and stood tall though slightly wobbly in these damn heels.

I started toward him.

And his eyes, they *followed me.*

They *kept* following me, too!

I pushed through short first-years and jumping first-years and drunk first-years who didn't seem to know I was alive, but this guy, *this* guy was watching me the entire time.

Could it be that I was saved?!

I shoved my way through the last of the crowd between him and me, and suddenly there he was and there I was, fluttering my long, lush lashes like my life depended on it. And it kind of did, honestly.

"Hello?" he said, and not entirely friendly either.

But I didn't care! I wasn't going to be picky!

"You can see me??!!" I screamed excitedly, even though he was standing right there, in front of my face, looking all handsome and tall and happy to see me. Well, or maybe he was just surprised to see me, but whatever. Details. "Yahoo!"

He took a step back, wincing. "You don't have to yell."

I waved my arms around in a wild dance, still unable to believe that after all this time someone was aware of my virtual existence.

He took another step back. "Um, stop trying to hit me."

I laughed. Well, maybe it was more of a cackle or shriek of unfettered glee. "I'm so not trying to hit you. Or hit *on* you. What's your problem anyway? You look pretty grumpy."

This observation did not seem to endear him to me. His frown deepened. "None of your business," he said. "I don't even know you."

"Ah, so it's girl trouble, is it?" I asked, bouncing up and down on my toes. I could sense girlfriend problems from a mile away. I knew I'd hit on the problem, too, from the way this boy's face got all scrunched up and ready to deny it. And I could see it in his eyes, the need to finally talk to someone about it. "Well, you're lucky to come across the likes of me," I went on, before he could get any words out. "I'm an expert in assisting with girl troubles." I put out my hand. "My name is Ree and I'm *so* happy to meet you. Like, crazy nutty happy!" I sang that last word alto and it rippled with a nice high and wavy bravado.

The boy looked like he definitely wasn't sure he felt the same way about me. But eventually he wiped his hand off on his jeans and he slipped it into mine. He hesitated another minute before finally, he spoke.

"I'm Adam," he said.

12

Skylar

faith

TWO HOURS LATER and there I was, setting my limbs into one of those cradles yet again. Lying in one of those horrible boxes.

Blinking up at Lacy, of all people. Putting my trust in her. I looked around, stared through the glass enclosing me. Putting my trust in this uncertain technology, too. Trust that, yes, it would help me cross the border without detection.

Rain would be so angry at me when he found out. But then, Lacy would have to handle him this time. After all, she said that she would.

"Are you ready?" she was saying from above me.

"Yes," I confirmed. I had to admit: I was impressed by

her. She was all business from the moment I arrived. "All right. I'm going to shift." I closed my eyes and took a deep breath, preparing myself to go under. Just before I began to drift I heard Lacy's voice again.

"Don't worry, Skylar," she said. "I'm going to take care of you. You can count on me. I promise."

Kit smiled.

I smiled back.

He put out his hand and I took it. We were on a beach, the day cloudy, but I didn't care. I loved the beach and the ocean no matter what the weather. This, and . . . Kit. I loved . . . Kit.

The two of us wandered across the sand slowly, like we had all the time in the world, leaning into each other, not speaking. Just being together.

I felt so happy.

But then I looked up and saw that the sky had become a murky green, a color I'd seen before, a color that was ugly and foreboding. I stopped walking and turned to face Kit. "Do you think we'll ever find our way to each other again?" I asked.

His eyes darkened like the clouds above. "I honestly don't know."

I nodded. My happiness fled. "I think I'm not supposed to be here."

"You are. You're supposed to be with me."

"But you just said you didn't—" I stopped speaking.

Kit had vanished.

I clutched at my chest.

What was I doing here? How did I even get here?

I started down the beach again. Far, far ahead I could see a group of people. Children. They were running in circles, skipping, and they were singing. No, they were chanting. I listened, trying to make out their words.

"Long live the king and queen of New Port City! King Rain and Queen Skylar!"

I halted. Turned around and walked quickly in the other direction.

It was starting to storm. Fiercely.

I put my hands up, trying to block the rain from pounding my face. A thought nudged at me and my brain drew it out, and as it became clearer and clearer in my mind, the torrent lessened until it was just a light mist.

Shifting.

I was shifting. I was crossing the border into the App World. That's what I was doing, and this was just the in-between-place. That's where I was.

I was just a little rusty. Rusty at shifting.

The more lucid I became, the more control I had, and I watched as the clouds cleared and the sun came out, and soon the beach was disappearing and I was in that long familiar hallway with the doors. I did my best to push away the unease I was left with after seeing Kit and reminded myself that it was only a dream. But still . . .

Focus.

I needed to focus.

There were so many doors. They seemed to have grown exponentially since I'd last done this. Trader's house in Loner Town was a logical enough place to cross into the App World, so I began to search for the door.

My attention was grabbed elsewhere. By a door that pulled at me, drawing me toward it. I let myself go to it. Stood in front of it, careful not to get too close. Bars crisscrossed it. Heavy and metal. Sharp spikes jutted out where the bars didn't cover the battered wood behind them.

It was a prison door.

It had to be. Why else would it look like this?

Rain had mentioned the possibility of virtual prison, but I'd never heard of the App World having a jail. No one had spoken of one during my years there. Then again, lots had happened in both worlds, to say the least. Whatever was on the other side of this door, I needed to see it. I could feel the certainty of this. It was where I needed to go. Before I could think better of it, I reached for the thick latch to see if it would allow me through.

At first nothing happened.

Then I heard the screech of metal sliding across metal.

It opened a crack and I stepped forward.

The hallway with the doors was gone.

I'd crossed the border into unknown territory.

The familiar feeling of static moved across my skin. Virtual skin.

Once again, I was a virtual girl. I pushed this thought away.

I blinked, taking in my surroundings. I was in an apartment—a nice apartment. How strange. I'd expected some sort of dank cell like I'd seen on the old-time Real World movies, dirty and ugly, with more of the same bars to pen me in—or to pen in whoever was imprisoned. But instead there were plush white couches everywhere like I'd grown used to at the Sachses' apartment, and clear evidence of Interior Decorator Apps. Pricey ones. Not at all what I'd imagined would be behind that door.

"I think I know you," someone said, sounding shocked but also kind of snarky.

And at the same time . . . elated.

I spun. There was a girl standing there. She couldn't be much younger than me. Before I had a chance to respond or even ask her name, there came another loud knock, this time from the hallway outside.

The girl turned toward it, jaw hanging open. She started to laugh, to giggle uncontrollably, her fiery red hair, the one feature that really defined her—fiery like Lacy's—swaying along her back. "All this time stuck by myself and now I have not one but *two* visitors." Her voice gurgled, the laughter bubbling into the atmosphere. "Maybe it's the government. Maybe they've come to erase me," she whispered, eyes wild, then went to the door and threw it wide. "You made it! You really came like you said you would! How did you get through? I can't believe you're here!"

As the girl rambled, she stood blocking the person who was standing on the other side of the threshold.

"Come in," she chattered happily, and finally stepped aside.

That was when I got my first good look at her newest caller.

Now it was my jaw that fell open.

"Skylar?" Adam said.

PART TWO

13

Kit

addictions

"MY SISTER WILL get over it eventually."

I sat up. My entire body ached. My head pounded. I couldn't see. But I knew whose voice was speaking. I'd gotten used to hearing it these last months. "Trader," I managed, his name slurred and thick on my tongue.

"She still cares about you," he went on. "I can tell."

Trader's features began to take shape as my eyes adjusted to the light and my surroundings. "Skylar is with someone else," I said.

He pushed his black hair away from his face, only to have it flop back down. "She is, but she isn't."

I tried to get up, but everything hurt. My muscles

refused movement. "What does that even mean? She is, but she isn't?"

Trader crossed the room and crouched down next to me. "It means that my sister and Rain have a lot of history and he's always there for her. Skylar knows she can rely on him, so she does. She cares about him, but whatever went on between the two of you is different."

I managed a laugh, but the effort nearly choked me. My throat was raw. "Yeah, different as in over."

Trader's moody eyes were steady. Maggie used to complain that I was brooding, but no one's really seen brooding until they meet Trader. "No," he stated, like this was an accepted and universal fact.

I tried to get up again and this sent my head spinning. "Skylar hates me."

Trader laughed. The sound made me wince. "It's quite the opposite. You're stupid if you think otherwise. Skylar has been moping for months about you, but unless you do something about it soon, she's going to move on. And then it will be too late."

I studied him, despite the pounding at the base of my skull. "You really believe that?"

"I do. And even though having a sister is new to me, I find myself wanting her to be happy." He laughed again. "I guess that means even I can surprise myself."

"Huh," I said, too tired to muster anything more coherent. But the heart inside my chest spoke otherwise with this new information, which had been conveyed with sincerity from the unlikeliest of sources. I let my head fall back.

Trader blinked at me from above. "I can tell you something else that you better listen to carefully, Kitto."

If I didn't feel so broken, I'd reach up and punch him in the face. He'd taken to calling me this nickname, and I loathed it. No matter how many times I told him to shut up and stop calling me that, he kept doing it. But he was letting me hide out in his place, which I appreciated. "What else can you tell me, T?" I asked.

He tapped the rest supporting my head. His hand swept across the contraption where I lay, immobilized. "If you keep doing this to yourself, you're not going to be around much longer and then you'll never get to make my sister happy. You don't want that now, do you?"

Something about hearing concern from Trader's mouth, Trader, who wasn't exactly a font of responsibility and virtue, jolted me enough that I managed to get up—slowly, carefully, and with a serious dose of pain throughout my limbs, my neck, my head. The effort paid off and soon I was standing.

"Good boy," Trader said.

I busied myself pulling a sweater over my head. It was freezing in here. "You'll stop with the patronizing remarks if you know what's good for you."

Trader leaned back his head with laughter. "Yeah.

Like you're in any shape to be sparring. Not after what you've been doing to yourself." He shook his head in disapproval, his eyes darkening. "Idiot."

I shrugged. "I'm fine," I said.

But we both knew this was a lie.

"Remember when you said you'd never plug in. *Ever*," Trader reminded me.

The two of us stared down at the cradle. It looked like something out of a horror film. "I thought I never would either." My heart still pounded in my chest, making me dizzy. "But that was before Skylar."

The house had grown dark.

Shadows fell across everything. A wave crashed outside and receded, until the roar of another one replaced it. I wandered around the room in circles, my bare feet scuffing against the cool wood of the floor. I forced my attention away from the cradle as long as I could, tried to ignore it. Tried to pretend it wasn't there.

But it called to me.

Eventually, I couldn't bear it any longer and my eyes went to it.

Trader had left hours ago, but his warnings echoed inside my head. He was right. I was being reckless. I knew what I was doing to myself wasn't good. Eventually, my body would give out from the abuse. I'd never imagined that coming to stay at this broken-down house would mean I'd start playing around with that Shifting App, but with the nights too long to do nothing, it wasn't that surprising that I'd found a new vice. Unlike with the whiskey, this addiction made me hate myself.

Trader had been right. I'd sworn I'd never plug in.

Yet lately, plugging in to the App World was the only thing that kept my mind off Skylar and the stupid decision I'd made, going to Jude instead of trusting that Skylar would keep her word and get Maggie free. I'd screwed up everything and I wanted to forget it.

Lucky for me, there was an App for that.

Lucky for me, there were several. Dozens. Thousands. And so far I'd only sampled a paltry few, courtesy of Trader's endless stash of capital at his house.

The cool night air floated through the open windows. The metal of the cradle was cold to the touch. My fingers ran across it. I wondered what Skylar would think if she came and found me plugged in. Would she even care? Seeing her nearly ended me. I'd imagined running into her a million times, I'd played out what would happen in my head over and over—what I wished would happen. Then I saw her like some dream and it wasn't at all like I'd imagined. In the fantasy she forgives me. In the fantasy, just by seeing me she can't help doing this because she can't help remembering what we had. Or what we'd started to have.

The reality of our meeting was something I could barely stomach.

Skylar couldn't get away from me fast enough.

The memory of her turning her back made me physically wince.

Trader's other words echoed inside me now.

Not the words of warning, but the ones about how Skylar still cared for me, how she'd been moping around without me. How even though she was with Rain, her heart was still mine. Maybe I should've gone after her that day I saw her. Maybe I should've tried harder to get her to stay, to talk to me. To hear me out.

I looked at the tattoo on my forearm. Even in the darkness it glowed, still bright with newness. I stared until the lines and colors blurred together and I couldn't recognize their shapes. There were nights when I'd regretted the decision to ink such a permanent reminder on my skin. Even Maggie warned me against doing such a thing. But I'd wanted the reminder because I wanted to punish myself by having a symbol of all that I'd lost right on my own body.

With this thought, I laid myself back into the cradle and picked up the little tablet next to it. With a few taps the Shifting App began to download and soon I was drifting off into a virtual sleep where everything, all that pain and grief, would soon be forgotten.

Long live the Mind Eraser App, went my brain.

And then I was gone.

14

Skylar

a diamond among apps

"WHAT ARE YOU doing here?" Adam asked.

I stared, unsure how to answer. I'd grown so used to seeing the Adam of the Real World that it was a shock to see him here. I'd nearly forgotten the virtual version of Adam. For one, his skin color was different. Instead of dark and rich, here he was pale and washed out, the standard tone of everyone in the App World, myself included. But now that I'd become accustomed to the differences among real bodies and real skin, it seemed wrong. Like the App World had taken something fundamentally Adam away, in exchange for him plugging in and getting to enjoy the downloads that virtual living promised.

I looked at the other girl in the room, then back at

Adam. "I could ask you the same thing." The name *Parvda* hovered on my lips. "Why in both worlds are you in this apartment?"

The girl was still laughing. Cackling, really.

I could already tell she and I were unlikely friends. Surely her parents were the type who'd fed her ideas about Singles living off the state, Singles eating up money and donations from families like hers. This apartment was more opulent than the Sachses' place. She probably took everything for granted. There were permanent virtual enhancements downloaded to her basic self, too, the kind that Lacy had when she was in the App World that kept a girl a cut above, appearance-wise, from everyone else. I wondered if she even remembered the downloads or if her parents had downloaded them to her when she was too young to realize.

"This is so freakin' surreal," the girl said. "Skylar Cruz in my house!"

Hearing my name sent tension through my code, my virtual skin going taut. If I was still in the Real World I would have goose bumps. I turned to her. "You already know my name. So what's yours?"

"Ree," she said. "It's Ree." She glanced at Adam, her eyes darting back and forth between the two of us. "You already know him, I guess."

I crossed my arms, eyeing Adam. "I do. But how you two met is a story I'd like to hear."

Adam was silent. He wouldn't look at me.

But Ree was more than willing to fill me in. "We met in Greek Life, College Edition. And now he's here to save me," she added, as if this was evident and totally normal. "You two are the only people who can see me, for some reason."

I nodded, taking this in. "A college party. Right. And he's here to *save* you. And we're the only people who can see you. Hmm-hmm."

"It's all true," she said. "And I'm guessing you're here to save me, too." Pure happiness danced in her eyes. "I can't even believe that all these months I've been by myself, no hope in sight, no one to talk to or hear me, and now the Real World cavalry has come to get me out of this place."

My mind kept snagging on the weirdness of finding Adam in some random girl's apartment, the idea that he's been meeting girls like Ree at App World Gaming parties while Parvda was weeping in bed at Briarwood. But I made myself focus on what Ree was saying, trying to reconcile it with the prison door I'd walked through to get into her apartment. "We're the only ones who can see you? Why?"

She shrugged. "I don't know. But I'm relieved you can. I've been stuck here forever, invisible, until you guys came along."

"You're imprisoned?" I asked her.

Ree nodded, her face still giddy. Champagne bubbles were bursting around her in the atmosphere. "The government has me caged because of what I saw and what I know. They promised my mother and me unlimited free downloads. But a girl can only download so many Apps by herself without going a little crazy, you know?" I opened my mouth to answer, but she got there first again. "Though you probably wouldn't really know about that, would you? Having been a Single your whole virtual life and all. It's a pity you would miss out on that . . . that . . ."—her face was alight with the search for the right word—"utter and transporting joy of the unlimited and unending download fest!"

"A terrible pity," I agreed, and wondered if she noticed the irony.

She waved her arm through the atmosphere. "Maybe you can still experience it!" She called up her App Store. It was enormous. The Apps filled the entire living room, leaving almost no room for Adam and me to stand. "I wonder if I can transfer my unlimited downloads to you. I mean, it's not like we're in a rush, right?"

"I don't think now is the time," Adam said, finally speaking a few words.

His virtual skin was the color of cherries, a strange hue on someone who, in the Real World, had the fortune of never having to worry about his cheeks visibly flushing red. I remembered another time I'd seen Adam turn this shade, but it was out of anger, not shame, because Parvda had been left on the other side of the border in the Real World. I think I preferred the Adam who raged on Parvda's behalf, as opposed to the Adam who was embarrassed to be caught meeting girls at college parties and showing up to their apartments afterward.

"Yes," I said. "I appreciate your offer, Ree. It's very sweet." I eyed Adam. His gaze fled the moment it locked with mine. "But I think now is the time for my friend Adam and me to do some catching up. And then we'll figure out what's going on with you and see if we can help. Right, Adam?"

Adam was staring across the room. Anywhere but at me. Hands dug deep into his pockets. He shrugged. "Sure, Skylar." He sighed heavily. "I suppose we should talk."

"Is there a place—" I started, but when I turned back to Ree her mouth was hanging open, eyes full of alarm.

She put a hand on my shoulder, the feel of it strange. Almost fizzy. "I know you guys want to talk." Her fingers curled tighter, though her eyes weren't on me. "But I think now is not the time for you to catch up."

I tried to follow her gaze. Her attention seemed caught on one of the Apps, but there were so many in the room, bouncing up and down and lunging at her, it was difficult to determine which of the thousands she could possibly have her eye on.

"Don't you see it?" Her voice grew hushed.

"Don't we see what?" Adam asked. "It's impossible to focus in this storm of icons."

"After all this time," she whispered. "I've been waiting for it and here it is, finally!"

"What are you talking about?" I asked. The atmosphere was so thick with Apps I nearly couldn't see the furniture. If Adam wasn't so close I might lose him in the teeming clouds.

Ree pointed.

I searched through the jumping mass of icons. "Which one?" I asked, getting desperate.

Ree seemed in a trance. "Just look. Once you see it you can't unsee it."

This time I started with the tip of Ree's pale finger and followed its trajectory carefully, passing the familiar icons with angel's wings and Apps for temporary changes in appearance, beautiful and grotesque. For a split second I was impressed by the number of Gaming Apps that flooded Ree's Store, and wondered if I was wrong before and she and I could have been friends, or even *would* have. I moved on and on until finally I saw what had caught Ree's eye.

I gasped. "What *is* that? I've never seen anything like it!"

Ree was nodding. "I know. It's difficult not to stare."

The two of us stood there, transfixed.

Soon Adam joined us. "It's beautiful," he said.

"Stunning," I agreed.

The three of us moved toward it, the other Apps jumping aside as we pushed through the throng, making a path toward the one that held us.

We stopped in front of it.

It was black, or maybe gray, a dark diamond gift box polished and cut with expert skill. It shone and sparkled and caught the light like the most precious of jewels. It put the Tiffany App to shame.

I wanted it.

I needed it.

It called my name. Beckoned me. It was nearly impossible to breathe.

Jealousy flooded my code. This was Ree's Store, not mine.

I reached out to it anyway.

It was a witch casting a spell.

I was about to touch it when Ree's arm came down across mine—hard and fast—swiping my hand away. "Ow!" I cried, turning to her. "That hurt!"

Ree stared at me, her eyes serious. "Not as much as touching that App would have."

I snapped back to reality. "What do you mean?"

Adam tore his gaze away from it. "Hurt her how?"

The three of us stood in a tiny triangle, the App in question floating a safe distance away from our virtual selves.

"That App is poison," Ree said. "Downloading it will"—she looked left, then right, then up and down, as though worried someone else was in the room, listening. She leaned closer.

Adam and I did, too.

She lowered her voice to a whisper. "Downloading it will virtually kill you."

15

Skylar

bits and pieces

THE THREE OF us circled the poisonous App, careful not to get too close.

At certain angles the sparkle was blinding.

It shone blues and pinks, greens and yellows.

Could it really cause virtual death?

Those two ominous words circled inside me, round and round, sickening my code.

I used to think virtual death was impossible. Or at least, very, very rare. Lacy had threatened us with it when we first met, warning that if Adam, Sylvia, or I told anyone we were about to illegally unplug, we'd be virtual goners. But I don't know if Lacy knew what she was talking about back then and if her threats had any substance.

Before, when I was a Single, virtual death was something that only happened when the real body died on the plugs, and on the plugs real bodies lasted a long, long time. But then the Race for the Cure was won and even that rare, eventual kind of death was eradicated, at least on a virtual level.

At least, that's what everyone was told.

Was it all lies?

The images of all those dead bodies in my mother's lab returned to me now.

Could this App have something to do with the people who were dying on the plugs?

With the virus?

"How do you know what this App does?" I asked Ree. "If it causes virtual death, then you must never have downloaded it."

Ree swatted at the Apps that buzzed about her head, her ears, diving at her nose and mouth. "Get away!" she cried. She couldn't call off her App Store without calling off the Death App, too, so there were icons racing and jumping around everywhere. They were nearly attacking Ree, they were so impatient. "Obviously I haven't or I'd be floating high up in Heaven 6.0, which, by the way, is apparently just a vacation resort for a bit of peace and quiet and *not* a place where anyone is supposed to end up permanently." An App dove through her hair and she waved it away. "Have you guys ever been there?"

"No," Adam said. "Vacations like that always required too much capital."

Ree actually had the decency to turn a little red. "Sorry! I don't mean to keep acting all privileged in front of Singles."

I turned my attention from the glittering App to study Ree. There was a look of sincerity in her eyes. Maybe I'd judged her too hastily. "It's fine," I said. My gaze automatically drifted back to the jeweled box hovering between us. It was magnetic. It *wanted* us to touch it, yet it also wasn't like the rest of the icons, desperate and needy for us to download it. In a certain way, that was part of its appeal. "Just tell us what you know about this App."

"Well," Ree began. "I call it the Death App, and its existence is why I've been jailed here by the government for months and months. The fact that I know it exists, and that I've seen what it can do." Her voice dropped an octave on her last few words.

Adam didn't take his eyes off the Death App when he spoke. "If you've seen someone download it, that means you've watched someone virtually die. Right?"

"Two people, unfortunately," she said. "My best friend first, and then my mother. The second you touch it, it starts to, I don't know, maybe destroy your code? The download makes you shriek in agony and . . . and . . ." Ree took a breath, gathering herself to go on. "And then it blackens your virtual skin until . . . well, it looks like you're

roasting and burning . . . my friend Char was like . . ."
Ree hiccuped, a strange sort of choking noise. "She was
seriously *charred*, and that is definitely not a joke. Then
you eventually sizzle into oblivion." She snapped her fingers in the atmosphere. "Poof! You disappear. And you
don't come back, trust me. My mother's virtual death was
recent. Maybe, like, just a week now? But Char's happened
ages ago."

I swallowed. Underneath the bright excitement on
Ree's face were traces of loneliness, of grief and loss,
something raw and frightened. Traumatized. "I'm sorry.
That must have been awful." I thought back to when I'd
left Inara behind in the App World, when I'd crossed the
border, and how upset she was that I'd lied to her. How
much I'd missed her later on—and she was still alive. It
had been awful to lose my relationship with Jude and to
nearly lose the one I had with my mother, and both of
them were still around too. I couldn't imagine what it
would be like to watch someone I cared about die. Even
a virtual death must be horrible to witness. "You must be
devastated."

"It's been . . . more difficult than I would have imagined." A swarm of icons had gathered in front of Ree's
face, so thick it was impossible to read her expression.
She screamed in frustration and with one powerful swipe
of her hand, lashed out, and they fled, leaving her alone
temporarily.

"You can call off the App Store," I told her. "We can look at the Death App again later."

"You don't understand." Ree walked over to the wall and stood against it, so at least the icons couldn't come at her from behind. "If I call it off, we might never see it again. I've been trying to get this Death App to appear for ages, and this is the first time."

"But you can't stay like this either," Adam reasoned. "The Apps are only going to get worse. Soon they'll cover you head to toe."

Ree shot a puff of air at an icon lingering near her mouth and it floated away backward, only to zip right back to her lips, nearly touching them. "Gross! Get away!"

"Call it off," I said. My eyes lingered on the Death App, marveling at its gloomy beauty. For a split second, I thought of Kit. "We'll figure out how to call it up again. I promise."

Ree led us onto the enormous terrace outside her apartment. "Let's have a bite to eat while we do our explaining and getting to know one another."

She called up a feast of virtual food, the likes of which I hadn't seen since Mr. and Mrs. Sachs threw a special party for their friends and allowed Inara and me to crash it. There were bowls of glowing fruits, so ripe and juicy they were nearly bursting. There were pizzas and dishes piled with pasta and towers of sandwiches stuffed with strange-looking vegetables. Lined up alongside everything else were tiny tubs of gelato in a variety of neon flavors. At the center of the table stood a tall, thin, nine-tiered wedding cake decorated to resemble a fountain, bright-blue waves of moving icing cascading down the side and running over the top of the table, some of them reaching all the way to the ground. They gurgled and splashed noisily.

I hadn't eaten App World food in ages. It all looked so delicious.

But while I knew I would enjoy trying the buffet of delights Ree had offered us, I also knew that none of it, not even the fanciful cake, would compare to what I'd eaten in the Real World. There was nothing like real food. Mr. and Mrs. Sachs had always been right about that.

The memory of the Death App flashed in my brain.

To how many people had it appeared? Could it hold the answers my mother was searching for in the Real World? About rumors of a virus?

Ree stood back, admiring her choices. "I haven't had guests in ages. All these free downloads and no one to share them with! I haven't had a feast like this in months."

I tore my eyes from the virtual food. "You've been locked in this apartment alone for months?"

She shook her head. "I wasn't alone at first. My mother was with me." Ree's face paled to gray and her eyes filled with virtual tears. "I actually miss her. I never thought

I would, but I do. She probably disappeared into virtual oblivion believing I hated her. I certainly acted like I did while she was still alive."

"I'm sure somewhere she knew you still loved her, no matter how you acted or treated each other while you were together." I said this, then wondered how much my words were spoken to comfort Ree or to comfort me about Jude.

Ree motioned for Adam and me each to sit in front of one of the place settings on the table. "That's a nice thought, but she and I treated each other pretty badly. Maybe too badly for our relationship to ever be redeemable."

Of the three chairs, Adam chose the farthest from me.

"No relationship is ever beyond repair," I said, realizing again how this claim could apply to so many people and situations in my life, too. My relationship with Jude, with Rain. Even with Lacy. My relationship with Kit, too. Maybe Kit more than anyone else.

Ree took her plate and piled it with a mishmash of things that, if put together in the Real World, would make a person sick. But here no one got sick and you could mix gelato with pizza and they would taste good together. "I guess if anyone had a reason to be optimistic about family relationships it would be you, wouldn't it?" The fountain cake kept dripping onto the terrace floor, but Ree didn't seem to notice. "You must seriously hate your sister."

Hearing Ree casually mention Jude and toss off how she knew the history between us made me wince. I'd just met her, and not only did she know who I was, but she knew all about my family. As did everyone else in the City, I supposed. That was the price of fame, as Rain was always reminding me. Other people obsessing over your life.

Had he noticed I was gone yet? Was he right now talking to Lacy? Were they having their heart-to-heart? Jealousy flashed through my code, searing it a bit, but then it passed.

"No, I don't hate Jude," I answered, my voice as steady as I could make it. "Let's go back to the Death App and why you haven't left your apartment."

"I already told you," Ree said, her mouth still full. She swallowed. "It wasn't by choice. The government jailed me because of what I know and what I've seen."

I put some food onto my plate to be polite. A glistening slice of pizza and a sandwich layered with something green and something blue. Then I picked up a tiny bright-yellow tub of ice cream and wondered if it might be lemon. "You really can't leave?"

Ree stared at me, the exasperation clear on her face. "No! Believe me, I've tried *everything*, and nothing, absolutely *nothing*, has worked. Until I met your friend Adam." She gestured at him with her fork. "He came here to try and help break me out. He's the first person other than my mother that I've talked to since this whole jailing business began. The first person to even see me or hear my voice and acknowledge my existence, App knows why. And I only met him because it occurred to me to go through the Gaming Apps to contact someone. It's, like, the only loophole I've found. That's how scared the government is that I'll tell people what I know."

Adam still hadn't touched anything. He kept glancing at me. "Yes, Skylar. That's why I'm here. The *only* reason. To help Ree. I promised I'd help her."

"It's been total solitary confinement for me," Ree confirmed. "Until now, with you *both*! But what if the government is listening and they know you're with me? They'll come for me *and* for you and then we'll *all* be stuck."

Adam leaned back in his chair. "That would not be good."

My mind began to do the math. People were dying in the Real World on the plugs. The government had sequestered Ree because she knew about this Death App. There were rumors of a virus. If the government was *that* worried about word getting out, then why wouldn't they be listening? Why wouldn't they have this apartment bugged? This thought chilled me so thoroughly my fingers frosted over the metal tub of ice cream in my hand.

This meant Emory Specter likely already knew I was here.

Or if he didn't, he certainly would figure it out soon.

"We need to go," I said to Adam, getting up so quickly I knocked over my chair, which crashed to the terrace floor behind me. "Now. She's right. It's not safe for us."

Ree stood too, tipping over her plate. Fountain cake spilled onto the floor in a great sugary splash. The blue of it was too blue, like the fluorescent blue of chemicals that should never be allowed to enter the body. She wore a look of panic. "But you can't go! Not yet! I shouldn't have said that. I'm sure it's safe. No one is listening. I was just being melodramatic!"

"You weren't," I said to her, then to Adam. "Let's go see Rain's father. He'll want to know what is happening."

Adam looked at me like I was mad. "Rain's father? But he's—"

I put a finger to my lips. "—exactly who we need to talk to."

Adam stood up from his seat. "Skylar, wait—"

"Now," I urged. I searched his eyes. "Please, Adam. *Please.*"

He glanced at Ree uneasily. Then he shrugged, in apology, I supposed. He followed me across the terrace and we made our way through Ree's living room.

She followed close behind us. "Don't leave me," she begged. "Come on!"

"Don't worry," I told her. "We'll be back."

Then Adam and I passed easily through the front door

and into the hallway.

When Ree tried to follow, she was held back as though by an invisible string tugging at her back. And with one single step forward on our part, Ree suddenly vanished. As if she'd never been there at all.

16

Ree

disappeared, officially

SKYLAR AND ADAM were gone for only a few minutes when they came for me.

The government.

Well, Mrs. Farley. But she *was* the government. She put me here, trapped me, then disappeared without another word. Who knew if she was aware that my mother was gone? She didn't even have the decency to knock. Maybe she hadn't needed to the first time either, but had just done it for show. To freak my mother and me out a little bit less.

I guess Skylar had been right, and the apartment might have been a tad bit bugged.

"And I thought you'd be satisfied with unlimited

downloads," a voice said from behind me. *Her* voice.

I spun. I'd been staring out onto the terrace through the screen door, trying to organize my thoughts, going over how I'd been alone for what felt like forever and then I'd had two visitors at once, one of them super famous, both of whom could finally see me, and somehow they slipped through my fingers without actually helping me get out of this overcoded hole. I gaped at Mrs. Farley now, wanting words to come from my mouth, but instead I only sputtered.

"Silly me," she said. "You had to be one of *those* girls."

Finally, I composed myself enough to speak. "What do you mean, one of *those* girls?" I asked. I tried to stay calm. I would have preferred the very cute Adam to fill the role of rescuer, but I couldn't be choosy at the moment, and I was fairly sure Mrs. Farley had the power to end my captured misery, since she was the one who started it.

She blinked from behind her big owl-eyed glasses, a fashion choice, since everyone in the App World had perfect vision. She cocked her head to the side, her tall updo tilted like the Leaning Tower of Pisa. Mrs. Farley wore a tweed jacket and matching skirt, which made her look like a frumpy grandmother, except for the part where the color of her suit was a mash-up of neon-pink, bright-green, and yellow threads. It made me dizzy to stare at it. "The kind of girl that can't be satisfied by downloads alone."

"You think that's a bad thing?" I grabbed for the screen

door handle. I wanted the option to get away quickly, even if I still couldn't get past the terrace.

"It's inconvenient," she said. Then she promptly walked up to me and peered around my back, a blur of bright and rosy colors. "Going somewhere?" She laughed.

I let my arm fall to my side and shrugged. "I thought I might need some air."

"Well, I'm not one to stop anyone from taking in the fresh atmosphere!" She popped open the door and stepped outside. Turned and looked at me expectantly. "Young Ree, did your mother not teach you that it's rude to keep your elders waiting?"

My virtual heart skidded at her mention of my mother. Slowly, I put one foot onto the terrace, followed by the other. The mess from the feast was melting onto the floor, ruined and ugly. A river of too-bright blue. To the left, my mother's sad and empty lounge chair was conspicuous. Mrs. Farley's stare followed mine. "Missing someone?"

"Yes. But you were already aware of that, right?"

She nodded. "It's strange when someone virtually dies. But your mother's death was a convenience for all of us. Wasn't it?"

I winced, my code squeezing itself into thin ribbons inside me. I'd known somewhere that my mother was really and truly dead. But I hadn't allowed myself to be 100 percent certain about it. I'd given her a slim chance of being around somewhere in the virtual ether, somewhere from which she could return with the right trick of a download. Hearing Mrs. Farley confirm she was gone for good made me hurt all over, like I'd just fallen from the top of a building without an App to protect me. I glared at her so hard I wondered if my eyes might be turning red with rage. "A convenience? How nice for you. But don't assume it's what I wanted."

"I know." Her smiled was satisfied. "But for us, it's far better when someone dies among the already sequestered, so I don't have to go through the mess of cleaning up after a more public death, like with your friend Char. It was very nice of your mother to go so quietly and privately. She made my life so much easier!" Mrs. Farley took off her big owl glasses. "Don't lie to yourself, Ree, or to me. You didn't like your mother much, and now you're free of her. Congratulations."

These words stung. I turned away and went over to the paltry remnants of the feast to distract myself, calling up a Cleaning Service App to take care of the mess. What was left of the fountain cake was vaporized into nothing in the atmosphere and the ice cream and everything else began to disappear, and Mrs. Farley spoke again after a brief silence.

"It looks like you were having a party," she observed. "Which is strange, since I set everything up so there would be absolutely *no visitors*, which I'm sure you already know well."

"I have no idea what you're talking about," I said dully.

"Of course you do. You managed to find a way to invite guests, which is mystifying. Very particular guests. Which is why I'm here, after all."

I shrugged, my back still to her. "Why don't you do what you came for, then, and shore up the apartment's prison defenses so no one else can ever come see me again."

She laughed and I heard the click of her heels on the terrace as she approached me. "But I'm not here to do that." The toes of her shoes squished into the bright-blue frosting that had escaped the Cleaning App. "Had your guests not been in your apartment, we never would have known about their presence in the City. They managed to cross the border without detection!"

Stupid, stupid me. I felt a bubble pressing against the walls of my throat, making it difficult to swallow. "How lucky for you."

"Yes. Very."

Skylar and Adam may have abandoned me, but I still felt guilty that I was the reason they might get in trouble for being here. "So what now?"

"I've come to take you somewhere else," Mrs. Farley said.

The bubble expanded. I coughed, grasping my virtual throat. As much as I'd longed to leave this place, this was not how I imagined doing it.

"I'm taking you to a far more secure prison." Mrs. Farley informed me, her voice low and smooth. "And this
time there won't be any downloads around to cheer you
up. It's just so unfortunate that you couldn't play by the
rules, isn't it now?"

She let this question hang in the air.

It formed a loop and dropped right around my neck
like a noose.

"So I hear you've met my daughter."

Rage built through my code until I was an anthill
overflowing with tiny red sparks, one swarming over the
other. They spilled onto the floor around me and disappeared. I wanted to scream.

I didn't. I breathed deeply once, twice, then looked up.

Emory Specter blinked at me from his chair. As if
my day couldn't get any weirder. Or more messed up.
First the government disappeared me from my sad little
apartment after abandoning me there for, like, forever,
and now I was sitting in a room with the Defense Minister. Though to call it a room was an understatement. It
was more of a grand hall. And Emory Specter's chair was
more of a throne, while I was sitting on a pathetic little
rickety thing that might break at any moment. The man
couldn't be more transparent. He needed to install himself like a king, when he practically already *was* a king,
and prove this to me by emphasizing my insignificance

down to the chair where I sat.

Maybe he was really insecure?

I studied the man. An Antianxiety App would be seriously helpful at the moment. "I don't know, have I met your daughter?" I kept my eyes steady on Emory. Or should I call him Mr. Specter? Defense Minister Specter? E. S. for short?

I nearly laughed.

Maybe he had Naples complex. No. Napoleon! A Napoleon complex! He was *a lot* shorter in person than on Reel Time and official broadcasts. Maybe his basic self was faulty, a little glitch in ways that only an App can fix. He always seemed taller and thinner when I'd seen him, but maybe he made himself taller when he appeared to the public for announcements, like the one about the Race for the Cure being won at that ginormous funeral. And when he granted the City a day of free Apping for everyone who refused to unplug after Skylar Cruz made her emergency broadcast about that stupid Body Market. The government sure did love giving out free downloads in exchange for our cooperation, now that I thought about it.

Emory was studying me. He hadn't blinked once since I'd arrived. It made it seem like he had fish eyes.

What a ridiculous man!

He frowned. "What's so amusing?"

Oops. Had I actually laughed out loud? Or had he taken some Superpower App that allowed him to read my thoughts? I shivered. That was a chilling idea. "Nothing is funny. You were saying I'd met your daughter and I was asking you if I had. Because, really"—I started counting the months I'd been *sequestered*, as Mrs. Farley put it, on my sad, pale little fingers—"I couldn't have, at least not recently. Unless maybe your daughter went to my High School 4.0?"

He tented his hands and adjusted himself on his throne with a little butt wiggle. "I didn't think you were that dense."

"I'm not."

"Sure," he said, not at all sounding convinced. He didn't seem about to give any hints who his daughter was either. He sighed and smiled. "Let's see . . . Ree . . . that's your name, right?" Before I could respond that *yes, it was*, he called up some sort of document and it appeared in his hands. He ran his fingers across it as it flashed, pages turning. "Ree Aristocrat." He burst into laughter himself. "I'm so sorry, darling. What a last name! Your mother was that transparent when she plugged in that she chose Aristocrat as her family name? As if that could turn you into nobility!" His laughter slowed and died. "The nouveau riche will always be lower class. Let's see . . . what else . . ." He scanned his finger some more. "Your grandfather made his money trading in black-market Real World goods, and then there was a mass exodus to virtual living by your relatives." He chuckled and clutched at his stomach. "I figured you must come from an ugly criminal element to have a last name like Aristocrat."

I crossed my arms, and the chair creaked in protest. "Are you done mocking me?"

"That depends," he dropped.

I was getting tired of his stupid game. "On what?"

"On what you can tell me about my daughter and why she's here. She's always mucking about in my affairs and I think it's time she and I had a heart-to-heart. Don't you think?"

"I don't give a flying App about your relationship with your daughter and whether the two of you make nice. I just want out of here." My shoulders slumped a little. "Am I *really* expected to guess who she is?" I was starting to sound like a brat, but I didn't care. I wanted him to think I felt all *whatever* about being in his highness's presence, even though truly, I wanted to run away screaming. Meanwhile my App-free brain tried its best to function without any downloads and go over every girl I'd ever met to try and come up with a candidate.

Emory's knees twitched. Every other part of his body seemed to twitch, too, as though the energy running through his code spilled over into the atmosphere, generating heat and electricity around him. "I suppose if I must, I'll tell you," he said. "Though the answer is right in front of you. You just saw her." He leaned forward. "Today."

"Whoa," I said slowly, drawing out the one syllable.

"No way. *She's* your daughter?"

He smiled. "Yes way, Ms. Ree."

"Skylar Cruz?"

He nodded and the smile faded.

I began to laugh. Hard. So hard I was clutching my virtual stomach and tears poured down my face until a little river of them was spilling onto the smooth marble floor like that amazing waterfall cake from earlier this afternoon.

Emory's face turned angry. "*Now* what's so funny?"

This time, I didn't dodge his question. "Your daughter is the same girl who also happens to be your nemesis? That's so perfect." I couldn't stop giggling. "Really. It's amazing. I like her better already!"

Emory rose from his throne. "You can laugh now, but you won't be laughing for long."

I shrank a little, regretting this admission. "I'm sorry," I stammered. "I . . . I . . . ."

His eyes narrowed. "Don't worry, Ms. Ree. I'm not going to do anything to hurt your boring, basic little head." His tone was serious. Scary serious. Deadly sounding. "You, my dear, are very important now. It's time Skylar and I took the time to get to know each other, and you are going to prove very useful as bait."

17

Skylar

holes

"IT DOESN'T MAKE any sense that you want to go see Jonathan Holt," Adam was saying. "He's not even—"

"—we're *not* going to see Rain's father," I snapped back. As we hurried through the City, I realized I was angry at Adam. Glad he was all right, but frustrated he'd stayed away from Parvda so long and made her miserable. And dismayed I'd found him in the App World at the apartment of some girl, regardless of his claims that he was just trying to help.

Adam took two long strides and parked himself in front of me. Even in the App World, he was tall. "Then where are we going?"

We were smack in the middle of Main Park. I stared

up into the now-familiar eyes of my friend. "We're headed to Loner Town."

"I hate that place," Adam said.

I shrugged. "It's not that bad."

"It's the worst."

"You get used to it."

"Why there?"

I peered up at him. "To access the stash of emergency capital at Trader's house. And his . . . App Store." I left out the part about how it was a Black Market App Store.

Adam let out a long breath and stepped aside. The two of us resumed walking. Main Park was buzzing with the usual activity of the City at two o'clock on a Friday. Most Under Eighteens were still in school, but there were always those who skipped out early. There were the rich kids on one set of benches, dressed in the blazers and skirts and pants that boasted their prep academies. The girls and boys were beautiful like models because, of course, they'd either each downloaded one of the Model Apps or had permanent enhancements threaded into their codes. Then there was a bunch of Over Eighteens playing World Cup Soccer. It looked like Argentina versus Spain from their jerseys. There was the regular assortment of others who were floating or flying above the trees or climbing through them, a collection of kids Goth Apping over in a shady, secluded corner, and parents taking their ones and twos for a walk on yet another of the App World's perpetually nice days. Snow and rain and wind and thunder only happened if you downloaded it.

Adam kept eyeing me. We crossed through the gates on the far side of the park and left it behind, heading into the seedier part of town. He finally spoke. "You're mad at me."

I looked left, then right, noting that the neighborhood had changed since I'd last visited. It was more . . . populated. A bit more fixed up. Someone had finally done some updates on the architecture. "Yes, I am," I told him. "Parvda misses you. Terribly." Adam huffed. I shot him a glare. "And I don't even know why you two fought or why you plugged in and abandoned her. Abandoned *all* of us. It was dangerous to come here, you know this, and yet you did it."

His huffing turned to scoffing. "She seriously didn't tell you?"

"She's been sobbing too hard to get any words out." We rounded the corner and the landscape became vastly different. The buildings and street and sidewalks were deteriorating. They seemed to crumble before our eyes, bits of virtual concrete tumbling to the ground, leaving behind gaping holes. The sun was an even paler yellow and the air turned chillier, as though the neighborhood was being punished by the City, left out of the eternal nice weather and light of the rest of the App World.

I glanced back, to the part that had been fixed up.

It was almost as if someone had fixed that part up for show. The buildings that ringed Main Park were the most traveled, and few people crossed into this part of town. But this part of town was worse than I'd ever seen it.

Adam kicked a jagged chunk of brick lying in the middle of the sidewalk and it went bumping down the street. "Parvda's been crying?"

I stepped around a giant pothole. "Yes, she's been crying. She hasn't stopped since you plugged in." The farther we got from Main Park, the darker the sky became. Thin red and purple lines pierced it in places. "What happened with you two?"

Adam kept his eyes on the ground. We walked in silence for a block, and passed what once must have been a tall apartment building that was now a pile of virtual rubble. Neither of us commented on this. "You have to promise not to tell anyone. Absolutely no one, Skylar. Not Rain, not your creepy brother. No-bod-y."

I halted and Adam stopped. When he looked up at me his cheeks were burning. I'd never seen him like this. Sympathy mixed with worry carried away my anger. I touched his arm. "I won't. I promise. You know you can trust me."

His eyes found the sky as he spoke. "I asked Parvda to marry me."

My eyes lit up. "What?!"

"You heard me," he whispered, voice hoarse.

"That's not what I was expecting." Parvda hadn't mentioned a single word about a proposal. "That's so sweet!"

Adam's face stormed. "No it's not."

"Yes it is!"

"She rejected me. She said no. That's why we fought and that's why I left."

"Oh, Adam, you poor thing!" I reached around his tall frame and squeezed as tight as I could. "I'm so sorry."

He sighed and patted my back. "Not as sorry as I am."

I pulled away and looked up into his stricken face. "Did she say why?"

The color in his cheeks deepened. "She said we were too young. I told her I didn't care and that I'd still love her years from now, so we might as well make things official."

"You are a little young," I observed. Adam immediately heaved a big breath to start a protest, but I got there first. "But I'm not criticizing! I just wonder if Parvda . . ."

"You wonder what?" he asked, eager. Hopeful.

I bit my lip. The two of us started walking again. "I wonder if Parvda regrets saying no. She's truly inconsolable. You shouldn't have left like that. Shifted without saying a word to anyone."

"Parvda knows where I am." Adam's voice was bitter.

I smacked him on the arm. "And she's suffering in the Real World because you left. The whole time she's been hoping you'd come back. And here you are, virtually moping around."

Adam bowed his head. "You're right about the moping. That's why I was at that party. It wasn't because I was trying to meet someone new. I just haven't known what to do with myself without Parvda. For some reason, I downloaded that stupid Gaming App and ended up meeting Ree. I only agreed to help her because, well, she seemed so desperate, and also, it would give me something to do." He glanced at me. "Why do you think we're the only people who can see her?"

"I was wondering about that," I said. "Maybe it's because we didn't plug in the normal way. The reason I shifted was because I hoped I could cross the border without the patrols realizing I was here."

"Interesting theory."

I shrugged. "It's the only one I can come up with. After all, you got through undetected—at least it seems that way. Though I am worried that going to Ree's was a mistake on both our parts. If we weren't detected before, I bet people know now."

The sign for Loner Town appeared ahead, flickering in and out of the atmosphere. "I didn't realize Ree was involved with some sort of government cover-up," Adam said. The two of us stopped and stared at the buzzing letters. "Is it just me or is that . . . disappearing?" he asked.

I took a step closer. From this angle, I could see through the words to the crumbling street and building behind it. "I think it *is* disappearing. First the Death App and now this."

The two of us took in our surroundings. It was as if, I don't know, the code of the City was off. Like, the code itself might be deteriorating. There was no one—absolutely no one in sight. Nobody sitting on a bench or on the sidewalk or even on a front stoop in an App stupor. Loner Town seemed totally deserted.

"What in both worlds is happening?" Adam asked.

"I don't know. That's why we're headed to Trader's house. To try and find out."

Adam shivered with disgust. "I never wanted to see that place again."

We continued, stepping carefully to avoid falling into one of the giant potholes or tripping over the broken bricks and rocks lying everywhere. "But Trader has certain . . . methods for accessing information that might hold answers. That's why I shifted—to see what I could learn about what's going on in the App World. Well, and to see if I could find you and make sure you're okay." I eyed him as we walked. "I didn't intend to end up at Ree's place, and I had no idea I'd run into you there. That was a fortunate accident. But it's good I ended up at Ree's, and not only because of you." Part of the street had caved in and Adam and I had to cross to the other sidewalk to get around it. "There are some terrible things happening with the bodies in the Real World and I think the Death App might have something to do with it. I'm worried the mass exodus we set off with the Shifting App last February might have done something to the fabric of the App World. I wonder—" I stopped midsentence.

I'd been wrong before.

Loner Town wasn't deserted.

There was a man just down the block.

He was taking in the wares of his App Store, but he hardly had anything to choose from. Among the few he did have were three shockingly brilliant icons—one black, one coal gray, and the other a sparkling silver. All of them in the shape of presents. Even in the weak light from the sky above us, which was scattered with looming clouds, the Apps were like little suns, beckoning.

"Are those . . . ," Adam started.

". . . Death Apps?" I finished.

We hurried forward.

The man looked from the coal-gray icon to the dazzling black one.

"Don't touch that!" Adam shouted.

But the man had already gone for the shiny silver, his hand closing around it tightly.

We were too late.

The two of us ran to him.

At first nothing seemed to happen and I wondered if

we were wrong about those icons. Or even if Ree had been lying, making up stories about witnessing virtual deaths because she was bored. But as we got closer the man collapsed to the sidewalk and began to groan.

He clutched at his stomach.

His virtual skin started to sizzle, just like Ree had described, and then it grew molten like the liquidy silver of the App itself. It seemed to slide off him.

That's when he began to scream.

Adam halted. "Holy—"

"—I know."

The two of us stood over the man, watching helplessly as he began to disappear.

There was a gaping hole where his stomach once was, and it spread across his body, opening out into his chest and down his legs, all the way up to his neck until only his face was left, racked with pain. His bulging eyes stared up at us until they were gone, too.

Until all that was left of him was virtual dust on the broken sidewalk.

"That was horrible," Adam croaked.

"One of the worst things I've ever seen." I clutched my nauseous stomach. "So Ree wasn't lying."

"I guess not."

The two of us moved on in silence. Gingerly, we stepped over the man's remains and continued down the block. Before, I'd been disturbed not to see anyone, but now I was grateful. I didn't want to witness anything like that ever again.

In the quiet, my mind raced.

Was this why Loner Town was so deserted? Could it be that people hadn't left of their own volition, but instead were victims of the Death App? Were things suddenly worse or had they been this bad for a long time? Adam and I were nearing Trader's house, but three blocks away from it we had to contend with another shock, one that might've caused the end of my own virtual existence if Adam hadn't grabbed my shirt and pulled me back.

"Skylar!" he yelped, yanking hard.

I was so lost in thought I didn't even see what made him grab me.

The two of us stood at the edge of a gaping hole in the atmosphere, an entire block of houses and buildings gobbled up by it. We stared down into it.

"Does it have a bottom?" I asked, my voice hushed.

Adam got on his knees and ran his fingers across the crumbling perimeter. Tiny pebbles and chunks of virtual concrete went tumbling into the empty blackness. "Not that I can see." We listened for the rocks to hit bottom. Adam leaned forward, his eyes searching the dark space. "Or hear."

Now I was the one grabbing his shirt and holding on. "Be careful."

Adam inched backward on his knees before getting

up. "Something bad is happening in the App World. How could I be here all these months and not hear anything about it?"

I thought about Ree. "A government cover-up?"

"But how can you cover up . . . *this*?" Adam gestured toward the massive sinkhole.

"I don't know, but let's get to Trader's," I said. "If there's any talk about Death Apps and other dark virtual disappearances, we'll be able to find out there."

Adam and I moved forward, slower this time, maneuvering carefully around the sinkhole so we didn't go plummeting into oblivion. After what felt like an eternity, I could finally see Trader's house. Most of Trader's block had survived whatever blight had befallen the rest of Loner Town. And weirdly enough, Trader's house looked better than usual. The blackened shingles weren't dangling and those that were usually missing altogether had been replaced. The tree in the front of the house seemed to be thriving.

A drop of water fell from above.

Adam's eyes shot toward the sky along with mine.

Another splashed onto my cheek. "It's raining?"

Weather was downloaded here. It didn't just *happen*.

"Let's get inside," Adam called over the torrent.

We ran the rest of the way, and when we reached Trader's front steps, we were dripping wet. I jiggled the lock like he'd taught me to do and it slid open. I flipped the light switch and Trader's living room grew bright—far brighter than I was used to.

Huh.

There were other changes of note. The old, splinter-ridden table was fixed. So were the rickety chairs. The mattress that was usually propped up along the wall was lying flat along the ground, sheets pulled tight across it. "Someone's been here."

Adam disappeared into the kitchen. When he came back, he was holding a plate in his hands. "From the look of it, someone's *just* been here."

The dish held the remnants of a sandwich. "The food download hasn't even drained away yet," I said. "Whoever it is, we must've just missed the person."

His eyebrows arched. "Trader?"

I shook my head. "No. He's been glued to the Real World, and Inara." The walls still looked as though they might fall down any minute and the floorboards were pocked with holes, but things seemed almost neat. Like someone was caring for the place.

A thought chilled me. "Hello?" I called out.

Nothing.

"Maybe Trader has a squatter," I said. The house had all but been abandoned for months, so it wouldn't be out of the question that someone would take up residence. As much as I didn't begrudge anyone who needed a place to stay, I didn't love the idea that there might be someone else lurking, listening to Adam and me. "Whatever is going on, I don't like this."

"Me neither. Let's get whatever we need and leave."

"It's not that simple," I said, and went over to one of the holes in the wall and began digging around inside it. This was where Trader hid things like his stash of capital and, most important to our interests, his Store of illegal Apps. I could feel the Apps tickling my fingers and I was about to call them up when I noticed something else that sent such a chill running through my code that my virtual skin turned blue. I retracted my hand from the hole.

A single glass jar. It was filled with virtual sea glass.

Adam bent down and picked it up. "This is pretty. At least whoever has been here has nice taste."

"It is pretty," I agreed in a whisper.

The thing was, the jar in Adam's hand was a virtual copy, identical in every single way, to the one Kit had given me as a gift last winter.

18

Lacy

tiny risks

I HATED HER.

Skylar twitched in her shiny glass box. She could be anyone right now. Just another girl, not special or important. With one little push of my finger I could send her into oblivion.

Well. No. I *could*, but I wouldn't.

I'd never *really* hated Skylar. Hate was a strong emotion, reserved for people who'd earned such an outpouring of energy. Skylar wasn't worthy. Maybe not until recently. She'd always been more of a gnat around my lovely face that refused to be swatted away. Speaking of my lovely face . . . I dropped slightly and used the glass as a mirror. I looked *fine* today. Just fine. Never gorgeous.

Never spectacular like I was in the App World, glorious in everything I put on my perfect body, sumptuous from every angle. In the App World I'd been famous and rich and a queen among the Under Eighteens, and in the Real World I was barely . . . anyone at all.

Was it possible that was why . . . ?

No.

Well. Maybe.

Maybe being a nobody for a spell was why I'd almost grown to *like* the little gnat stretched out doing Apps-knows-what back home where I belonged.

But wait.

I dug around in my brain a bit. It was true, despite all evidence to the contrary and what my Haters had always wondered: *Lacy Mills did have a conscience.*

Does. Does *have a conscience.*

I did. I *do.*

Our last conversation about Rain won Skylar a lot of points. I was surprised she was capable of it. I surprised myself, too, by being capable of it. Zeera kept telling me to give her a chance, but—

"Hmm," Skylar groaned.

I jumped away from the box. Then I crept back and peered over the top. From the moment Skylar shifted, she couldn't stay still. She seemed somehow . . . like she was in both places at once. Here and there. Or at least, hanging on to here while she was still over there.

I sighed.

Skylar just had to be unique in all things.

"Can you hear me?" I whispered, feeling a bit crazy talking to a lifeless body. *Mostly* lifeless. "I'm not going to let anything happen to you. I promised and I meant it."

"Lacy, I thought I'd find you here. Who are you talking to?"

I turned, startled.

Rain. Of course, Rain. He was probably looking for Skylar, because he was always looking for Skylar. And she was always avoiding him. Or playing hard to get? I could never decide. He stared at me from way down the aisle, which was a good thing, since I made a promise to this Real World princess and I intended to keep it, despite our unhappy past.

"Nobody! You must be hearing things!" I raced over to him before he could get close enough to see that it was Skylar. Rain, the sole reason I'd stayed in this world. I smiled my most dazzling smile at him, as dazzling as I could make it in this clunky body. It was time I took advantage of the deal I made. I was still Lacy Mills, after all. I hadn't changed completely. And I definitely wasn't going to allow this moment without Skylar around to pass me by. "I'm so glad you're here!"

"Really." He sounded unconvinced. "You've been angry at me for months. What are you doing down here anyway?"

I put on my best innocent face, lips pouted, eyelashes fluttering. If I was alone I'd pinch my cheeks to redden them up and give a nice flush to my skin. It was shocking, the things a girl had to do to brighten her real self, when what would make the most sense would be to download the right App to do it. "Just doing some thinking. Besides, I like it in this place. It's so quiet."

Rain looked at me. "Since when do you like the quiet?"

"I *do*," I protested. "And I know I've been a little standoffish."

His eyebrows arched. "Standoffish?"

I cocked my head. "Annoyed?"

"Try enraged."

I blinked. Maybe now wasn't the time to broach the subject of whether Rain still had feelings for me. Then again, who knew how long Skylar would stay plugged in and I'd have him to myself? "It's true. I have been upset with you, but . . ." I suddenly couldn't speak. All the haughtiness went out of me, replaced by sheer need, want, *hope* that I could fix things with Rain. Whatever that meant. I swallowed.

Even if it meant we would just be friends.

Rain touched my cheek with the back of his hand. "Are you okay? You're so pale."

"Hmmm," I barely managed, because every cell in my real body was turned toward the place where Rain's skin touched mine. He took his hand away and I blurted, "Are we still at least friends?" Now my cheeks flushed all on their very own.

The surprise on his face was illuminated by the glow of the plugs. "Yes. We are. We'll always be friends, Lacy."

I stopped myself just in time before asking, "*Just friends?*" My heart plummeted to the jagged rocks below the cavern to the ocean floor. Why did I have to go and provoke Rain to declare our undying friendship? This wasn't going where I wanted it to. "You were looking for me. Any particular reason? Can I help with something?"

Rain leaned against the glass wall of the plugs and nodded. His expression grew serious. "Yes. Listen." His tone had turned serious. "I need to tell you something important."

That you love me?

These four words sang out inside me like the gorgeous pop star I was back in the days when I'd download the American Idol App, when I was a young twelve and all tween-like. But as I watched Rain now it didn't seem like he was about to profess his undying love.

Sadly, I was right.

"It's about Skylar," he said.

My chest tightened. Pain. I felt pain inside it.

Of course Rain wanted to talk about Skylar. When didn't he?

"We got into a fight," he began.

"Oh?" The pain lessened, though only a bit.

"She's determined to plug in, and I can't let her. But she's stubborn—"

"—I know, isn't she?"

"—and I'm afraid she's the kind of person who's going to do it regardless of the risks. But she absolutely cannot."

"She'll survive," I said, despite the chill that ran up my spine. "She always does."

Now Rain blinked at me. He was hesitating. I knew him well enough to tell when he was debating if he should trust me with whatever secret information was in his possession. He took a deep breath, seeming to decide that yes, I *was* trustworthy, which sent a tiny streak of glee through my veins. "There's something wrong in the App World, Lacy. People have been dying on the plugs. Children. The elderly. Sixteens. There's no rhyme or reason to it. Not that we've figured out yet. But I'm worried it might have to do with the Shifting App. And so is Skylar."

"That's horrible." I resisted the urge to glance back at her right now. Then I resisted the urge to roll my eyes in utter and total exasperation. That girl. She always had to meddle when things got dangerous. She must have a death wish. "But what does this all have to do with me?"

"Well, I thought maybe Skylar might go to Zeera for help, and now that you're friends with Zeera, I'm hoping you can make sure that she won't help Skylar."

I rolled my eyes and groaned. Skylar was smart, I had to admit it. Rain would never guess she'd come to me of all people. And if only Rain had spoken to me sooner, I'd have known not to listen to stupid Skylar! It wasn't like I could force her back to the Real World, because what if shifting really did cause a problem? A teensy little death problem? And I somehow made the situation worse?

"So I can't rely on you then?" Rain asked, his words clipped with frustration.

My hands balled into fists. "No! I mean, yes. Yes, you can rely on me. I'll make sure Zeera doesn't help her," I said, which wasn't a lie. I just didn't tell him that *I'd* helped her.

"Good," he said. "Thank you."

"You're welcome," I said.

We stood there awkwardly.

What I *should* do was go check on Skylar. Truthfully, now I was a little worried. Well. Only a little bit of that worry was actually for Skylar, and the bulk of it had to do with what Rain would think of me if Skylar went and died on my watch. Before I could decide to send Rain on his way so I could go check on his precious girlfriend— even thinking the word in relation to someone other than me made me gag inside—Rain decided this for me.

"I guess I'll see you later," he said.

"Okay." I was unable to mask my disappointment. "Bye, I guess."

He gave me a quick nod. "Bye." Then he turned and walked away.

And I watched him go.

Every step that took him farther hurt my heart.

I was wasting my chance.

Um, why was I wasting my chance?

"Wait!" I shouted and ran after him. "Can we, um, talk?"

He halted. "About what?"

I could tell from his tone he knew that I meant to talk about us. "At least face me," I said. "Can't you give me that much respect?"

When Rain turned around, shame was written onto his face. "I'm sorry. I wasn't trying to be rude. I'm just off to . . ."

"Look for Skylar?" My eyes sought the floor. "Wait for her? Propose marriage to her?"

Rain grimaced. Even still, he was gorgeous. "Actually . . ."

I dug my toes into the hard cavern floor and waited for him to tell me the inevitable.

". . . no."

I raised my gaze. His eyes had softened. He was looking at me in a way he hadn't in months. I soaked it up like sunlight. "Well. I'm glad."

He studied me back. "Okay."

I twirled a lock of my hair, a habit from the App World that transferred to the real one. The familiar green sparkle of my nails gave me the courage I needed. It was now or never. "There are some things I need to say to you," I said. "And some questions I have."

The softness in his eyes faded. "Lacy."

My name from his mouth sounded like a warning. "Rain." My finger was still twirling, my courage growing rather than receding. "I'm just asking for a conversation. Don't you at least owe me that much?" As I spoke the question, I knew I was right. Rain *did* owe me at least that much. And then some.

For a moment he went still.

Then he nodded. "You're right. I do." He looked around the cavern, dark except for the eerie glow of the plugs, as though searching for someone. Or wondering if someone else was listening. After a minute, he asked, "Where do you want to go?"

19

Skylar

city death

I COULDN'T TEAR my eyes from that jar of glass.

I shook my head.

"Sorry," I said to Adam. "I don't know what got into me. I need to focus." I stuck my hand back inside the hole in the wall and out came Trader's Black Market App Store. I'd known about such Stores for ages, everyone in the City knew about them. Trader warned me once what to expect if I ever called up his, but it was one thing to hear rumors and descriptions and something else to be at the center of one. "Have you ever—" I began, but my voice dropped off as I took in the icons now hovering and darting about in Trader's living room.

"—seen one of these?" Adam supplied. "No." He

swallowed. "And I can't say that I ever want to see another one after today."

The two of us alternated between staring and shielding our eyes.

Some of the icons were violent. Horribly so. They depicted images that I wished I'd never seen but would be burned in my memory forever. Some of the icons screamed and cried. The people they depicted were subjected to various forms of torture, the images repeating vile acts as the icons replayed the horrors they promised. There were Apps for every kind of vicious thing you could imagine and a million things you would *never* imagine unless you were deranged. They filled every corner of the room and flitted into the adjoining kitchen until it was impossible to turn away and not see another one.

Trader told me once that before the App World came into existence, when the virtual was still something you accessed only through those little devices and tablets, back when people still referred to it as *the internet*, there was something called the dark web. The dark web was the evil underside of the normal, public virtual sphere. Criminals operated it and used it to trade everything from weapons to slaves and so many other terrible things. You had to know how to access the dark web in order to use it, and lots of people didn't even know of its existence. The Black Market App Store was modeled after it, apparently.

Not exactly the kind of thing you learn in Real World History Class.

"I don't see a Death App icon," Adam whispered, sounding choked.

I nodded. "I suppose that is *one* good thing."

There were nonviolent icons too. If you were seeking classified information, conspiracy theories, government cover-ups, you also went to the Black Market App Store. There were Black Market Apps that specialized in underground chatter and traded in illegal information. This was how Trader had become aware that the borders were going to close between worlds before it was announced to the rest of us; how he'd known to get working on an App that would allow people to illegally cross from here into the Real World, and to have it ready once Jonathan Holt made his emergency broadcast announcement that Service was canceled.

I searched the storm of horrors populating Trader's living room for the icon he told me was the best of them. The scenes only seemed to get worse and I didn't know how much longer I could take witnessing such horrible images. "We need to find an icon with a man's blond head and an hourglass next to it. There's a globe inside the top half of it, dripping toward the bottom half." When I turned to Adam, his hands covered his eyes. He was usually so brave. "Adam, I know this is awful, but I need your help!"

He groaned and removed his hands from his face. "I

really don't want to see any more of this. It's almost worse than having to watch that man download the Death App."

"But as soon as we find the right icon the others will go away!" I began to step through the Apps, studying each one. They were a tornado of debris, ready to hurt and maim the eyes and mind of anyone who came into contact with them.

My foot caught on one of the holes in the floor, and I nearly tumbled into an App so vile I screamed a scream I'd only heard during the Horror Flick Apps Inara and I used to download when we wanted to scare ourselves, back when feeling terrified seemed a fun break in the monotony of so much pleasantness in the City.

Adam reached out just in time to stop me from touching it. "Skylar, careful!"

"I know. Thank you," I said between heaving breaths, my arms gripping my stomach. The act of vomiting was supposedly another of the terrible capabilities exclusive to the real body, but now I wondered whether the virtual self might become so nauseous with fear and terror it could happen here, too. "Help me search!" I called to Adam, and we moved around the room quickly now, ducking and sidestepping as some icons hovered nearly motionless while others tried to slam into us. Then, finally, I saw a flash of white-blond by the staircase, the icon itself seeming to drip an entire world down to the floor.

"There it is," I said, full of relief.

The Wicked Leaks App.

I rushed to it, desperate to make everything else go away.

"Skylar, wait!" Adam was shouting. "Don't you think we should—" he tried.

Adam's voice died midwarning.

The rest of the Black Market Apps blinked out.

For a moment, there was blissful calm. A silence that was total and complete.

The two of us breathed.

But soon the voices started. They filled the atmosphere, one on top of the other, some so loud they were shouting and others barely a whisper.

Then the mouths appeared.

Hundreds, no, thousands of mouths, detached from their faces and virtual bodies. Mouths just hanging in the air, lips moving as they spoke, some revealing rotted teeth. Depending on where you stood, you could home in on different types of chatter, different illegal conversations. By the staircase I heard a snippet about illegal Apping and how to find communities of criminals who would do it with you. I moved closer to the now-fixed table and chairs and heard a man's deep voice explaining how to hack the code of someone's basic self, and then another, a woman, extolling a plot to take over the government. Trader had warned me there were a lot of plots brewing, each one of them more fervent than the other.

We could be here all day trying to find the information we needed. Weeks, even.

I thought back to that night in my bedroom when I was still a Single and needed information about Lacy Mills; how I'd whittled down the millions of possible scenes I could choose to view from her life. It was as simple as searching for moments she'd spent with Rain and sorting them by price. So what was the magic combination of search terms that would lead me to the right thread of chatter now?

Mysterious virtual disappearances?

No. Too vague.

The Death App?

No. That was probably just the name Ree had given it, and if it was, it would be useless among this mess of possibilities.

An image of that dark and bottomless hole that nearly swallowed Adam and me entered my mind, and the way that Loner Town seemed to be deteriorating. Could the deaths of the bodies on the plugs and the virtual death we'd witnessed *and* the crumbling of this neighborhood be connected? Could the City itself be dying? The entire App World fading from existence?

Was that even possible?

And could all this have to do with a virus? That little "bug," as Trader called it?

A particularly ugly mouth started shouting nonsense

in my left ear and I swatted it away.

"Skylar." My name was strangled in Adam's throat.

My mind was stuck on those chilling thoughts. "What?"

"Come here," he shouted. "Please."

Adam was crouched in the corner. A mouth painted with neon-pink lipstick was whispering words at lightning speed in between giggling and laughing. The lips were razor thin. "Did you find what we're looking for?" I asked.

"Not exactly," he said.

"We don't have time to get distracted by information we don't need."

"This isn't a distraction! You need to hear this!"

I went to him and dropped down so we were level. Adam listened close and I nudged in next to him. At first the words came too quickly for me to catch anything, but then I began to hear a name repeated over and over between everything else.

"Skylar."

"Skylar Cruz."

"Skylar, Skylar, *Skylar*."

"They're talking about me," I breathed.

Adam nodded. "And it's not good. You've got Haters."

"I have Haters?" Lacy Mills was the kind of person who had Haters. Rain had Haters. Basically anyone and everyone with any fame whatsoever had Haters. It was one of the many things Rain told me he'd loathed about being famous and that had made him desperate to unplug, and it was one of the things Lacy was good at shrugging off, or enjoying, since she'd loved soaking up attention, *any* attention. But the notion that somehow *I* could acquire Haters was nearly incomprehensible.

"Listen carefully," Adam said. "They're almost worse than Haters."

I moved closer to those neon-pink lips, so painted there were deep cracks in the thick layer of shiny makeup. The voices were not only fast, they were layered, one over the other, making it difficult to follow a single conversation. Then I heard my name again, *Skylar*, and I strained to hang on to the string of words that followed with everything in me.

"There's a virus in the App World," said that one line of chatter.

Every zero in my code jumped to attention.

To talk of a virus in the Real World with Trader was one thing. But no one in the App World would ever utter that word unless there was something to it, not even on the Black Market. The word *virus* was verboten, even vaguely illegal. I'd never known anyone who'd ever said it out loud, except in reference to the tragedies of the real body. But a virus that spread virtually could mean complete and total extinction of life as everyone knew it in the City.

Given the Death App and the state of things in Loner Town, this would make total sense.

The voice kept going. "Skylar the Plague launched a virus into the App World during her emergency broadcast. The government is trying to keep this quiet, but there's no doubt that it's spreading and spreading fast. Too fast for anyone to contain it."

Skylar the Plague?

This wasn't the only name people were calling me.

Skylar the Virus Spreader. Skylar the Bringer of Virtual Death. Skylar the Destroyer. They sounded like titles one might acquire while gaming, titles that would strike fear and revulsion in the hearts of all players. There were even plots to kill me. But the real question I had was this: *Did* I launch a virus into the App World with the Shifting App? Had my mother been wrong about those bodies and why they'd died?

"Virus, virus, VIRUS," went the mouth, lips curling and cracking.

"You need to leave the City," Adam said. "It's not safe. People want you virtually dead, really dead. Dead in every way you could possibly be dead. They're blaming you for whatever is happening here."

"I'm less worried about me than I am about a virus," I whispered, nervous to say that word out loud into the atmosphere. "And the thought that maybe it's our fault. *My* fault," I corrected. Adam was about to protest again, but I gestured for him to wait. A new set of search terms had popped into my head and I wanted to try them out. "Wicked Leaks, show me *Death of the City* and *Death of the App World.*"

Adam's mouth formed a quiet, shocked O.

The two of us waited.

One by one, and then in groups and bunches, the mouths around us began to disappear. I'd hoped that maybe all of them would, that my search would come up empty, but soon the disappearances slowed until about thirty mouths remained. They crowded closer around us.

One of them was louder than all the others. Its voice was clear and strong and confident, a single string of words repeated over and over in warning.

Adam and I turned to it together and stared at it in horror.

"The App World is dying," it cried. "The App World is dying."

20

Skylar

the tug of regret

WITH A FLICK of my hand the mouths that remained disappeared.

I looked at Adam. "Come back with me to the Real World. Please. There's so much we need to figure out."

"No," he said, quiet but firm.

I gritted my teeth. "Adam!"

"*No*," he repeated, louder this time. Adam was shaking his head, his whole body swaying. "You can't believe everything you hear on the Black Market."

"This from someone who was just telling me *I* needed to leave because of threats from Haters. You'll believe that, but you won't believe the possibility that total virtual death is on this City's doorstep? Not to mention the fact that *we saw that man virtually die.*"

Adam sat on the floor and rested his back against the wall. A strange-looking bug scuttled out from a crack in the wall near his left arm. It glowed red and orange and yellow and still managed to look menacing. "I don't believe the App World is dying. It's too crazy."

I joined him on the ground, careful to avoid the creepy insect. "You saw what I saw. That giant hole in Loner Town? The Death App in action? The way Loner Town seems to be, I don't know, *disintegrating*?"

"But what about the people whose bodies were sold on the Body Market? If the App World really is dying, then wouldn't they just cease to exist forever?"

I'd already had the same thought. "I don't know." I rested my arms on the top of my knees, the pale color of my virtual skin so foreign after the deep golden brown of my real body. "If the App World is dying, then the Body Market has to close permanently, so nobody else loses a body they might want to return to. I need to shift back to the Real World immediately. Adam, shift with me. Come *on*."

He just sat there, silent. Being stubborn.

"What if you stay and you die? What would happen to Parvda?"

He lowered his head. "Then she'd finally be free of me."

I wanted to pinch him. No, I wanted to punch him. "You're being absurd."

"I don't care. Stop trying. I'm not doing it. Besides, what about Ree?"

I'd nearly forgotten about her. There was a pocket inside me, tucked deep and hidden like a secret cabinet, that pulsed with guilt at abandoning her to that prison of an apartment. I knew that we owed her for that essential bit of information she'd offered about the Death App. But the rest of me just shrugged. "Ree can wait. We'll help her later."

Adam gaped at me. "You used to care about everyone and making sure they were okay."

I avoided his stare, sensing the way my code was hardening, my very makeup turning solid, so solid I wondered if the blood had stopped pumping through the real veins of my body. "And I still do. But unfortunately, Ree is just one person, and right now there are hundreds of thousands of others to consider."

A look of disapproval flashed on Adam's face. "That's awfully utilitarian of you. Maybe you're more like the rest of your family than I thought."

Adam's words seemed to have sharp metal hooks, and they pierced my virtual skin. I looked down at my arms and expected to see them bleeding. I stood, leaving Adam alone on the ground. "Look who's talking. You're the one who cares about Ree more than your girlfriend."

Adam opened his mouth to protest, but nothing came out.

"I'm leaving," I told him.

Then I turned my back—on Adam, on Ree, on the mysterious owner of that jar of sea glass beckoning me—and I began the process of shifting back to the Real World.

"Bye, Skylar," Adam whispered.

I stepped out the front door of Trader's house, willing the room with the doors to appear. Shifting involved taking control of the virtual scenery, becoming the conductor of the landscape, the architect of the pathways from here to there. But the pathway back to reality was always through the room full of doors. I never knew if it was a trick of the mind or an actual place.

The floor underneath me seemed to tilt, and I saw the now-familiar long hall, though the doors themselves changed each time I was here. The one closest to my left was covered in white fur, the pelt of a great and beautiful animal, and I shivered in disgust at the thought of something so majestic shedding its skin. Another was covered by a rushing waterfall, yet one that left the wooden floor beneath it dry. A few were simple, doors you might find at the entrance to a modest house or a small apartment, but most had at least one enticing, unusual quality—the glitter of endless diamonds, the smell of ripe and juicy peaches, the plush softness of fluffy blankets. The last two made me wonder how much my own needs could conjure what I saw, since my stomach was growling with hunger and all I wanted was to crawl beneath the covers of a bed and go to sleep.

I noticed a familiar door to my right.

The door to Ree's apartment.

But this time the locks were broken, the bars across it splintered. I walked on until it was far behind me, willing myself to forget about it, searching for the signpost that would tell me I'd safely crossed the border between worlds and was ready wake up in the real body again. My heart stuttered and skipped with the rhythm of my steps, curious what that sign would be and if it would be different from the one I'd grown used to all those months ago.

I wanted it to be different.

Maybe it would have to do with Rain.

Maybe it would be the terrace outside his room with the beautiful nighttime view of the stars. Or that spot on the beach where he liked to sit and watch the ocean as it rumbled in to shore during a storm. Or even the table where he ate lunch in the cafeteria, the one by the tall windows that looked out onto a grove of pine trees. Or maybe the signpost would have to do with my mother or Parvda, or even Zeera and Sylvia, all of whom had come to represent my time and life in the Real World.

Ever so gradually, almost imperceptibly, the wooden floor underneath my feet became sand and the white walls between doors became the pale outline of dunes that rose up on either side of me. Seagulls called out overhead and the faint sound of the ocean waves roared and then receded, soothing my tired senses like a sweet song. My skin was warmed by the sun and my muscles loosed in relief, the tension flowing out of them at the thought of home, at the way the beach and the ocean and the tall wild grasses that framed the coastline gave me a sense of true belonging, just as the promise of the real body did as well, the sight of the brown skin that matched my mother's and a heart that was flesh and not a long string of meaningless code. I expected to see Briarwood off in the distance, and once I did, I'd know I could wake and find myself safe and sound in the dark caverns underneath the mansion.

But as I kept going, the shore became rockier, less easy to cross. I picked my way along jagged boulders and wide, flat sheets of slate, slippery with seaweed and neon-green moss, tide pools so big I had to step through them carefully since going around them would require wading into the churning sea.

There are no rocks like this near Briarwood.

Only beach.

A road appeared that hugged the shore, cresting like an angry wave ready to pull everything in its path under. I knew by now I would not see Briarwood around the next bend, and when I saw the familiar tree and the cottage perched alongside of it, my heart and mind absorbed what this meant, even as a voice inside me whispered a truth I wished I could avoid.

Kit is still the signpost to your real self.

Trying to sit up after shifting was like wading through something thick and viscous, like the air around me was made of batter. My limbs were heavy, my body exhausted, and my stomach seemed to have climbed onto a merry-go-round. I wasn't sure how long I lay there, immobile. Maybe hours. But when the dizziness finally subsided and the pounding in my head dulled to only a faint hammering, I opened my eyes.

The memory of Kit's cottage and the way my pulse jumped as I reached for the door to his house was so vivid I half expected to find out I'd awoken there, to see him across the room, the edges of his tattoos visible beneath the sleeves of his shirt, his back to me making dinner.

But, of course, that's not what I saw.

I was still in the cavern beneath Briarwood in the very same spot as before, alive at the very least, amid the eerie now-familiar glow of the plugs.

Lacy was nowhere in sight.

21

Ree

glitches

BEING BAIT WAS so totally boring. And unlike with the sequestering in my apartment, it didn't come with unlimited free Apps, which was so totally annoying.

If Char was still alive she would virtually die all over again with jealousy over my current predicament, though. I mean, me, ending up in a bizarre and elaborate throne room with Emory Specter, who thusly informed me first, that he has a daughter, and second, that his daughter is also his nemesis. It was just amazing on so many levels. The best gossip ever.

A bird landed on my windowsill.

It was about five different shades of the brightest greens, with a long, thin, sharp beak. It cocked its head and looked at me. I got up from the couch slowly, hoping not to scare it away.

"Here, little birdie birdie," I called. I took one careful and quiet step forward, then another, but by the time I got close enough to reach out and touch it, it chirped loudly and flew off, leaving me alone again. "Oh, lovely," I said to nobody and nothing aside from the rather attractively decorated walls and tastefully furnished room.

I had to admit, as far as prison cells went, this one was pretty lush.

If I could download an Interior Decorator App right now, I wouldn't be averse to this very same design scheme. With its big all-white canopied bed and matching puffy chairs and couches slipcovered in soft white fabric covered in tiny blue flowers, any girl could be happy here for a spell. There was even a white braided rug on the floor.

Jail might be deadly boring, but it sure was nice.

I went to the window for the twentieth time in the last couple of hours, touching the sill where the bird had been perched just moments before. Emory Specter and Mrs. Farley and whoever else ran this place obviously weren't worried about me climbing through the window. It was already open wide when they locked me inside. The first thing I did was try and figure out if there was any possibility of escape.

The answer: no freakin' way.

I was so high up that puffy clouds floated by, so close

I could nearly put my hands through them. There would be no jumping, not without any Apps to break my fall or fix me immediately afterward. Good thing I was used to flying-related Apps, otherwise I might suffer from vertigo. Main Park was barely a speck below, a little green square I could squeeze between two fingers. The City stretched on and on as far as I could see, an endless grid of buildings and apartments and streets. I'd climbed to the top of the Water Tower about a million times before to take in the view, but it paled in comparison to the one I had from here. I kept racking my brain trying to think if I'd ever noticed a building this tall in the skyline of the City, but I couldn't come up with anything so high that it spiked through the clouds. The possibility that maybe I was in a tower coded to be invisible crossed my mind, but that seemed too crazy, so I dismissed it.

And then I sighed.

The view hadn't changed since last time I checked.

I leaned my stomach onto the sill and tipped forward.

My feet rose off the floor until they were dangling in the atmosphere. The farther I stretched, the more I could see about my location. Though even if I could pinpoint where I was, it likely wouldn't do much good. I could scream all I wanted and no one would hear unless I somehow managed to download a Megaphone App, and that wasn't going to happen anytime soon. Besides, Mrs. Farley probably had this place coded like my apartment, to prevent me from getting out or to prevent anyone from being able to communicate with me.

I leaned a little farther, so much I was angling toward the ground, my feet rising higher than the sill, high enough that I could easily slide forward and end up touching those clouds floating below the window. And not in a good way. More in a falling-to-my-death way. Still, what did I care what happened now? Emory Specter claimed he wasn't going to hurt me, but why should I trust him? Once his nemesis daughter got here, if she even came for me, which I highly doubted, given the way she'd abandoned me once already, what would stop good old Emory from virtually killing me afterward? I leaned a smidge more to the right, twisting my virtual self in ways it probably shouldn't be twisted, hoping I could see a little farther beyond the edge of the skyscraper.

My daredevil contortions were soon rewarded.

I noticed something new. Though I wasn't sure exactly what I was looking at.

A large black circle covered part of the City below. Maybe Loner Town? It was like someone had blotted out the landscape. Or, you know how when an architecture download starts to deteriorate and sometimes the fabric of the atmosphere gets glitchy and little holes appear? What I was seeing was kind of like that, but on a massive scale.

Wait. Could that be, like, a giant glitch?

The hugest glitch ever?

It looked as if someone had detonated a bomb in a game. But that was impossible, since this was the City I was seeing. And even if this was an enormous glitch in the fabric of the App World, why hadn't anyone come along and fixed it? Wasn't that what the government was for? I mean, the hole might be in Loner Town, which nobody really cares about anyway, but a glitch that big is a risk to let fester. Glitches were like wounds. If neglected too long, they could infect wider swaths of code. Everyone knew this. It was basic information technology, the kind of thing people learned in App World History 1.0.

A gust of wind blew and pushed just hard enough that I tilted a little farther.

I screamed, unable to right myself, desperately digging my fingers into a crevice between the stones, my breaths heavy. When I was steady again I pushed upward until my feet reached solid virtual ground.

Whoa. That was close.

My virtual heart was throbbing like I'd just downloaded a new and improved boyfriend.

No girl wants to go virtually splat by an App-free fall from a skyscraper. Surely I could be fixed with the right downloads to my code, but I didn't relish the thought of having to go through all that pain. Plus, what reason would Emory Specter and company have to fix me? They might just allow me to suffer.

I glanced at the door, hoping nobody heard me scream.

Then I looked out the window once more, this time with new purpose. A Binocular App would be an excellent enhancement at the moment, but I'd have to make do.

And now I knew what to look for.

I searched the landscape of the City below for other black spots, and my code soon roared with a static so forceful I could hear it.

I began to count. *One, two, three, four, five*, and so on and so forth.

Seriously.

I counted once more, to be sure.

There must be at least twenty-seven black spots across the City, and these were the ones that were visible without any downloads to help. None of the holes were as big as the one I could see in Loner Town. In fact, most of them were fairly small in comparison. But still, I could identify them with the naked virtual eye. They reminded me of the dots that appeared across your virtual vision if you kept staring at the Sun 8.0 directly for too long.

I took one step to the left and looked again.

One, two, three, four . . .

This time I counted a total of nineteen black spots.

Different black spots.

I did the same thing again, this time taking two steps to the right. Then one step backward. Again, and again, from slightly different vantage points, I counted the black spots on the landscape. I even tried squinting my eyes and opening them wide to see what changed. What I learned was soon clear: depending on the angle, a person could identify *different* glitches in *different* places. Maybe the government *was* trying to repair the holes in the fabric of our world, but wasn't able to do so completely. And the one in Loner Town was just too big to fix.

Or maybe they weren't trying to repair them at all.

Maybe they were irreparable and the government was just trying to hide them instead?

I stepped away from the window and turned my attention to the room, alternating between squinting and opening my eyes wide, studying everything from different angles. The bed, the couch, the chairs, the side tables. Even the rug. Nothing seemed out of the ordinary. No black spots, not big ones or even tiny ones. Everything seemed in perfect downloaded order, without any glitches that I was able to find.

I plopped down onto the puffy couch. "Harrumph."

I sat there awhile doing nothing, because there was nothing to do. I didn't even know if I was waiting for something, or if Emory Specter would call me down to talk again, or if he'd already forgotten my existence and would only remember again if his nemesis daughter showed up. Then, because I was bored, I decided to examine the room one more time.

This time, I tried to alter my angles of observation, but it was difficult since there wasn't a way to mark my previous viewpoints. Nothing that a Hansel and Gretel App wouldn't fix, but alas, there would be no bread crumbs to indicate my previous steps so I could avoid them in the future.

Seriously. How did people get by before there were Apps for, like, every single thing?

It was truly a mystery.

I was spinning one way and the other, frustrated, when something caught my eye.

By the door.

Was that a black spot?

I tried one viewpoint after another and came up with nothing—at first.

I went closer, then closer still, until I was practically crouching against it, my eyes level with the lock.

You have to be kidding me.

"A glitch, a glitch, a glitch," I shrieked, before it occurred that I should shut up in case somebody was listening to the happenings in my room.

The glitch was right next to the lock. A round black spot, large enough for my fist to push through it. You had to look at it just so to see it, but there was no doubt that it existed.

I reached out one single finger and poked at it.

My finger went through easily and came back totally intact.

Curious, I stood and took a step back. The hole

disappeared from view, like the virtual wood spontane-ously repaired itself somehow. I remembered where it was, though, just an inch and a half to the left of the lock. Once again, I placed my fingers in that spot.

They disappeared like ghosts that could pass through something solid.

I retracted my hand, then made a fist and plunged it into the glitch. I felt around on the other side of the door until my fingers touched the cold metal of a key. Care-fully, I turned it until I heard a click.

A bolt sliding open.

I retracted my hand again, studying it.

"Huh." It seemed totally unharmed.

A part of me wondered if putting my arm through a glitch would mess with my code or do some other horrible irreparable damage, like melt my virtual skin or turn my fingers into black spots. When I was satisfied that all was well, my fingers closed around the knob on this side of the door and tried it.

It turned easily.

I pushed it open wide.

Then, after looking left and right, I stepped into the hallway.

22

Skylar

selfish

THIS IS WHAT I saw when I went to find Rain:

A girl and a boy on a terrace. They were staring into each other's eyes, eyes that were full of longing and confusion and division. They sat at just enough distance from each other that they couldn't touch. But everything about their bodies announced that this was all they wanted to do.

The moment my gaze had landed on Lacy and Rain, I knew they were meant to be together.

The sand slipped and slid underneath my feet as I stood there, watching them. I'd taken the path around the mansion that led to Rain's room from the outside. My body had craved the real air, the real sea, the real warmth of the real sun after so much time amid the pale virtual imitations of these things. I didn't want to be indoors once I managed to get my limbs moving and steady enough to walk. The only stop I made was to glance inside my mother's lab, but she wasn't there.

Lacy and Rain were so engrossed in each other they hadn't noticed me.

I waited for the tears to come. For jealousy to rage inside me, informing me of the truth of my feelings for Rain, and of what I had lost when I took the risk of making that deal with Lacy. Of allowing her to come between us.

But I felt none of this.

Their lips moved quickly, first Rain, then Lacy, deep in conversation, murmuring words I was too far away to understand. My toes inched forward and I took another quiet step. I should have turned around and left them alone, but I kept moving toward them instead of away. I'd nearly reached the steps of the deck before I was able to catch snatches of what they were saying.

Or, rather, confessing.

"Skylar . . . special to me . . ."

This, from Rain.

"But she . . . our history . . . and you and I, we . . ."

This, from Lacy.

There came a long pause. I didn't dare look up, worried they would sense my presence. I kept my attention on the rough gray wood of the terrace steps as I listened.

"Rain, I still love you." Lacy was saying. "And I think you still love me. I can tell from the way you look at me. Are you ever going to be honest with yourself and admit this? Be honest with me, too?" Her voice was strong and clear, so I didn't miss a single word.

I can tell from the way you look at her too, Rain, I found myself agreeing.

I waited for Rain to answer.

Another long silence passed.

"Yes," he said eventually, but nothing more.

"Yes *what*?" Lacy sounded frustrated.

"Yes, you're right," he said quietly. "I do still love you."

My breathing stopped.

I heard rustling.

I looked up.

Once again I saw the boy and the girl on the terrace, but now I saw that the boy was sliding closer to the girl and taking her hand into his, her face radiant with joy.

For a second, I stood there frozen, knowing I should leave but rooted to the ground like the cattails swaying in the grasses behind the dunes.

All I could think about was Kit.

How I wished for a moment like this with him.

Lacy's eyes shone.

I pivoted, the balls of my feet digging into the rough sand, and walked in the other direction, down toward the other end of the beach.

* * *

I stopped short of the refugee camp. I wasn't in the mood to answer more questions about plugging back in to a world that might be dying. But Andleeb had been out for a walk and she found me there, staring into the distance, watching as evening fell and tiny bonfires began to pepper the sand, people gathering around them to cook and warm their hands. The temperature was dropping fast.

"You look like you just lost a friend," she said.

I shook my head. But had I? Maybe I'd lost Rain as a boyfriend, but maybe this didn't mean I'd lost him as a friend, too. "I'm fine."

Her dark eyes were unblinking. The way her head scarf framed her face made them seem even bigger. "Are you sure?"

I didn't trust myself to answer this question without honesty, so I changed the subject. "Where's Rasha?"

"Rasha's napping, and you never want to wake that girl when she's sleeping." Andleeb laughed. "In the App World, she became a bear when she was afraid, which is pretty appropriate since she growls if you rouse her."

I laughed in response, which sent the world into a spin. I was still dizzy from shifting. Andleeb grabbed me before I could fall. For a second I thought I might pass out. Sometimes I wondered if those incredible App World–related skills that I brought back with me when I'd first unplugged also drained away from the real body eventually, just like they would from one's virtual self. I stood there for a full minute, waiting, until finally the world stopped spinning. "Do you feel like company on your walk?" I asked, now that I thought I was steady enough to move again.

Andleeb was studying me with concern. "Sure," she said eventually, and dropped her hand from my arm.

"It really doesn't bother you, having to wear that scarf over your hair all the time?" I asked as we headed closer to the water.

She adjusted it, pulling it tighter. Today it was the bright-green color of the lawn outside the library in New Port City, with tiny yellow polka dots. "No," she said. She told me about her family's culture and faith and how it had been affected by everyone plugging in, and what it was like to return to the Real World and have to adjust yet again. "I like the way my head scarf makes people notice me. It makes me feel visible in a way that I never was in the App World. The scarves make me into a mystery. Like, a secret waiting to be discovered."

"That's a nice way of seeing it," I said. "But I don't know about the being stared at part. I've always hated having people stare."

Andleeb's face darkened. "People stare at you for different reasons."

My feet dug through the packed sand with every step. My legs weren't as steady as I'd thought, and I grasped for grounding. I needed to get ahold of myself. There were things that had to get done, but I wasn't yet in a state to do them. "Yes. And not all of them good. I am not Queen Skylar to everyone."

Andleeb didn't respond.

For a while the only sounds were from the waves crashing into shore. My body was exhausted, and by my third stumble Andleeb grabbed me again, holding me up. "Skylar, what's going on?"

I bent forward a little, hands on my knees, just trying to breathe. "I'm tired, I guess."

"Tired, yes. But I would say that you look like someone who just unplugged."

I straightened and stared over the dunes at the mansion rising up behind us. The windows reflected the last rays of the sun before night fell completely.

"Skylar?" she pressed.

I turned to Andleeb. She had the eyes of someone I could trust. "Before I answer, tell me something first."

The wind buffeted her scarf and flowing long-sleeved shirt and pants. She nodded.

"Do you think the situation with the refugees is improving or getting worse?"

Andleeb's eyes traveled down the beach toward the camp. "It depends on who you ask. But I'd say people are losing patience. Life is difficult in the body, even more difficult than most remember. Like we've discussed before, if there was a way for people to plug back in safely, I think a lot of the refugees would jump at the chance."

The bonfires were bright spots of orange in the sand. "I was afraid of that." Shadows gathered around them, and laughter traveled down the beach toward the place where we stood. The laughter gave me hope. "What if there wasn't a choice? And not because we couldn't negotiate a truce with the App World, but because . . ." I trailed off.

"Skylar, what?"

"Because the App World was . . . *is* no longer safe. Not just because of the border patrols." There. I'd said it. The claim *The App World is dying* echoed in my head.

"You did plug in," Andleeb whispered.

I nodded. "The news isn't good."

Andleeb reached for my hand. "I'm listening."

"I'm going to need all the help I can get with the refugees." An idea was forming as I spoke. "I think we need to identify ambassadors from among the refugees to be go-betweens, both to help with the Keepers resisting your presence and to help smooth the transition to life in the Real World." I squeezed Andleeb's hand. "Do you think you and Rasha might be up for such a role?" My question hung in the evening air—the only sound around us was a seagull crying overhead.

Andleeb squeezed my hand back. She grew taller, shoulders back. Regal and strong. "You can count on me. And I think I can say the same for my sister."

"Good," I said. "I'll be in touch again soon. We're going to need to call a meeting." I took in a deep breath. "And I'm going to need your help."

"Of course," Andleeb said. "We'll be ready."

I leaned in and gave her a grateful hug.

Then we said our good-byes and I headed off to find Trader.

Trader was walking away from Inara's room when I saw him. I picked up my pace, nearly breaking into a run so I could catch him before he rounded the corner.

"Trader," I called out.

He stopped and turned. "Hi, Sis," he said, with a dark grin.

"I went to your house," I said.

His face grew alarmed. "Why would you do that when I'm right here?" He was trying to joke, but there was something else underneath his tone.

I studied him. "I meant your house in the App World."

"Oh. You shifted? Hmmm. You haven't done that in ages. You shouldn't. It takes a lot out of you and, well, it's dangerous." His words were dark, but his face had cleared of worry. "Maybe that's why you're such a weird shade of gray."

"Things are far worse than I ever could have imagined," I said, ignoring this last comment.

Trader's expression was impassive. "So?"

"You were right about the virus—but it's not just a little bug. I think it's big, Trader. And regardless of what started it, the App World seems to be, well, *disappearing*."

This got Trader's attention. "What do you mean?"

"When Adam and I went to your house—"

"—Adam?"

"He and I ran into each other. But that's not the point. We found Wicked Leaks in your Black Market App Store. Aside from several plots to kill me, there are *a lot* of rumors about a virus—a terrible virus. And one of the rumors is that it's *killing* the App World. The chatter is that the App World is dying. Those were the very words we heard. *Dying*."

"It could be just a rumor."

"I don't think so." The memory I had of the sinkhole was vivid. "Enormous swaths of the City have literally just *vanished*. It's crazy. And there's this thing called a Death App. If you download it, you're virtually dead. Adam and I watched a man die before our very eyes."

Trader's face paled even more than usual. "That's not good."

"Definitely not."

"Inara's parents . . ."

"I know. So many people, and none of them safe, but all of them believing they live in the perfect safety of the City, an eternity on the Apps."

"All of it one big lie," Trader said.

"There's more," I went on. "People are dying on the plugs. My mother—it's a long story—but she's trying to figure out why. The dead are being delivered to Briarwood so she can study them. She thinks the problem is coming from the App World and not from their real bodies." This information I'd been keeping hidden rushed out in one big release. "I'm worried that whatever is happening, it can't be undone."

Trader glanced back at the door to Inara's room. "You don't know that yet. Maybe it can be fixed. I'll need to speak to Zeera."

I bit my lip. "I think Rain already has her looking for information. But I'm not sure she'd be in favor of anyone plugging in to go and help."

"But you just did," he said.

"Yes, but *she* doesn't know that. Rain doesn't know either. He was really against me going."

Trader rolled his eyes. "Just talk to him. He does anything you want."

I shook my head. "Not anymore. At least, I don't think so."

"I'll believe that when I see it," Trader said. "But let me talk to Zeera. She'll listen to me. We speak the same language."

"Okay. That would be great."

Trader studied me. "I can tell there's something else on your mind, Skylar."

The comment he'd made earlier nagged at me. "What didn't you want me to see at your house in the Real World?"

"Nothing," he tried.

"When I was at your house in Loner Town, I saw something unusual," I pressed. "A lot of unusual things, actually. A half-eaten sandwich. A jar of sea glass."

Trader slumped against the wall. "You wanted to ask me about a bunch of trash?"

"I wanted to ask you about your virtual guest. Who is it?"

Trader flicked away the lock of hair that had fallen across his brow. "Oh, Sis."

The white paint of the wall seemed to shimmer behind him. "Whoever it is has also been fixing up the place. *Trader.*"

His eyes sought the floor. "It's the same person you're probably thinking."

"But he said he would *never*," I said, still disbelieving.

"You wanted to know, so now you do. I can't control whether or not you believe it." Trader closed his eyes and shook his head. Then he dug a hand around in his pocket and pulled out a set of keys. He slipped one from the ring and held it out to me. "He's been staying at my house in the Real World. I'm not supposed to tell you this, obviously. But . . . oh well. And you *know* there are certain facilities just sitting around, and he may have decided to take advantage of them." He trailed off.

I took the key and stared at it. The metal was old and worn, splotches marring the face of it.

"I'm going to see Zeera right now, and then I'll be the one to have a little chat with Rain about the situation in the App World. You're not alone in this." He leaned down and planted a kiss on the top of my head. "I know you feel that way sometimes. But you have allies, and you don't have to figure anything out by yourself. Or always be the one in charge." I opened my mouth but Trader shook his head. "Let me handle at least one part of this. I am quite capable myself. Leadership runs in our family."

"More like dictatorship," I muttered.

"Perhaps," he said. He pointed to the key. "Now go. We'll need his help anyway. I have a feeling things are going to get serious fast." He waved me away. "Good luck." Trader lumbered off without looking back.

My fingers closed around the key, the jagged edges biting into the skin of my palm.

23

Skylar

honesty

TRADER'S HOUSE IN the Real World had been painted recently. A light gray that blended in with the color of the rocks behind it, pale in the moonlight. Gone were the broken shingles and roof tiles, the siding patched up. Just like with his house in Loner Town, someone was taking care of this one. Light flickered in the windows.

I took the key out of my pocket and climbed the front steps.

My hand shook as I held it to the lock. It made a loud click as I turned it. My eyes went to the windows. I half expected to see a face there, wondering who was outside, or for the light to go out, or even for the door to swing open. None of these things occurred, so I dropped the key back into my pocket, turned the knob, and pushed.

The door creaked open.

Everything was silent. Not a shuffle or even the sound of breathing. The room was swept clean. It was nearly bare except for the soft light of a lamp and a small table and chairs in the corner.

But then I heard a groan from the next room. The one with the view of the rocks and the sea. The one where Trader kept his lab and workplace.

I went to investigate.

There, on the floor in the very center of it, was Trader's makeshift plug, the tablet he'd used to create the Shifting App lying next to it.

Right alongside Kit.

His eyes were closed, his limbs unmoving, the color in his cheeks a deathly hue. His chest was still. Had he stopped breathing? I ran to him and crouched down, put a hand to his forehead, worried I'd find it cool and only growing colder. His skin was warm, but his lungs didn't seem to be taking in air. I grabbed the tablet from the floor and studied the screen to see at what stage Kit was in his shift, only to see he'd completed it and should be awake again.

But he wasn't.

The tablet fell to the ground with a loud crack.

I hovered over him unsure what to do.

"Kit, please don't die on me," I whispered. "Please,

please, please, I couldn't bear it. I don't want to be in either of these worlds without you in them."

There was no movement, not a breath, not even a twitch.

Tears burned my eyes. "Please don't be gone. I still love you."

Coughs erupted from Kit's lungs, his breath in heaved as though he'd been drowning under water. I sat back, my breaths coming just as quickly.

Eventually he stopped coughing.

His eyes flickered open.

A weak smile appeared on his lips. "Skylar, you came for me," he said, barely audible. His hand found mine. "Finally."

I pulled away and stood.

Stormed into the next room and slammed the door behind me.

I sat at the table, debating whether I should leave. What felt like an eternity passed before Kit dragged his body into the room to join me. He nearly fell into the chair next to mine. It rocked precariously and he grabbed the table to hold himself steady, then leaned onto his elbows. There were dark circles underneath his eyes. He looked far worse than last time I'd seen him.

"I worried you'd left," he said.

I turned away, staring out the darkened window. "I thought about leaving."

"I'm glad you didn't."

"Maybe I should go now."

"Don't."

"I can't believe you," I said.

"You can't believe what about me?"

I looked at him. "You've been shifting. You've been plugging in."

One of his hands thumped onto the wood, as though his arm couldn't hold the weight of it. "Obviously."

"Shifting is dangerous!"

"I've been doing this for a while," he said. "I know what my body can handle."

"You look horrible, so maybe you don't."

He managed a grin. "Thank you for the compliment. You are looking lovely yourself tonight, Skylar."

My cheeks grew tight. "I'm not here to play around, Kit."

He yanked himself up until he was standing and slowly made his way toward the kitchen. He filled two glasses with water and ambled slowly back. He placed the second glass in front of me. "Then why did you come?"

"I don't know," I said, even though I did. Or at least I thought so. *Because I can't live without you.* "You used to be the only person I knew other than my Keeper who'd shunned the App World."

"People change, I guess."

I placed my hands into my lap and stared at them, my fingers curled tight into fists, nails biting into my skin. A chill had fallen over the room. "Yes. But not you."

"Don't be disappointed in me, Skylar." He sounded sad. Pleading. "I'm only human."

"I was there, Kit. I was at Trader's house in the App World and I saw the jar of glass—I saw it and I *knew*, even though I didn't want to believe it. We just missed each other there. Did you know that?"

He didn't respond.

I looked up. "What's so appealing about the App World that you'd break your vow to never go?"

Kit didn't answer. He sipped from his water glass, staring into the bottom.

I thought about the tattoo Maggie told me about. I searched for it on his skin but saw nothing. His long-sleeved shirt covered his arms to his wrists.

"Trader said I could stay here," Kit said finally. "I couldn't stand to be at the cottage anymore. I think he felt bad for me. He's a better person than I originally thought, your brother." Kit took another sip and swallowed. His eyes shone. "I've never been good at resisting temptation, and here I was, surrounded by technology, and that contraption of his."

"You mean the plug," I said.

"Yeah, that." He chuckled. "I'd never seen one up close. I'd looked at pictures of them, drawings my sister did. But pictures are one thing and to see the real plug, to be able to study it, is really something else."

The room had grown dark around us, the glow of the lamp soft on Kit's face. "I remember the first time I saw one, too," I admitted, then gulped down half of my water.

He nodded. "I became curious. I was bored and I was lonely and I wanted to escape."

"Escape what?" I pressed, when he trailed off.

"What do you think, Skylar?" He'd turned his head so I could no longer see his eyes. "One night, Trader came by and I asked him how it worked, and he showed me."

My mouth went dry. Trader hadn't mentioned that part. "My brother helped you to shift?"

"Yes. The first few times." He gaze returned to mine. "He told me it was dangerous to do on my own and didn't want me getting hurt. He helped me until I could do it by myself."

"But you're not supposed to do it on your own," I said, my stomach sick. "Not ever. Someone should always be there to monitor you, or at least to check in on you."

"Well, yeah, he told me that, too, but I've had a lot of time to myself, and he can't exactly control what I do when he isn't here." Kit took another long sip and set his empty glass onto the table. "Besides, I told him not to worry what happened to me, since you'd written me off for good, and if I disappeared from this world it wouldn't make a difference."

"You know that's not true," I whispered.

He inched closer. "No?"

I inched away. Dropped my gaze to my lap. "Why do you keep doing it? Why do you keep going back? Is it really just to escape?"

"Why do you even care, Skylar?"

"I don't know."

"I was searching for my parents," he said, as though this was nothing.

I looked up. "Oh!" I was a little ashamed for this not occurring to me before now. So many families were torn apart by this division in worlds, and Kit's wasn't an exception by any means. In fact, I knew that his parents plugging in had nearly destroyed him.

Kit shrugged. "Don't get too excited. I didn't find them. Maybe I never will."

"But didn't Maggie know where they were?"

He shook his head. "She never found them either. I don't think they ever wanted to be found by their children. I've even wondered if they changed their names, just in case the two of us found a way into a virtual future."

I reached across the table. The second my fingers touched Kit, all I wanted was to pull him close. "I'm so sorry. That's horrible—"

"—Skylar," Kit interrupted.

"What?"

"I know what I heard when I was waking up," he went on. "Was it the truth or were you lying?"

I was grateful for the dim lighting. "What did you hear?"

Kit's gaze didn't waver. "You said you loved me. Do you?"

"You were dreaming."

"I don't think I was." He watched me, unblinking. His eyes were full of hope. "Why did you really come here, Skylar?"

I knew what I should say, what he wanted me to say. What I wanted to tell him.

Because it's true, I love you. And things with Rain are over. For good.

But my earlier confidence had waned.

"I'm here because I need your help," I said.

Then I began to explain all that I'd learned.

24

Ree

negotiations

"WELL, AREN'T YOU uncharacteristically clever, Ms. Ree."

I froze, midstep, like in one of the Cartoon Apps I used to watch when I was an innocent little five. I'd barely made it to the elevator bank on the floor where I'd been imprisoned when this voice rang through the atmosphere. I looked around for its source. Left, right, up, down, but couldn't find it. I didn't need to see it to know who was speaking.

Emory Specter.

God, that man's bulging eyes were truly everywhere.

"Actually, not *that* clever if you thought I wouldn't be monitoring you," he went on.

A spark flared out of nowhere. Then a shower of them.

A hologram appeared, enlivening the nondescript white walls of the hallway.

I'd been right about Emory Specter making himself appear taller for broadcasts and various other projections. He'd grown at least a foot since we met in his weird throne room. Today was casual day, though. He was wearing jeans. "Hi, Minister Specter," I said, figuring that it wouldn't hurt to be polite, seeing that he'd just caught me trying to escape.

"Are you going to tell me how you did it?" he asked.

My shirt was beginning to fray at the neck from a lack of updates. I resisted pulling at the threads. "Don't you already know the answer? I thought you were monitoring me."

The hologram moved closer. "It's not like you're a star on Reel Time, Ms. Ree. I don't have time to monitor your every move. Nor do I have the interest. I'm a busy man with an entire City to defend."

I smiled. "And I bet you've been *very* busy defending our City lately."

Emory frowned. "What's that supposed to mean?"

"Why don't you do the guessing this time?"

More sparks flew and the hologram disappeared.

This made me wonder if there was another glitch. I half expected to see a black hole where the figure of Emory Specter had just been. Instead, one of the elevators dinged, followed by the doors opening. The real

Emory Specter emerged from it. His face was red with anger, his height definitely much shorter than in the hologram.

I tried not to laugh.

"I don't play guessing games," he said.

"Yes you do. You tried to make me guess the name of your daughter." I batted my eyelashes at him. "Feeling a little forgetful?"

"You're awfully unafraid."

"You promised you wouldn't hurt me," I snapped.

"Perhaps I've changed my mind."

"Whatever. I don't care." I sighed and studied my virtual nails. I *did* care, of course, but Emory Specter obviously loved games, and I could play them too, when required.

"Tell me how you got out," he barked up at me, because he sure was short in person.

"Give me a reason to and I will," I barked back down at him, because it sure was fun to be taller than the Defense Minister. "I'm open to any and all exchanges."

He stamped his little foot. "I'm not negotiating with you."

"Then accept the fact that you'll never know." I turned on my heel and headed toward my pretty flowered prison. "Ciao!"

Emory's footsteps followed after me. Two to my every one. "Explain yourself, now!"

I halted. "I already told you. Not unless you make it worth my while. Why do you even care? What are you so afraid of me finding out?"

Steam was rising from his neck. "I'm not afraid of anything!"

I laughed. "You should really download a Chill Pill App, Minister Specter. I'm a little worried about your virtual blood pressure."

Tiny flames flickered in the pupils of his eyes. "What. Do. You. Know."

I pretended to consider answering. "Gee, I've thought about your offer, and I don't accept."

Steam simmered in his shoes, the vapor filling the atmosphere like when those magicians use Dry Ice Apps to make everything they do seem mysterious. For a moment his attention seemed elsewhere, in a way that made me think he was mind-chatting. Then Emory closed his eyes and began to take long, slow breaths. His virtual skin turned a pale Caucasian 4.0 again and the fog began to fade. "Lucky for you, Ms. Ree, I've reconsidered my earlier comments and I'm willing to do an exchange. Your answer for your freedom."

Excitement surged through my code. "Seriously?"

Emory cocked his head. "Yes, seriously," he said, in a mocking tone.

If he wasn't the Defense Minister of the App World and I wasn't at his mercy right now, I might have smacked him. "What's the catch? I thought you needed me for bait."

He breathed deeply. "Plans change. This deal expires in exactly thirty seconds, so take it or leave it. No more irrelevant talk."

I stuck out my hand. "Information about how I got out of that tasteful and comfy prison room in exchange for my freedom."

He took it and shook. Yuck. His palm was clammy from overheating with rage. "It's a deal. Now speak."

I leaned against the wall behind me and crossed one ankle over the other like I had all the time in the world. I watched as his cheeks started to burn again. I was good at annoying my elders. Before he could get angry enough to take back our deal I started to talk. "I know about the holes in the atmosphere. The glitches in the fabric of our world. And I suspect they can't be repaired or I wouldn't have been able to see as many as I did, and I also suspect they must be related to that Death App that killed my mother and my poor friend Char." I drew in a breath. "That's how I got out. There was a hole in the door, big enough for me to reach a hand through." I wiggled my virtual fingers in front of his face as demonstration. "And so here I am."

Emory Specter nodded. Then he beckoned me back through the hallway to the elevators. He pushed the call button and soon one of them was dinging. The doors opened. He shooed me inside. "Off you go. The floor that exits onto the street is marked with a zero." He rolled his eyes and shook his head. "I know that's confusing, but the building was designed by a European."

I put an arm out to stop the doors from shutting. "So that's it? I'm free?"

He tapped his foot impatiently. "That was our deal. Hurry up."

My hand clamped against the wall. "I'm confused. Aren't you afraid I'll tell people what I know? Isn't that why you imprisoned me in my apartment in the first place?"

Emory Specter's eyes went blank again. Someone was definitely mind-chatting him. When his attention returned he answered me. "It doesn't matter much if you tell people at this point, Ms. Ree. I'm afraid it's too late for that." He sounded so fatalistic.

Alarms rattled through my code. "What do you mean *it's too late*?"

The Defense Minister of the App World began to pick my fingers away from the frame of the elevator one by one. When only my pinky remained he looked me straight in the eyes. "You'll know soon enough, Ree." Soon my pinky was peeled away too and the doors began to close. Before they shut he said one last thing. "Everyone will."

25

Skylar

ruins

I STEPPED OUT of Trader's house.

Kit had gone ahead and pulled his motorcycle from wherever he'd hidden it. His hand was on the back of the seat, keeping the bike steady. He looked up at me. "You're coming with me, right?" he asked, then eyed the car I'd parked along the edge of the grass, on the old broken and potholed street.

It was Rain's car and Kit knew this.

I wanted to get on the bike with him and drive off, like we used to.

But the very second I'd seen Kit, it sent everything in me off-kilter. My lungs couldn't get enough air, my skin was flushed and tingly, my heart pounded so hard it made me dizzy, I was sure I could hear the blood pumping through my body. Kit made me feel out of control, and I hated feeling out of control. Plus, I needed to be steady. There were things to be done.

"I'll drive the car," I told him, glad for the shelter of the dark.

The ocean had grown angrier during our time inside the house. The waves roared as they slapped against the rocks. Kit looked away, staring off into the black of the night. Then he climbed onto the seat of his bike and the motor roared to life.

I got in the car and waited until he pulled in front of me and took off.

He didn't look back. Not once. Not even to see if I was following.

The lights in New Port City were dark.

It was late, the sidewalks deserted. Kit navigated the shadowy cobbled streets with me doing my best to keep up behind him. He knew them better than I did.

We'd already driven past the Water Tower and the library, still with the glowing white banner across the entrance that read, *REFUGEES GO HOME*. I rolled down the window of the car and breathed in the salty air. If the App World was truly dying, then this place would have to be everyone's home soon, like it or not. With the moon and stars glowing above, it didn't seem like such a terrible fate. The Real World held a certain kind of decadent beauty that virtual living could never duplicate.

Kit veered left and soon we were pulling up alongside a decrepit building.

The Body Market rose in front of us like a gray ghost against the night. It looked empty.

I turned off the ignition and the car went silent.

Kit slid off the seat of his bike and stood there next to it, back toward me, waiting.

I got out and went to him.

We stood close.

I wanted to touch him.

He looked like he wanted to speak. Words on his lips he refused to say.

"What aren't you telling me?" I asked.

His eyes landed on mine, a hardness in them I hadn't seen since we'd first met and he'd grabbed me away from this very sidewalk and imprisoned me in his house. "What is it that *you* aren't telling me, Skylar?"

"I've told you everything I know. The dead bodies. The Death App. The rumors of viruses and the App World dying. I told you what I needed from you, your help."

"That's not what I meant." His voice was as cold as the chilly night air.

I looked at Kit. Took him in. The tension in his stance, the angularity of his jawbone, nothing about him relaxed. Everything about him unhappy. I was pushing him even further away than he already was. It took everything in me not to take my hands and place them on either side of his beautiful, anguished face. To pull him close and kiss him like I'd dreamed of doing every night since we'd last been together. But I couldn't. Now wasn't the time. "Then what is it that you want me to say?" I asked, though of course I already knew.

Kit just shook his head. Then he shrugged. "Follow me."

The Body Market was in disarray.

"What happened here?" I asked, my voice hushed.

It looked like a storm had struck. A tornado, with gusts of wind knocking down displays and ripping up the once lush red carpet, leaving it torn and frayed. The doors weren't even locked—we walked right in. A bolt hung broken and twisted from the handle.

"You happened. And your friends," Kit said.

"This is all from us?"

Kit shined a flashlight he'd taken from the pocket of his jacket over everything. "I gather you haven't been here in a while."

"I've been by, but I haven't ventured inside." My face was reflected in a pane of glass, cracked down the middle. One of the coffins, once gleaming, now empty. "Not since the day that we woke everyone up." I ran my hand against the jagged edge. "I knew there was chaos, but I'd assumed that everything had been fixed up by now."

Kit stepped over a broken piece of marble that had fallen and smashed. "It was never the same again."

"But I thought it was up and running. At least part of it."

He continued down the aisle. "It was. Not anymore, though. It died a slow and painful death."

I wound my way through the now cluttered space. Only a few plugs remained, and those that did appeared damaged, useless for their original purpose. They were cracked, some reduced to a series of sharp spikes, a series of bent and misshapen spiders sticking up from the bottom of the coffins. I kept going until I arrived at the very center of the Body Market, a place that had sent shivers of disgust over my skin as I waited in line to see my best friend, Inara, for sale and on display as punishment from my sister. The coffin where she once lay was gone, the dais reduced to rubble, the carpet shorn from the ground.

"Skylar," Kit beckoned.

I joined him, the flashlight shining a bright ray ahead of us, until we reached the opposite-side entrance.

The hotel stood tall against the night. Not a single light on in any of its windows. The dirty and tattered remnants of flags and banners hung limply from their posts. A pang of guilt pinched me at the sight of my sister's hopes and dreams so thoroughly destroyed, even though it was me who led their destruction. Jude had once been so fearsome, but there was something painful about the most arrogant and terrible among us when they were laid low.

"This way," Kit said, and waved me toward the door.

I didn't move. The entrance looked ominous. And beyond it, deserted like everything else. "Inside here?"

He nodded and pushed through the door.

Reluctantly, I followed him into the darkness.

Kit went straight to the staircase and started to climb. He didn't stop or hesitate. He obviously knew his way around. I suspected he didn't even need the flashlight that swung this way and that with each step, illuminating our way up. We must have gone five or six flights—I'd lost count—before he led us onto one of the floors and down a long hallway.

At the end of it was a room.

From here I could see the glow of a chandelier. Make out the soft murmuring of voices.

I halted. "You're sure that this is a good idea?"

"You said that you need my help pulling everyone together. Even the former New Capitalists. Your sister might not be here running things anymore, but there are still plenty of them left in this city." In the darkness it was difficult to read Kit's face. "I'm not going to leave you alone, Skylar. Not for a second. Trust me," he added.

I looked away from him now, toward the end of the long hall. "Okay."

He started toward the room. I joined him and the

glow grew brighter as we got closer. Kit didn't wait or stop before the doorway.

Three people were bent over a series of screens and notebooks and strange machines set up across a long black table.

"Hello, Jag," Kit said.

I winced. Jag was my sister's second-in-command. The man Kit had betrayed me to.

Jag turned, surprise crossing his face at the sight of me. "I haven't seen you in a while," he said to Kit.

Of the two others in the room, one was unfamiliar.

At first, neither one of them looked up from their work. But then, the one on the right, the one I knew as intimately as the sight of my own eyes in a mirror, turned to see the guests who had arrived so late into the night.

"Mom?"

26

Rain

discord

"YOU'RE THICKER THAN I thought," Trader said.

He was glaring at me.

Zeera was looking between the two of us, uncertain.

Parvda was standing there with panic raging on her face.

Lacy stood off in the corner, trying to seem inconspicuous, playing on her tablet.

The five of us were in the weapons room, for the first time in ages.

"We need to at least listen to what he's saying, Rain," Zeera said. "It's potentially disastrous. What if the App World really is dying?"

I looked at each one of them. "I just think we need to be careful."

Zeera's face filled with sympathy. "I know you're worried about Skylar feeling she needs to go back, how dangerous it would be."

A strangled sound emerged from Lacy's throat.

Was I worried about Skylar? I suppose I always would. Regardless of Lacy. And even though Skylar had left without telling me what's going on or what she's doing. Yet again.

Lacy's eyes found me. They were full of anger. And pain. She was waiting for me to contradict Zeera. "You'll never let her go, will you," she said. Her words formed a question but they sounded like a statement. Then she marched out, heels storming along the ground.

Zeera glanced at the doorway. "Rain?"

"I'll talk to Lacy after we settle this," I said. Lacy might never believe Skylar would leave my heart, but she seemed to have no idea how big a place she already occupied. And for how long she'd been there.

Trader sighed and crossed his arms. "You can't live without the drama, can you? You court it. Yet the drama that really matters, you refuse to acknowledge."

I returned his glare from earlier. "I'm here, aren't I? Listening to you."

"Yeah, but not taking in a word I've said."

"You're wrong. I've heard all of it. You said that

Skylar shifted and came back—"

Trader snickered. "Of course that's all you heard."

"—she saw Adam," I went on. "People are dying on the plugs, there's likely a virus, the App World is deteriorating."

"—dying," Parvda said, voice full of fear. "He said *dying*."

I put a hand on her arm. "I know you're afraid for Adam, but for now it's just a rumor."

"And what if it isn't?" she asked, yanking her arm away. "I'm going to check on him. I can't take this anymore," she added, running out like Lacy.

I shook my head. "We can't allow things to fall into chaos."

"They already are, Rain," Zeera said. "We need to pull together. This is not the time to be divided."

"And by pull together you mean do whatever reckless thing Skylar wants?" I could hear the bitterness in my voice.

Trader's eyes were cold. "She's not yours to protect or control. You've decided what she did was reckless because she did it against your wishes. What Skylar did was *brave*. At least now we have information."

"I never wanted to control her," I spat.

Zeera banged the table with her fist. "Everybody, stop fighting!"

Trader closed his mouth. The two of us turned to her.

"We need to call everyone together. Rumors or not, it's time to tell people what we believe is going on and form a plan." Zeera grabbed her tablet and began punching the screen with her fingers. "There. It's done. I sent a message to everyone at Briarwood. We're meeting bright and early tomorrow in the training gym. Meanwhile, I'll see what I can find out about the App World from here." She busied herself powering up the screens that had lain dormant since February.

"And how are we going to let Skylar know about this?" I said to Zeera's back. "You said it yourself—we need to pull together and figure out a plan. She never checks her tablet."

Trader's eyes slid from mine. He pulled out his own device from his pocket, razor thin and glowing, and began to tap the screen. "I know how to find her."

I went to see Lacy.

She answered her door without a word, without a glance, turned her back on me, and climbed onto her bed, pulling her knees tight into her chest. When I sat next to her, she edged away. She seemed so fragile, so unlike the fierce and fiery girl I was used to.

"Lacy, please." I reached out to her.

"Don't touch me," she snapped.

I sighed. "What about our conversation from earlier?"

"Exactly," she said. "What about it? What did it really

matter, since it will always, always, *always* be Skylar. Everything is about Skylar."

I placed a hand on her shoulder and she jumped up from the bed and went to stand across the room. Her eyes were bright and angry. "Lacy—"

"—she cares about you," she interrupted. "But not like you want her to. When are you going to accept that? Skylar is in love with someone else and you can't see it. You refuse to."

A sharp pain spread beneath my rib cage. I breathed slowly, willing it to subside. "I know," I said quietly. "I've known for a while."

Lacy stilled, as though if she moved even slightly, my admission might break apart and disappear forever.

"I need you to hear me." Carefully, I got up from the bed. I didn't want to send Lacy fleeing from me again. "It's true, I care about Skylar. I worry about her taking risks—any more than she already has. It's taken a toll on her and we both know it. She's not the same as when she first woke up in this world and I . . . I feel responsible."

Lacy shook her head. "Skylar does what Skylar wants," she said, but the venom was gone. "You're not responsible."

"But I am. My father is. My family. Her place in this whole situation, this war between worlds, began as a pawn. She was a tool for barter between all of us, between realms. No one considered she might have a will of her own, that she might resist or even that she was capable of it. Me included." I took a step closer to Lacy, encouraged when she didn't take a step away. "I'm as guilty as anyone. I didn't even really think of Skylar as human until that day when she escaped from her sister on the cliff. I've been trying to make up for this ever since," I confessed—so many admissions tonight, making me feel lighter, even as hearing myself say them made me feel pain. And shame.

Lacy's hands felt for the wall behind her, as though she didn't trust them not to reach for me. "Your love for her," she began, hope in her voice. "Was that you making up for all that you've just said?"

I shook my head. I didn't want to lie. Not anymore. "No. That was real. *Is* real."

Lacy seemed to deflate, her shoulders curling forward, her chin tilting downward.

"But it doesn't work," I went on, quickly, hating to see Lacy so upset. "Skylar and me—we've tried. *I've* tried. It's just not meant to be," I said, yet another admission. Painful, but true, and one I'd known for a while now, even if I hadn't yet spoken it out loud. I crossed the rest of the distance between Lacy and me. She didn't seem to be breathing. "And it's also true, even though I've avoided saying it, that I love someone else. That I have for a long time. For years." I placed my hand gently underneath Lacy's chin. Tilted her face upward toward mine. "And the person she's become since arriving in the Real World has only confirmed it, Lacy."

Her eyes were watery, a tear leaking down her left cheek.

I pushed everything else from my mind. Before she could say anything in response, I kissed her.

27

Skylar

distrust

"HI, SWEETHEART," MY mother said.

She came to me and pulled me into a tight hug.

Kit hung back by the doorway.

"What are you doing here?" I asked, still stunned to find my mother in this place with Jag, of all people. Of course, my mother knew him, since he'd worked so closely with my sister. But flashbacks to so many unpleasant surprises the night I first saw Jude at the mansion and all the horrors that followed filled my mind and made my stomach churn.

She let me go. "Things are getting worse. Far worse. And quickly."

I pointed at the large man staring at me with unfriendly,

suspicious eyes. "But why are you with *him*?"

"Keeping enemies now will only serve to destroy us and hurt everyone else, even if they don't know it yet." My mother's expression was grim. "There's been more deaths. A lot more."

Dread bottomed out in my stomach. "How many?"

"Dozens."

The other woman in the room approached. She was tiny. Her hair was shiny and black, cropped short along her chin. "Seventy-two more at last count. And rising."

I gasped. "Seventy-two?"

The woman bobbed her head once. "Things are deteriorating quickly. We can't keep up with all the dead."

"Skylar," my mother said. "This is Grace. She and I trained together to be doctors. Grace is my contact here at the Body Market."

"What's left of it," Grace said. She strode forward until she was close. "It is nice to finally meet you."

I hesitated. "You work—worked for my sister?"

Grace glanced at my mother. "As I'm sure you know, many of us had no choice."

My mother turned to Kit. "And since we're doing introductions, who is this?"

He stepped forward and extended his hand. "Hello, Mrs. Cruz," he said politely. "My name is Kit."

She shook it, but her eyes were wary. "This is the boy who kidnapped you and held you hostage during the blizzard," she stated, then arched her eyebrows at me. "Isn't it?"

Kit's hand dropped to his side. I suddenly wanted my mother to like him. To approve of him. "That was a long time ago."

"But Skylar—"

"You don't even know him. All you know is what Rain told you about him, right? And I'm sure he's poisoned you."

My mother didn't deny it.

"Well then," I went on. "Forget everything he said. Kit's on our side and I need you to treat him that way. And besides, he's . . ." I trailed off. I was about to say *my friend*, but that wasn't right. "I care about him," I said instead.

There was hope in Kit's eyes again. Hope and something raw. Pain. Or need.

My mother stayed silent.

But then Jag stepped forward. "Hello, Skylar."

My eyes became slits. "You speak to me as though we've met when we haven't. Though I've heard plenty about you." I glanced at Kit. "That you're in charge of what's left of the New Capitalists and those who chose to remain plugged in and forfeit their bodies."

"I forget sometimes that you don't know," Jag said.

"Know what?"

"That of course I do know you. Intimately." He smiled. "You were just unaware for all that time, plugged in."

Kit moved so he was standing between us. "Jag," he said, a warning.

Jag put up his hands in a gesture of apology. But his eyes remained cold and calculating.

A shiver raced over my skin. The thought of this man standing over me, while I lay there unconscious, was unsettling to say the least. "We figured you would know the status of those who remained plugged in," I said, moving the conversation onto more pressing matters. And from the state of things downstairs, it doesn't look like they're here anymore."

Jag's mouth was drawn in a straight line. "No. You made sure the Body Market failed."

"And I'm not sorry I did," I said. "Especially now that the App World is becoming so poisonous to some."

"But we're not here to debate the Body Market," Kit reminded me, and perhaps Jag, too.

The light fell across Jag's face, but it was difficult to read what he was thinking. Or if he could be trusted. Ever. "We really do need to set aside our differences, old grievances. We're facing death, potentially on a massive scale." I turned to my mother. "Did you tell them about the possible virus?"

She nodded.

"In theory, it's a rumor," I went on. "But I don't think it is. There's too much chatter. And I saw with my own eyes the ways that parts of the City are deteriorating. We need to see if whatever is causing it can be fixed. But in the meantime, we can't just let people go on living virtually as though nothing is wrong." The five of us stood in a circle in the dimly lit room. The black of the night coated the windows in further darkness. It matched the mood of our conversation. "I think it's time that we warn the citizens of the City. This isn't about choices anymore, of whether to stay or go. This is about basic survival. If people stay in the App World, they are risking their virtual existence, not merely their bodies."

Grace nodded. "We need to get citizens of *this* city on board first. They're unhappy with the refugee situation now. What you're talking about is a whole new level of influx. We're facing the restoration of the Real World as it used to exist before the exodus. New Port isn't big enough to handle this alone. We'd have to repopulate the old cities."

"Then that's what we'll have to do." I eyed Jag. "And where is my sister? If you're suddenly on our side, then why don't you get in touch with her and help us negotiate a meeting time for everyone to talk. Safely."

His eyes swept across the ground. "Contacting her is not an option. She's . . . out of communication."

My mother lowered her gaze as well. "Skylar, your sister . . ."

Grace stepped forward when she trailed off and looked at me, without hesitation. "What no one wants to tell you is that your sister plugged in permanently."

I still didn't understand. "So, why don't we just unplug her then?"

"We can't," Grace said. "Her body was destroyed."

My mother visibly winced.

The breath went out of me. "Destroyed?"

"Per her request," Jag confirmed. "She decided she was never coming back. She didn't even want to retain the possibility."

My brain did the math. "But that would mean if the App World is dying . . ."

"Then your sister would die with it," my mother filled in. "Just like anyone else whose body is gone. Those unlucky citizens will have nothing to come back to in the Real World. Literally." Tears pooled in my mother's eyes. "Skylar, there's nothing we can do. What's done is done. Not only for Jude but for lots of people."

"Jude decided she wanted a virtual life or no life at all," Jag offered. "That's what she told us before she left. *Very clearly.*"

Flames of rage licked at my skin. "And you just went along with her and destroyed the only connection she had to the Real World? You destroyed any hope that she had." I let that sentence dangle there, unfinished. Any hope she had of what? Any hope *we* had of fixing our relationship? Was that what I really meant? I breathed deep, trying to calm myself. "I don't trust you," I told Jag now. "Not at all."

Jag opened his mouth, but my mother put out a hand to silence him.

"Don't blame him for carrying out your sister's wishes," she said. "Jude is not someone many people can say no to."

"Skylar, your mother is right," Kit said.

And you would know, I thought, but managed not to say. "So what next then? There are so many things to take care of. The relationship between the refugees and New Port City. The Death App. The possible deterioration of the App World and the threat of this to all its citizens. Bodies dying on the plugs. Which one do we deal with first? We need far more help than just the people in this room." I thought of Rain, of Trader, of Zeera and Parvda. Inara and Lacy. Andleeb and Rasha. My Keeper. "We're going to need anyone and everyone who's able and willing to be on our side."

"Skylar, sweetheart," my mother said to me now, soft and pleading. "You're right, and there is a lot that needs to happen. We do need to recruit as much help as we can. But I know what needs to be done next, done now. As soon as possible," she went on, then stopped.

I tried to read her. I knew I wouldn't like whatever she was about to tell me. "What?"

"I'm going to plug in," she said. "It's time your father and I had a talk."

"I'm going with her. The two of us will shift together. It's safer that way," I told Kit as we descended the stairs of the hotel and started across the lobby. "I'm certainly not letting her go to the App World alone, or allowing her to just plug in and end up in the hands of the border patrol. Maybe it's time I met with my father, too." I swallowed, the words thick in my throat. "And saw my sister," I added. *For the last time?* My strides were long. My heart pounded.

"Skylar," Kit said, catching up. The tiny rectangular tablet was lit up in the palm of his hand. "You're wanted at Briarwood." The screen of Kit's tablet went dormant and he slipped it back into the pocket of his jeans.

Since when was Kit communicating with people at Briarwood?

"A message from Trader," he explained.

"Oh. I see."

Kit shrugged his shoulders.

We pushed through the exit of the hotel and into the chilly night air. The stars shone bright above us and I thought of the ones on Kit's shoulder. Wondered what else had joined them there on his skin. I longed to see. We made our way back across the rubble of the Body Market. "Well, let's go to Briarwood then," I said.

Kit's flashlight beamed across the ripped-up carpet. "You want to take *me* to Briarwood?"

"I told you, I need your help. And you heard my

mother. We all need to work together, so we shouldn't separate. There isn't time to go chasing after each other in the morning."

He turned to me, halting. I could feel his eyes burning in the darkness. "But I can meet you in the morning somewhere just as easily. There's no need for me to stay at Briarwood tonight. Unless you want me there with you. Do you, Skylar?" he asked. "Want me with you?"

"I don't," I began, hesitant, "want you *elsewhere*," I finished.

Kit didn't respond and we continued, crossing the rest of the Body Market to the place where the car and his motorcycle were parked in the deserted street. "Are you still with him?" he asked when we reached them. Kit didn't need to say Rain's name.

I had to think about this. Was I still with Rain? Technically, we hadn't talked about our status or discussed what I'd overheard with Lacy. But in my heart I knew that Rain and I were over. For good. "No," I told him, which was the truth. What I didn't say out loud was that I hadn't been with Rain in ages, not really, not in my heart, at least. Not since the blizzard and all those nights Kit and I spent huddled around the fire at his cottage. My heart had belonged to Kit from then on, regardless of what else I said and did. And despite how I'd done my best to forget him.

I looked at Kit now in the moonlight, and I decided to stop trying.

"Ride with me, Skylar," Kit offered. "We'll get the car tomorrow."

His words comprised a command, but his tone betrayed a question. His eyes, pleading. And there it was again in them: hope, and longing.

Without a word, I climbed on the seat behind him.

After a beat, I leaned forward and reached around his waist. Inhaled the familiar scent of his jacket, my eyes peering over his shoulder.

Kit reached for the handles of his bike.

The sleeve of his shirt rose up along his forearm.

I saw the edges of the new tattoo inked on his skin.

My breath caught.

Snowflakes. Starting at the very edge of his wrist. Continuing upward. A swirl. A storm.

A blizzard of them.

28

Ree

a lady knows best

ADAM WAS SITTING outside the door of my apartment when I arrived, head leaning against the wall. Eyes vacant.

The code of my virtual heart went all jumpy with joy. "What are you doing here?"

His face came alive. "Ree?"

"I'm so impressed! You came back for me!"

He pulled himself to standing. The color of his virtual skin was gray. He could really use a download to fix that. "I told you I would. I've been here a long time, but you were gone. Or I thought you were, since you didn't answer the door. But I also wondered if maybe whatever it was that allowed me to see you before had worn off and you couldn't hear me from in there. So I decided to wait. But honestly, I also just didn't know where to go to next."

Adam was rambling. It seemed like he'd been through something, and not something good. I unlocked the door with my virtual fingerprints and it popped open. "Home sweet home." I laughed. "I never thought I'd be happy to be back here! But shockingly, I am." I waved Adam inside. The place was a mess. The last time I called up my App Store, when the Death App finally showed its glittery face, the icons were so zealous and numerous they'd knocked over furniture and shattered a light hanging from the ceiling. I righted a chair and a table.

Adam stood there in the doorway, looking dazed.

I shook my head. Boys could be so useless.

"You could at least help me." I brushed the glass from the broken light into the corner with my foot.

"What?" He seemed to wake from shutdown. "Oh! Sorry."

The two of us cleaned and straightened what we could without the assistance of a download, since I doubted my deal with the government for unlimited Apps still held at this point.

"Where's Skylar?" I asked Adam after we finished.

"She went back to the Real World."

"Huh," I huffed. I *knew* she wouldn't keep her word. The girl always wanted to save everyone, and leave it to me to be the only exception. "Why didn't you go with her?"

"I told you. Because I promised to come back for you."

I waltzed up to him and studied his face. "Yup, nope, not sure I believe you." He opened his mouth but I put a hand up to silence him. "The truth now," I urged.

He lowered his eyes. "Honestly, I just wasn't ready to go back. And I really did come here because I promised. But I'm not sure it was a good idea to stay. A lot has happened since I last saw you."

I whistled, something I'd always been able to do since I was small, even without the help of a download. "You're telling me! Boy, have I had adventures, and they were not all fun and games like in that ridiculous college party where we met. Who first—you or me?"

"Skylar and I went," he began, then hesitated. "We went to a . . . *place* . . . where we could access information. Top secret information. Well, and rumors."

"Of course you did." That Skylar chick *would* have access to classified info somehow.

"And what we learned and saw was distressing," he said, then laughed a little. "To say the least. We saw the Death App in action, for one."

"Oh, poor you! No wonder you look like you have an App Hangover. Why don't you sit down." I led him to one of the couches and straightened the cushions, puffing them. Then I pushed him until he was sitting, since he couldn't seem to do anything on his own. "Wasn't it *dreadful*? Seeing the Death App in action has scarred me for eternal life."

"Yes." He was nodding, that dazed look coming over him again. "But there's more. There's a hole in Loner Town. A *giant* hole. Like, it's unimaginably big."

I gasped. "I know exactly what you're talking about!" I clapped my hands. "My turn to share!" I plopped onto the couch next to him and crossed my legs underneath me. "I saw that hole, too. It's gigantic. But it's not the only one!"

Adam turned to me, the vacant look in his eyes gone. "What do you mean? There's more than one?"

"There's, like, a gazillion of them. There are holes in the atmosphere all over the City. None quite as big as that one. But if you know how to look for them, you'll see that they're everywhere." I got up and began investigating everything in the room, every spot, every corner, every piece of furniture, from every angle I could manage for a girl of my height.

"What in both worlds are you doing?" Adam asked.

"Searching for one right now, obviously." I got up on my toes to peer at a shelf on the wall. "It's all in how you look." My voice tapered as something flashed after I got down on my hands and knees. "There," I said triumphantly, crawling toward the coffee table. If I bent low, I could see it. A hole about a foot long and vertical. "Come here," I told Adam.

He pulled himself off the couch and crouched next to me.

"May I?" I gestured at his hand.

He nodded and I took it. Then I thrust our clasped hands into the black gap in the atmosphere and they disappeared.

"Holy—"

"—I know."

The virtual skin of my hand grew cold and tingly. The longer I held us there the colder it got, until I thought icicles would form along our fingers. When I pulled out our hands they were nearly blue.

Adam snatched his back and investigated it. He seemed surprised it was still there. "This is not good."

I scrambled to my feet. "Tell me about it. There's probably others all around us. If we spent a little time searching, I bet we'd find a bunch more."

"Ree," Adam began. He looked up at me from the place where he still sat crouched on the carpet. "How did you learn this? Where were you?"

"If I told you now you'd have *so many* questions and there isn't really time. I only came back here to grab a few things and change before heading off."

"But—"

"—no buts." I checked my capital account and was pleased to see that I had at least something left. Just enough for my purposes. "Let me download us some new clothes with what little capital remains to the Aristocrat family name. I can't go anywhere in these worn-out rags. I need to look my best. And you could use a little outfit change yourself. That is, if you want to come with me? You do look like you could use some rest, but it's your choice."

"Where?" Adam asked.

I called up my App Store. "Pathetic," I muttered, when I saw the paltry number of icons that appeared now that I no longer had unlimited downloads at my fingertips. I found the App I needed and touched it. "Tell me first, do you want to join me or not?"

"I can't," Adam said. "I have to unplug and warn the others in the Real World."

"Your girlfriend, you mean?"

"She's not my girlfriend," he said quickly. There was something raw there, as raw as a still untested prototype App. "But yes, her. And the rest of my friends. I can't stay here any longer. They need this information."

I shrugged. "Suit yourself."

"Just tell me where you're going, so I know how to find you later."

The App began to transform my clothing, and soon I was dressed like the proper lady I needed to be for what lay ahead. "I actually believe you when you say that," I told him. "Since you've come for me twice now. You're a good person, Adam. A boy of your word."

"Thank you, I think," he said. "Are you going to tell me or not?"

"Yes," I sighed, as the prim heels appearing on my feet lifted me nearly to his chin. Adam was a tall one. "I'm going to see Lady Holt."

"Lady Holt," Adam stated. "Rain Holt's mother. Jonathan Holt's wife."

"The very same," I confirmed.

"Seriously?"

I imitated the shocked tone in Adam's voice. "Yes, seriously!"

Adam was gaping at me. "What could she possibly do to help?"

"Oh, plenty, I suspect. More than her inept husband, I'm sure. He was just a puppet anyway, in my opinion." I called up a Mirror App and took in my appearance. I looked so ladylike in my pink tweed skirt suit, pearls, and stockings. Perfect. "Because, as my late and much-missed mother always told me, which I think she learned from some women's self-help App she used to download: you should never trust a man to do a woman's job."

29

Skylar

gathering forces

"GO LEFT," I told Kit.

He hesitated, then leaned the bike in the direction I'd asked.

The graffiti along our route intensified.

GO BACK TO YOUR VAPID VIRTUAL EXISTENCE.
THE REAL WORLD IS FOR REAL PEOPLE.
YOU ABANDONED US, NOW WE ABANDON YOU!

The slogans and protests expressed rage and judgment, dismay that the quiet and orderly life the Keepers had worked hard to achieve had been disrupted, maybe permanently. I understood the resistance, the fears and the anger behind it, but how were we going to get everyone on board for what was to come?

The night was chilly, cold, even, and I wasn't dressed to be riding around like this. My teeth chattered, but I resisted the urge to grip Kit even tighter than I already was. I knew he and I needed more time to sort things out between us. Diving back into whatever we'd started in February without having talked to Rain, without Kit and me truly facing all that had transpired since then, was not a good idea.

But the heart wants what it wants as well. And mine wanted Kit.

"Here," I told him, and he turned down the drive where I pointed. "I need to run in for a few minutes. Then we'll head on to Briarwood."

He cut the engine so we could coast without noise, without waking every single person sleeping in the tall, imposing mansion that cut a shadow across the night. There was a flicker of light in one of the highest floors, but otherwise the windows were dark.

Kit pulled to a stop and set his feet on the ground, steadying the bike. "You're freezing," he said, once he realized I was shaking.

I rubbed my hands up and down my arms, trying to warm myself. "I'm fine," I lied.

He let this go. "Who lives here?"

I swung my leg over the seat and hopped down. "My Keeper."

Kit parked the motorcycle to the side of the drive in the cover of a long tree branch. He'd tugged the edges of his sleeves tight over his wrists. Maybe he didn't realize that I'd seen what they covered. "Doesn't she have a name?"

"Yes," I said. "Though she's never told me and says she won't. As I'm sure you know, it's forbidden for Keepers to tell their wards their real names because the word, *Keeper*, was ideally supposed to carry the same meaning as *mother* or *father*."

"Did it work?" Kit asked. "Do you see her as a parent?"

I thought about this, remembering how the feeling that she regarded me as though I was her child had passed through me on many occasions since I woke up in her care. "Yes, actually. I do see her that way. Or at the very least as an aunt. Someone I can depend on, no matter what."

"That must be nice," he said softly.

"It is," I admitted.

There was an exhaustion in Kit's eyes that he'd kept well-hidden until now, and I wondered if it was thoughts of his lost parents that put it there, or if it was all that shifting. Shifting could wreck your body, regardless of how young or strong you were. *Maybe it could even wreck an entire world. An entire virtual civilization*, I thought. But then again, so could family. Well, mine, at the very least. "I'll just be a minute," I told Kit, worried that he might fall asleep while standing.

This seemed to snap him out of it. "You're not going in there alone."

"It's safe, I promise," I told him.

He shook his head and followed me inside.

I opened the door as quietly as I could, not wanting to startle or scare my Keeper awake. But when we entered a soft light greeted us from the kitchen. My Keeper stood over the sink, washing more dishes than I could believe were contained in the cabinets.

She turned. "Skylar?" She looked and sounded nearly as weary as Kit. "What are you doing here so late?" Her eyes slid to him, but her expression gave away nothing. She wiped her hands with a towel and came to give me a hug. "It's been too long since I've seen you," she whispered.

"I know," I whispered guiltily back. "I'm sorry."

When she pulled away, she returned her attention to Kit. "Hello," she said, not unfriendly. But not overly friendly either.

"This is Kit," I said.

"I figured," she said.

There was no motion to shake hands or greet each other formally, and I let this go. For now. Everyone in my life seemed to have an allegiance toward Rain. I pointed to the giant piles of dishes. "What's that all about?"

My Keeper glanced back. "Oh, you know. Feeding

those people who never learned or forgot the skill of feeding themselves."

"The refugees staying here? You're cooking for all of them?"

She sighed. "As much as I can."

"I know you're a Keeper, but one person isn't enough to Keep all the people staying at the mansion."

"No," she said. "But we have to make do. There are too few of us to go around for so many people. As you know, there are a lot of Keepers very unhappy with the arrival of our new citizens. Eventually things will get better. I hope," she added.

"They're going to need to get better soon. Like, immediately," I said.

Her eyebrows arched. "Skylar, that's unrealistic. My fellow Keepers are—"

"—I know, I know," I interrupted. "I don't have much time, but let's go sit for a few minutes. There's a lot I have to tell you."

She closed her mouth and nodded.

The three of us went to the room with the couches and the great chandelier overhead, the remnants of another, glitzier era when the Real World was all anyone had. After I'd said everything that needed saying, explained all the theories, the possibilities, the unknowns, my Keeper sat back and contemplated the information in silence. The weariness on her face seemed to deepen, but I could see her brain working behind those familiar eyes.

When she leaned forward again, they were still working. "Skylar, I know what we should do. But I'm not sure you're going to like it."

"It doesn't matter what I like," I said. "Just tell me. Whatever it is."

"Why don't you wait to hear what she's thinking before you decide," Kit warned.

I shook my head. "If it's something that could work, I don't care what it is."

"I think your friend is right," she said, eyeing me.

And then she began to talk.

By the time we arrived at Briarwood, it was the middle of the night. When the sun rose over the ocean in the morning, the fate of both worlds would be decided. But before then, all there was to do was wait, and I needed sleep—as much as I could manage. My body was near collapse, and from the look of it, so was Kit's. I slid off the bike and was already headed inside, desperate for rest, dreading the thought of likely having to shift once more by tomorrow's end.

Kit hung back by his motorcycle. "Are you sure this is a good idea?"

"Yes," I said, without hesitation.

But the second we passed through the doors I wasn't so sure.

Rain was waiting for us. He slipped into sight from around the corner, arms crossed, wide awake. He stood at the mouth of the entryway.

How did he know of our arrival?

Oh.

My mother. Surely she sent a message informing him I would be on my way.

And that I'd be accompanied.

"Skylar," he said with a nod.

"Rain," I replied, breath drawn in, poised to continue, when Lacy came around the corner, carrying two glasses and a bottle of wine. A stab of jealousy burned through my rib cage, but it faded quickly.

"I found the vintage you wanted," she began, then abruptly stopped. "Oh!" she exclaimed when she saw us. Her gaze lowered to her hands and their contents guiltily. I could see her considering turning and going back the way she came.

"Hi, Lacy," I said. I suddenly wondered if Rain orchestrated this meeting of all of us without informing Lacy my arrival was imminent. If this was his plan, it only made me feel sad on Lacy's behalf.

"Hi, Skylar," she said, her voice small and still uncertain.

My gaze returned to Rain. "There's a lot to be done."

"I know," he said. "Trader was here. We met to discuss what you learned when you shifted." His voice lacked emotion, but there was a storm in his eyes.

I nodded. "My Keeper had an idea about how to handle informing everyone of what's happening in the App World, even those resistant to the refugees." I could feel Kit tense beside me. "And the influx of more, if our suspicions are right about its future."

"And . . .?" Rain urged. "What was her idea?"

My eyes returned to the glasses and wine in Lacy's hands. "Let's talk about it first thing in the morning at the meeting. You had other plans and I don't want to interrupt."

Rain seemed as though he was preparing to contradict me, opening his mouth to protest, but he grew silent instead. "All right," he said softly.

"When I wake up I'll go get Andleeb and Rasha and bring them here," I told him. "We'll need them too."

Kit still hadn't spoken. He stood at my side, frozen and barely breathing. I couldn't decide if this was because of sheer exhaustion or because he hated Rain and always would. "I'll show you where you can sleep," I told him now, making it obvious to everyone that it wouldn't be in my room.

The disappointment on Kit's face was unmistakable, but quickly erased. "Okay," he agreed.

"Let's go, Lacy," Rain said.

Lacy glanced at me, uncertain. I found myself wanting to reassure her that it was fine to be with him, but the circumstances prevented it.

Later. Later I would.

I made this silent promise to Lacy.

"Good night," I told them, and without further hesitation, I slipped past the two of them and Kit and I made our way silently down the hall to a room where he could stay the night.

When he hesitated in the doorway, I spoke before he could say anything first.

"Sleep well," I said, and then hurried away.

30

Skylar

risks of the heart

SLEEP REFUSED TO come.

I lay there in bed, my mind awhirl. Rather than thoughts of meetings and plans and the possibility that an entire world was dying and its virtual way of life with it, my thoughts were for Kit. That he was close. Just a few twists and turns away. All the questions I wanted to ask him, all the things I wanted to say, rose to the surface and inked themselves on my skin like tattoos.

Kit's tattoo.

I wanted to see it. Needed to.

Maggie's belief about its meaning pulsed through me.

I got out from under the covers and threw on a sweater. I didn't even look in the mirror before I was out of my room and rushing through the darkness of the mansion, retracing my steps from earlier, the purpose of my route pulsing through me. I knocked on his door gently, the sound a soft thud. The click of a lock sounded and the door swung open before I could prepare myself.

"You're back," Kit said. One of his hands rested high along the frame of the door, the other still gripped the handle.

I fought the urge to step into his open arms. "Did I wake you?"

"No," he said, and stepped aside.

A narrow bed, nearly too small for one person, was pressed against the wall with little room to maneuver around it. The window beside it was dark with the night. The one small lamp next to the bed was lit, but it barely gave off any light. Kit's jacket and sweater were draped over a chair. He still wore his jeans and his arms were covered by his long-sleeved shirt.

Kit shut the door behind him. He gestured at the bed. "Would you like to sit? Unless you're not staying long?"

"I don't know yet," I said. But I sat down anyway. I clasped my hands in my lap tightly.

Kit walked the few steps between the door and the bed and joined me there, though he sat as far away along the edge as he could. The sheets and comforter were still pulled tight. He hadn't even tried to sleep. "So, what's keeping you up at night, Skylar? The Keeper's idea? The prospect of further unrest in the Real World?" He paused. "The fact that Rain was drinking wine with another girl?"

"All those things," I said. "And also none of them."

Kit leaned against the headboard, and it creaked under his weight. "What's that supposed to mean?"

An image of Maggie made its way into my mind, the way she'd looked at me at the cottage. Her claims about Kit's newest tattoo.

"I met your sister," I said.

He immediately sat up, his back rigid. "Maggie? When?"

"I went to your house," I confessed. "You weren't there, but I know where you keep the spare key and I decided to go inside. I surprised her."

"I bet you did." Kit's voice was quiet.

"I decided I wanted to talk to you. So I went to the cottage," I admitted.

"You came to find me," he whispered once more, as though he couldn't believe this.

"Twice now," I confirmed. I was tired of hiding my feelings. Hiding served me no longer. "The first time to your house and the second to Trader's."

"But I thought—"

"—that I'd gone to find Trader?" I shook my head. "He told me you were there and gave me his keys. I went because of you."

The tension in Kit's back eased. A look of relief washed over him. "You came to find me *twice*," he repeated.

"Maggie made me lunch."

Kit smiled. "You and my sister had lunch. Wow. Was it edible?"

"It was the same pasta dish you always made me. It was good, though I didn't eat much of it. I wasn't very hungry."

He chuckled softly. "It's the only dish she knows how to make. She probably wanted to impress you."

I took a deep breath. "That's not why I brought her up. She said something to me. She claimed a number of things about you and . . ." I stopped.

"And?" he pressed.

My eyes went to his wrist, the cuff of his shirt pulled all the way to the base of his knuckles. "She told me you have a new tattoo."

"I have a lot of tattoos." He shifted uncomfortably. "You know that. You stabbed one of them, remember?"

"Kit," I urged. "I'm not talking about the ones I've seen. I'm talking about the one she inked for you recently. Maggie insisted I see it. That I convince you to show it to me."

Kit tugged the sleeve farther, gripping it tightly in place with his fingers. "What did she say about it?" he asked darkly.

I inched closer. "Won't you just show me? Please? I think I already know what it is. I saw part of it when we were on your bike."

Kit was silent. Every slight movement of our bodies, every breath, seemed loud in the quiet. I waited for him to make a decision, wondering why he was so worried to let me see, or why he was so intent on hiding it from me. Maybe Maggie was wrong and the new tattoo had nothing to do with me or with us. Maybe it was just Kit adding on to the images that already graced his shoulders. Maybe—

Kit held out his arm and started to tug the sleeve of his shirt up over his wrist. Little by little, he exposed his skin all the way to his bicep.

I leaned forward, studying the tattoo. "It's beautiful," I said.

And it was.

At the base of his wrist were snowflakes, just a flurry of them. Each one a tiny masterpiece, the blue of the ink bright as ice. But as they moved up his arm they grew more numerous until they became a storm that collided with the stars at the base of Kit's shoulder.

"Maggie is a talented artist," he said.

"Very."

Kit pulled his arm away and began to roll his sleeve back down over his skin, his eyes as intent on this process as if he were performing surgery. The tattoo disappeared from view. "Are you going to tell me what Maggie said or not?"

"Well," I stalled. My cheeks grew fiery. I worried their blaze told Kit everything he might wonder. "She said . . . she implied that . . ." It seemed ridiculous to say what she'd told me out loud now. Like it was something that would only happen in a story, but never real life, or with an App that would last for a few hours but would later fade to oblivion. That a boy—a boy I *loved*—would ink something on his skin that represented his love for me seemed impossible. That he would create evidence of it for all the Real World to see. Finally, I just said it. "Did you . . . is that tattoo"—I drew in a deep breath—"for *me*?"

Kit's eyes were steady and unafraid. "Answer me one thing first," he said. "At Trader's cottage, when I was waking up, did you say that you loved me or did I dream it?"

My eyes slid to the wall, which was shadowy and surreal in the dim lighting. I couldn't hold Kit's gaze while I answered. "Yes," I said eventually. "You heard me say that I love you. Still. Despite all that's happened."

He sucked in a breath. "Skylar—"

"—that must've taken Maggie forever," I interjected.

"A couple of months," Kit said quietly. "To finish it."

"Did it hurt?"

"It always hurts."

My eyes flickered back to his. "Are you going to make

me ask you again or are you going to answer me like you said you would?"

"Yes, it's for you. Of course it's for you. Every time I look at it I'm reminded of when we met and how we grew closer despite the situation. I'm reminded of falling in love with you. And what I did to push you away. I had Maggie do it so I would never forget." His voice was anguished. "Skylar?" he pressed, when I didn't say anything.

"I love it. I love that you did it," I whispered. But I got up from the bed and went to the door. The narrow room felt like it was closing in on me. I grasped the handle.

"Where are you going? Don't run away," Kit pleaded.

"I just need some air," I told him. "Some space. More space than there is in here. With you. I'll see you in the morning."

"What are you so afraid of?" Kit asked before I could leave. "Just tell me."

"Betrayal, Kit. I'm afraid you'll betray me all over again."

He met me at the door, but was careful not to get too close. "But I won't," he said. "I won't, Skylar. I promise."

I turned back slightly. He was near enough that I could feel the slight rise and fall of his chest. "You promised me things before and then you broke your promises."

"Things were different before," he said.

"And how are they now?"

"Different," he repeated. "Very."

"I'm not ready to trust you," I told him. "I'm just not."

"Then I'll wait."

His face was close. I wanted to kiss him. I took a step outside the room instead. "You might be waiting a long time, Kit."

"I don't care, Skylar," he said. "I'll be here when you're ready."

I nodded. I couldn't speak. My throat was too tight. Then I turned and left the way I came. I could feel Kit's eyes lingering on my back.

31

Lacy

allies once more

WHEN RAIN WAS asleep, I slipped away.

Down I went, one floor, then another, grateful that no one else was awake, everyone doing their best to rest before tomorrow. I thought I would make it all the way to my destination unseen until I rounded a corner and ran smack into Skylar.

"Lacy," she hissed, startled. "What are you doing up?"

"What are *you* doing up?" I returned, before I realized where we were standing. "Oh! Forget that question. I already know." I smiled a little, pleased to find Skylar emerging from Kit's room. But my smile faltered when I saw that her big blue eyes were shiny with tears. "Are you all right?" I wondered aloud. Despite everything, sympathy niggled its way into me for Skylar. Pain experienced on behalf of love was the worst kind of hurt, far worse than any pain in the real body. I'd wished on many an occasion for a Mind Eraser App to ease my heartache about Rain.

"I'm fine," Skylar said.

But she was lying. That much was obvious. I nodded at the door down the hall behind her. "Was he being a jerk or something?"

She shook her head.

That's a relief.

But was it a relief because I wanted Skylar's heart to belong to Kit and not to Rain? Or because I actually cared whether she felt bad, regardless of them both?

"I just had some questions I needed answers to," she went on, growing distant.

"Don't we all," I agreed.

The two of us locked eyes.

Skylar and I were sharing *a moment.*

Miracles did happen, I supposed.

The moment passed. Curiosity crept across her face. "Where were you headed?"

"Um, nowhere?" I replied, as though this would suffice.

Skylar's dark, thick, in-need-of-plucking eyebrows arched. "Um, try again?"

"To get a snack?"

"Lacy." The patience in her voice had grown thin. "Spill. I caught you sneaking somewhere, and if I had to guess it was down to the plugs, since there's nowhere else this hallway leads."

"Fine." I tapped my fingernails against the wall behind me. A nervous habit I could never seem to break. "I'll tell you what I was up to if you promise not to tell anyone else. Not *anyone*. Not yet at least."

"I don't know if I can promise that." She looked at me like I was some crazy person and not Lacy Mills, sought-after young starlet of the App World. Which I supposed I wasn't anymore, but whatever. Details.

I retracted my fingers and stood straighter. "Then why should I tell you anything?"

She seemed to think about this. "So you're not alone in it," she said.

And she said it with *kindness*.

It was real, too.

Ever since I'd heard talk of a virus, I assumed that *eventually* we might need to get people out of the App World. Like, to the tune of *everybody*. I started imagining possibilities that made *me* the heroine this time, rather than Skylar—or at the very least, alongside her. Shockingly enough, I actually thought of something quite good. But could I actually trust her with what I'd been thinking about? What I'd decided to do? Or at least, *try* to do?

Would she be willing to share the spotlight with me, her longtime nemesis?

Because right now, Skylar, the heroine herself in the flesh, was taking a risk by reaching out to me.

So I decided to take my own risk and reach back.

I told her my thoughts. How I believed I might be able to help.

When I finished, I tried to read the expression in her eyes. The tears had dried as she listened to me. But was it disapproval I saw? No. Definitely not. The way she looked at me, it was almost with respect. Admiration, even. Was that possible? Could Skylar Cruz, so long my nemesis in this world, actually have a change of heart about me?

Could I have a change of heart about her, too?

She kept staring like she'd never seen me before and my confidence faltered. Maybe I'd misread her reaction. My fingernails bit into my palms. "You hate what I want to do," I stated. "You think it's stupid. Unnecessary."

Skylar shook her head. "No," she said slowly. "I don't think it's stupid. Far from it. I think it's a great plan, and if I had to bet, we'll be grateful you thought of it."

Air puffed my lungs and seemed to lift me up. "Really?"

"Yes, really. And given what's likely ahead, it's smart, and I have a feeling we're going to need exactly this. I'm sorry if I've underestimated you in the past."

I nearly couldn't believe my ears, hearing these things from the mouth of Skylar the Great herself. "Seriously," I said, the word forceful and disbelieving.

She nodded. "But Lacy, what is this *really* about?" she asked, still sounding a bit suspicious of my motives.

The pesky fleshy heart inside my chest pounded against my rib cage like a child throwing a temper tantrum. "You're not the only one who can be heroic around here, you know!" I shot back before I could stop those words from flying out of my mouth.

Understanding dawned on her face—understanding that I wished I could erase with one swipe of my hand. "So this *is* about proving yourself to Rain."

I tossed my long locks to one side. "What if it is?"

"I'm not judging you," she said. "I'm really not. People do all kinds of things for love," she added carefully. Maybe she was afraid I'd lash out at her again, or maybe she was careful because she knew this subject between us was as delicate and thin as the very real and permeable skin of our bodies. "I respect you for it. Though I promise it's unnecessary. I see the way he looks at you, Lacy. You don't need to prove anything to anyone, him least of all."

"But you're not going to stop me," I said, choosing to ignore her last comment.

"No. I won't." She looked around, but there was no one

else in sight, no sounds to indicate anyone approaching us. We were totally alone. "In fact, if you really are serious about this, I'm going to help you instead." She blinked once. "If you'll have me."

32

Ree

high tea

"EVERYONE KNOWS YOU were always the brains behind this operation." I lifted my teacup and took a small sip. The warmth sent relaxing shivers through my code, and I was grateful for it.

"Oh?" Lady Holt said, displaying her trademark modesty. "What an interesting thing to insinuate."

She had invited me in to her palatial penthouse, but only to be polite. But that didn't mean she wouldn't usher me out long before I could get to the point of my visit.

My mother had been her number one fan—a fact Lady Holt knew well, given that my mother won a "Day of Shadowing Lady Holt" in a special contest that invited the winner into the virtual world of the City's honorary queen.

My mother had downloaded all the advice and opinions Lady Holt had ever recorded and was always going on and on about her bountiful "wisdom." My mother had bought into all the conspiracy theories swirling around her as well, the biggest one being that her husband was really only a puppet, his wife holding the strings and running the government single-handedly from behind the scenes. Before these last months I wouldn't have believed it, but then the entire App World watched Jonathan Holt crumble before the obvious dominance of Emory Specter, not to mention the chaos unleashed by his son, Rain, and Rain's favorite sidekick, Skylar. To say that such events raised questions was the understatement of the App century.

My coming here was a belated way of honoring my mother's surprising judgment.

But the question remained: if the rumors were true about Lady Holt, then where had she been these last six months? Why hadn't she stepped forward to rule in her husband's absence? The rumors were that he'd abandoned her and was somewhere in his real body with his son. So why in both worlds had she remained silent and out of the picture?

I smiled at her now. And decided to be honest. "I've learned a lot about this world in the last few months. Things that perhaps you already know, being who you are and all"—I fluttered my lashes, glad that I'd spent precious capital on a Mascara App to add to the effect—"or perhaps things you'd be very interested to find out?"

"I'm listening," she said, ever composed.

She took a sip of her tea.

I told her everything I knew. Everything I'd been through. About the holes in the fabric of the App World and about my ominous encounter with Emory Specter and the tidbit he'd dropped about the dark-seeming fate of our City. The steam from her tea curled up and around her virtual face, the elegant bell of her sleeves matching that of the skirt of her dress. She really was every bit the lady. When I finished, I was forced to endure a long silence, during which I fidgeted because I couldn't help myself. I drained my cup even though it was so hot it burned through my code. I wasn't raised for elegant meetings with App World royalty.

"Why come to me with this?" she asked finally.

I set my cup back onto the coffee table. "I just . . . I have suspicions about you."

She eyed me skeptically. "Yes. You said that earlier. And what suspicions are those?"

"That you might know what to do to save all our virtual lives from oblivion."

"And why should I do anything to help this world, when all it has done is taken my family away? My son and my husband are no longer here to give me any incentive to care."

"But you're a Holt!" I protested.

"Only by marriage," she countered.

"Good point," I admitted.

She huffed daintily.

"I have something else to offer you in return for any advice, solutions, help . . ."

"What could you possibly offer me that I would care about?"

"Access to your son," I dropped. "How does *that* sound?"

33

Skylar

acts of faith

"I'LL HAVE EVERYONE there by noon," Andleeb was saying.

The headscarf she wore today was a fiery purple. Vivid. Royal. It was perfect. "Do you think you can mobilize people that quickly?" I asked.

"The key people we need, yes," Rasha said with a nod. Rasha's hijab was a bright hot pink, and it set off the beauty of her olive skin and dark eyes. "As long as you provide us the transportation."

"I'm taking care of that," Sylvia said. "You'll have it."

I turned to Zeera. "You alerted everyone here and in the city?"

"As many as I could reach, with the limited technology

people have access to." Her eyes were on the tablet in her hands. She finished tapping on it and looked up. "I still wish we could wait awhile, until I can gather more intel on the App World. We don't really know what we're getting into."

Trader peered over her shoulder at the screen, reading something. "But we can at least cross the border undetected if we use the Shifting App again." His eyes flickered to mine. The Shifting App was powered by yours truly, so the burden of this plan would fall to me.

Rain kept glancing at the door, as though waiting for someone to walk through it and join us. "We *think* we can cross undetected," he corrected, distractedly.

He was wondering about Lacy. Worried about her.

I hope she's okay.

Parvda was nodding. "And we have no idea if and how shifting affects people in the long run. Adam is . . . Adam is so far under I can't pull him out." Her voice cracked. "What if he never wakes up? What if . . . what if he dies on the plugs?" She turned to me. "Shifting is hard on people, isn't it Skylar?"

"Skylar is fine," Trader cut in.

I hesitated. Parvda was right. I didn't know what the long-term effects were of shifting. "I am *technically* okay, it's true. But it's also true that shifting takes its toll on the body. A big one."

"Skylar is right," Kit confirmed.

Everyone turned to him.

"I've been shifting these last months, probably too much, and it's a destructive habit. I don't think the real brain is equipped to handle that kind of back-and-forth." He turned to Trader. "But you're right, too. Shifting allows us to enter into the App World undetected. I can't prove it without a doubt, but I've done it enough to believe that it's the case."

Rain was gaping at him. "*You've* been shifting."

"Yeah. So?" Kit challenged.

"I'm just surprised. I've been told you hate the App World." Rain looked at me as he said this.

"I do hate it," Kit said. "And I won't be sorry to see it go if it does."

Parvda and Zeera gasped.

"Don't say that," Parvda said. "Not while Adam is still there."

"I didn't say that I hated the people in it and I wanted them dead. Just the world itself."

Andleeb adjusted her scarf. "For some citizens, their real identity and their identity in the App World are so intertwined they're one and the same. If the App World dies, they'll die with it."

I thought of Jude, who'd had her body destroyed. And all the others whose bodies were gone. "And for many, regardless of the how intimately their identity is tied to their virtual existence, if the App World dies they'll die with it because they'll have nothing to unplug to."

The weapons room grew quiet.

Rasha spoke first after the silence. "Let's not forget the people who do have bodies to reclaim, and the ones who already have reclaimed them. There's hope for a lot of us. And that hope rests on Skylar's Keeper's plan today. We need to do our best to get all of New Port City on board or else . . . or else I have no idea."

"We're doomed?" Zeera suggested, but she wasn't making a joke.

"I'm still not sure her Keeper's idea is a good one," Rain said. "She is making a big bet, and a very, very risky one."

I took a deep breath. "Yes, it's a gamble. But it's also the right thing to do. Our worlds need this. It's the only way to restore some order and . . ." I searched for the right word.

"Some faith," Kit supplied. "The people of New Port City need faith in each other, in us. This is a way of asking for it. The only way, I think," he added.

"It's getting late, guys," Sylvia said.

Zeera tapped her screen. "She's right. We need to get moving."

The eight of us inhaled a collective breath.

Rasha and Andleeb were the first to leave. "See you all soon. Fingers crossed."

Before the rest of us could make our exits, Rain posed one last question.

"Has anyone seen Lacy?" he asked.

There were shrugs and people shaking their heads all around.

I left the room quietly, before a lie was required of me.

The cliff was the same as I remembered it.

And yet it was different.

Like so many things lately.

It rose up from the rocks and the ocean, the roar of the waves providing a distant soundtrack. The sun was behind the clouds, the sky gray and brooding and crisp with the air of fall. The peninsula was barren as before, except for the large expanse of grass that covered it. The podium was still there as well, but gone was the curving glass wall that separated the people of New Port City from the stone dais that jutted up at the center of everything, the glass wall that had separated me from everyone present the day that Jude put me on display, heralding the official arrival of the New Capitalist movement and all that it promised, including the Body Market.

Shortly after the hour passed eleven, people began to arrive.

There were the refugees who'd left the mansions and apartments where they'd made their makeshift homes, walking on foot from the outskirts of the city, following the line of Keepers who claimed a lifetime on this series of islands connected to the mainland by bridges. There were those of us who'd come from Briarwood, seventeens, now eighteens, abandoned to the Real World when the borders closed, and those who'd unplugged illegally and crossed despite this. Andleeb and Rasha arrived, with Sylvia and a few select others helping her ferry refugees from the camp on the beach. I recognized some of Jude's people, New Capitalists—even they still called themselves this—led by Jag and several of the guards who'd worked alongside Jude.

Soon I saw my mother making her way across the grounds. Zeera, Kit, Trader, and Inara trailed after her. Followed by Rain.

And Jonathan Holt.

He'd emerged from seclusion. He'd barely appeared in public at Briarwood since Rain had unplugged him in February. I was grateful he'd somehow convinced his father to be here today. His role would be an important one.

"Skylar, sweetheart," my mother said when she reached me. "But are you sure?"

"No." I tried to ward off a shiver as the appointed hour crept toward us. "But I think it's the right thing to do."

"It may be, but I'm not sure it's going to end up helping the App World."

"We'll have to hope that people see why they should help. Why they *must*."

"Oh, darling," she sighed. "You're young and idealistic, but you have to know that the right thing for you may not be the right thing for others. Not everyone is going to want to be so altruistic."

"But maybe enough will," I said.

She squeezed my hand. "Let's hope so."

As these words emerged from my mother's mouth, I noticed signs going up, posters and banners dotting the crowd, an assortment of now-familiar slogans painted on them.

REFUGEES GO HOME!
GO BACK TO YOUR APPING LIFE.
STOP CLOGGING OUR CITY!
DOWN WITH APP WORLD CITIZENS!
THE REAL WORLD DOESN'T WANT YOU HERE!

My only consolation was the absence of signs that made claims about body snatchers among us.

Andleeb broke away from her group and came over. "This is not good, Skylar."

"Just wait," I said, with more confidence than I felt. "We haven't yet said a word to them about the situation. Today is our chance to address everyone."

"And it's their chance to address each other as well," she said darkly.

A ripple went through the crowd.

My Keeper was making her way up to the podium.

I breathed deep.

It was time.

She nodded my way and I nodded back.

Kit and Maggie, Parvda and Rain, Zeera and Sylvia, Trader and my mother, everyone I'd grown close to in this world, gathered together now as we waited for her to speak.

My Keeper's voice rose loud and strong. "Thank you for coming," she began, and launched into a series of formal greetings, noting each group that was present. At the mention of the refugees, there were a number of boos and jeers. She called for quiet and, eventually when the noise died down, she turned to the matter at hand.

"A difficult question has been laid before us and the time has come to face it and answer with honesty. Are we, the Keepers of the Real World—those of us who were left behind because we had no other choice and those of us who made the choice to remain in New Port City in order to preserve the old ways of living in our bodies—willing to welcome back those people who abandoned our world for a virtual life? Are we willing to help reintegrate those refugees already here and the others who still may come? Or will we abandon them in their time of need as they abandoned us?"

The crowd erupted into hushed murmurs and whispers.

My breath caught, my heart knocking against the

cage of bones surrounding it. I'd prepared myself for my Keeper's question, for the quandary she put before all the people of New Port City—the *choice*, not the requirement—that one feasible and reasonable option would be for the Keepers to let the App World and its residents die, if it was truly dying without our intervention or assistance. My Keeper believed that only by offering a *real* choice to the people, a true one, and abiding by their will whether we liked their decision or not, might we have a chance to help those who remained vulnerable in the App World.

The matter of helping and intervening—or not—was to be put to the residents of New Port City as a *vote*, a democratic *vote* today. I'd known this was the right thing from the moment she suggested it. It was a brilliant plan, really, and the only one that might ease the incredible tension that had grown and crested among the Keepers of New Port City because of the refugees.

My Keeper was wrapping up her remarks.

She turned the podium over to Andleeb, who would make a plea on behalf of the refugee community. When she was done, she would offer the podium to whoever wished to speak next. We would stay all afternoon and into the night if need be, until anyone with words to say had spoken them and was heard by all. One by one, people emerged from the crowd, some of them moved by Andleeb's words, some of them by my Keeper's foresight that New Port City had needed this forum, but many of them angry by the changes here, by all that had transpired, urging people to turn away from these "others" who suddenly needed our help.

"Why should any of us care if the App World is dying? They reap what they sowed," bellowed one man to great applause.

"They barred us from a virtual life," said a woman who'd gone up to the podium to cheers from the crowd, which only seemed to grow larger and larger as the day wore on. "Now it's our turn to bar them from a real one!"

My heart sank at these statements and their strong approval.

But we'd committed to this process. It was too late to back down.

When Jag spoke on behalf of the New Capitalist movement, the crowd went silent, surprised, I was sure, to hear his plea to welcome citizens of the App World into this city again.

Finally, after it was evident that no one else was going to approach the podium, Jonathan Holt made his way there, steps uncertain, everything about him slow, careful. He seemed an old man after merely a few months in the Real World, his decline swift and unyielding. I saw Rain wince as he watched his father stumble.

Jonathan Holt reached the podium after what felt like an eternity.

"Greetings, everyone," he began. "Many of you only

know my name but would not have reason to recognize me. I am Jonathan Holt, former Prime Minister of the App World."

Surprise and anger swelled across the crowd.

"And I'm here today," he went on, "to apologize for all the wrongs you've suffered at my hands." The surprise grew more pronounced. He bowed his head. "Now I must ask for your forgiveness on behalf of every current and former citizen of the App World who needs you more than ever. And please, let me be more specific: I am not just asking, I am here to *beg*."

Rain's eyes were steady on his father's as he spoke to the crowd, as he groveled, pleading with them to hear his apology, to believe in his remorse, and to somehow move beyond the urge to punish a world full of virtual people for the actions of a mere few, like himself, who'd held all the power.

Tears sprung to my eyes as I listened, not only because Rain was forced to see his father, once a great man, brought so low, but because in Jonathan Holt's words and demeanor I could still see traces of the former leader in the emotion of his speech.

I hoped that enough people in the crowd were as moved as I was.

Then, at last, after Jonathan Holt ceded the podium, it was my turn.

After one final glance at Kit, I took a deep breath and climbed onto the dais.

The very same place I'd once lain out on display, and where I'd risen up and grabbed a dagger of stone, plunging it into the body of a man. A living, breathing man, whose existence I'd ended with a single, violent gesture.

I was here today as someone very different than before, and it felt important to be standing on this spot as the girl I was now. Back then, back before, I was full of energy and life, of hope and yearning, even as I was also full of fear and confusion. But today I was someone who'd killed, who'd been betrayed, who'd made so many mistakes, who'd won certain battles but had lost so many others. As I rose from my crouch to stand tall and face the people of New Port City, I now knew love, real love, the complicated, layered kind that disappoints as much as it exults, and friendship, too. Right then, my eyes locked with Inara's. She stood off to the side, not far away, and as we looked at each other, she nodded. I drew strength from knowing she was close and from her encouragement as I began to speak.

I told the crowd so many things.

About the people dying on the plugs. Rumors of viruses and the potential obliteration of an entire world. About the Death App and the holes in the City. About what we would likely need to do if these rumors, these theories, proved to be a reality. That I knew that the citizens of New Port were already struggling to accept and integrate the App World refugees, and that they would have to decide how they felt not only about the presence and future of the refugees already among us, but about the many, many others who might soon need our help. All this truth fell from my mouth and floated out to the people of New Port City, like fall leaves caught by the wind, piling up as I spoke.

The breeze whipped my hair, knotting it.

My heart pounded, my muscles tense.

Soon I came to the end. Said all that I could.

All that was left now was one final plea.

"Today, democracy returns to the Real World," I said. "It's up to you to decide the fate of this city. Will it open itself up to welcome strangers as its own people, or will it, too, like the App World, close its borders to those in need?"

34

Lacy

origins

I NEVER THOUGHT I'd come back here.

Not to the App World—I always imagined I'd come back *here*.

I stretched out one long, shapely leg, admiring the perfection of its skin, virtual skin, *my true skin*, taking in the shining edge of the scandalously short Luna Lazy dress I'd downloaded the second I woke up. The thrill of it, the sheer and total relief of the App coursing through my code, was beyond all I could have imagined after so much time in the vastly imperfect and deficient Real World.

But by *here*, I meant the Mills family penthouse.

The door to it, covered in virtual jewels because my

parents were ridiculously showy, blocked my entry no matter what I did. I practically offered the lock pad my virtual eyeball for entry and it still rejected me. My parents may have barred me from home, but they forgot to clean out my capital account, I was pleased to see, which is why everything about me still shimmered and tingled from that glorious download shower I took the moment I arrived in the lobby of our apartment building. How I'd made it nearly a year without any Apps was beyond me.

Love could make you do unbearable and shocking things.

I shivered.

Then I smiled.

I'd never felt better in my entire virtual life.

Skylar went overboard warning me about the price of shifting, about the harms that could come to the body, about Death Apps and dead bodies on the plugs, on and on and on about the darkest things, to the point where I'd nearly regretted accepting her help crossing the border undetected. Now that I was back, now that I was gloriously virtual again—now that I was *me* again—the *real* virtual Lacy Mills!—all those warnings and worries faded like a tired old App draining from my code.

Virtual Lacy was invincible.

Virtual Lacy could do anything!

I laughed, basking in the sound of that familiar but long-lost code-induced giggle of mine.

Virtual Lacy was going to save the App World from ruin!

Or virtually die trying.

This thought made me shiver too. But not the good kind this time.

"Lacy," said a hushed whisper from down the hall, breaking the silence. "Is that you?"

I turned and looked at the slim virtual man in a shiny red business suit looking back at me like he was seeing a ghost, thinking that the salvation and future of the App World, courtesy of Lacy Mills, was about to get started. "Hi, Daddy."

35

Skylar

democratic process

THE VOTING LINE snaked on for what seemed like forever. It wound up and down the peninsula and all the
way back to the trees that separated this place from New
Port City.

My Keeper and a few others, including my mother,
received the ballots. The rest of us, everyone from Briarwood, all the refugees, looked on, doing our best to pass
the time and tolerate the anxiety of whatever the citizens
of the Real World decided, however they chose to vote
about their future and its relationship to everyone else.
Only those who were born here were allowed to partici-
pate in the voting process.

This was also the right thing, and I knew this to my

very core. What was happening today, now, was about restoring power and voice to the people who'd stayed behind in the Real World, either because they weren't economically well-off enough to pay their way, or because they had rejected that life. These were the people who'd gotten stuck taking care of a world that had rejected them, barred them, shunned them. They'd been robbed of a voice for far too long, subject only to the wishes and rule of those who governed the City.

Today was about restoring power and voice in the form of a vote.

But my mother had also been correct in saying that not everyone would agree what the outcome of this vote should be, and this, frankly, scared me. The fate of everyone in the App World hung in the balance, and it depended on the capacity of the people of New Port City to decide to help those who had treated them as though they did not matter, and despite so much division between our worlds for so long. How the tables had turned. The once powerful citizens of the App World were now dependent on the forgiveness and mercy of those they'd treated as lesser, as disposable.

I watched as Kit stepped up to cast his vote.

After what seemed like hours, the last people to vote were those who'd overseen the process, my Keeper and, finally, my mother.

Then, the count started.

The moon shone high overhead by the time it was finished.

Much of the crowd had stayed, hovering, waiting. Some people went home, for dinner I supposed, and trickled back to continue the wait. Finally, after what felt like a hundred years, my Keeper made her way to the podium one more time.

Everyone hushed.

"The outcome was very close," she began. "Separated only by a few votes. Eleven, to be exact." She took in a deep breath. So did the rest of the crowd. "But I am proud to announce that today New Port City has proved itself to be a place that throws open its doors, its homes, and its hearts to those in need from wherever they may arrive, even if that place is a virtual world that many of us have only dreamed about visiting but will never see during our lifetimes. Or, perhaps, nobody will, ever again."

PART THREE

36

Skylar

virtual togetherness

"SHE ASKED ME not to tell you," I said. "She made me promise."

Rain halted ahead of me and turned around. "Skylar, what do you know?"

"I know that she loves you very much. And that she can be brave." I hesitated, but then went on. "And I know that you love her."

Rain lowered his gaze. "I'm sorry."

"It's okay," I said.

He glanced up, and our eyes met. "Are you sure?"

I nodded.

"You love *him*," he stated.

I nodded again.

Rain sighed. "Are we friends then?"

"I hope so."

"I hope so, too," he said. Then, "Please tell me that she's all right."

"As far as I know."

"Skylar! Just tell me what she's doing."

"You'll find out soon enough. She made me *promise*, and you of all people know about promises." But the look on his face was of such pleading, such desperation, I couldn't help adding, "She's in the App World—that's all I'm telling you!"

The noise from Rain's throat was anguished.

"Lacy can take care of herself and you know it," I reassured. "She's fine."

I hope.

"Let's go," he said. "We need to get there. *Now.*"

Everyone was gathered together around the plugs when we arrived.

Sylvia and Zeera, Parvda and Rain, my mother, Trader, even Inara.

We would all go. Kit, too.

I didn't know what to make of meeting the virtual him. I wasn't sure I liked the idea. I wasn't sure I liked the idea of meeting my virtual mother either.

Zeera grimaced in the glowing light of the plugs. She was preparing the Shifting App—something I'd hoped I'd never have to use again. But shifting was the best way to enter the App World undetected.

"Are you sure this is a good idea?" Inara asked.

"I'll be fine," I said.

Inara glanced at me, worried. "But why can't we each shift on our own? Why does Skylar have to be the one to lead us into the App World?

Zeera looked up. "It's the only way to guarantee we'll all arrive at the same time and place. And we also know she can do it. We don't have time to test another way."

My Keeper put a hand on my mother's shoulder. "I'll be monitoring Skylar the entire time." She looked around the room at each one of us. "I'll be monitoring all of you."

Zeera began showing her how to use the tablet and work the Shifting App.

"Are you sure that everyone needs to go?" my mother asked. "We know it's dangerous to plug in at this point. Maybe—"

"Everyone has people in the App World they need to see," I reminded her. "Plus, I'd rather not go alone," I admitted.

Kit crossed his arms. The edge of his new tattoo was visible as his shirt rode up his forearm. "You won't be. I wouldn't let you be."

"Who knows?" Trader laughed weakly. "We may get good news and not the terrible kind we're anticipating."

I eyed him. "You didn't see that hole in Loner Town."

His expression darkened, but he forced the smile on his face to stay put. He turned to Zeera and my Keeper. "Are you two ready?"

My Keeper nodded. "Zeera is a very clear teacher. So that's a yes."

Without another word, I slid myself into the glass box we'd designated as mine and settled onto the cradle.

And, one by one, they joined me.

This time, as with the others, I dreamed of Kit. Snow fell from the sky, but each flake, when it landed, seeped into my skin like ice-blue ink. Soon my arms were covered with inked-on snow, just like it covered the ground. Strangely, I didn't feel cold. Instead, with each new tattoo I grew warmer, happier.

"Kit?" I called out.

I was standing there admiring the new wintry scenes on my arms, wondering if he would call back to me, when I remembered why I was there, that I had to take control of the dream and conjure the room with the doors. One foot in front of the other, I began to make my way through the steep drifts. With each step I was more alert to my surroundings, more aware that this was not a moment for me to enjoy but one with a very particular purpose.

People were depending on me. Waiting.

As the snow drifts diminished, the warm, happy feeling abandoned me as well, replaced by a shivering and shuddering all the way to my bones. The lighter the snow, the colder I became, until the snow disappeared but I was still freezing. I looked around and found myself in the room full of doors. I rubbed my hands over my arms, trying to warm up, a dark, hollow feeling opening inside me as I saw that the beautiful snowflakes tattooed on my skin were gone. I wandered from door to door aimlessly. Lost. A tall blue one, painted like the ocean. A round arched one made of stone that looked medieval. There were so many, all of them different.

"Sis, are you okay?"

I turned, teeth chattering. The virtual version of my brother was standing there. "I think so," I told Trader. "I'm just so cold. Are you?"

"No, I'm fine. I worry about you, though. Shifting doesn't seem to—"

Right then, Inara appeared, with a great sigh of relief and a smile on her face. I was thinking how strange but how nice it was to see the virtual Inara again, to feel the familiarity of this, when Sylvia, Zeera, and Parvda appeared, the three of them clutching each other. I was tempted to fold myself into the middle of them, hoping for warmth, but then my mother appeared.

"Hi, sweetheart," she said. "Well, this is strange, isn't it?" She kept staring at her hands, her arms, the rest of her virtual body.

"Hi, Mom." I couldn't stop staring either. She was my

mother, but she was someone else. Technically, she looked like my mother. She had the same hair color and style, the same eyes, just like mine, even the same height and same shape of her face, oval and long. But her virtual skin was washed out, washed of its normal golden hue, and it made her seem less *living*, less *alive*, like a vampire had drained her of blood and left behind a shell.

"I always wondered," she whispered. "But I don't really know how to feel about this, this . . . *me*. I nearly don't feel anything, like I've been flattened out." She shook her head, her arms, like she could shake off the virtual and replace it again with the real.

"It's just for a short while," I told her.

"One can hope," she said. "I always wondered about you, too, sweetheart." She peered into my face, my eyes. Looked me up and down. "At least now I can say I've known what my virtual daughter was like all those years."

Before I could respond, Rain appeared.

Then, finally, the last person we were waiting for arrived.

Kit came from down the hallway, walking toward us, passing door after door on his way, a virtual version of Kit I never dreamed I'd meet, nor had I really desired to. His face was basically the same, recognizable at least, but—as with everyone else—this Kit was like a pale copy of the real person.

He didn't stop walking until he was standing in front of me.

At least his eyes were identical to the ones I knew.

"It's nice to meet you, virtual Skylar," he said softly.

I nodded.

In that moment, I made a decision.

We would get back—we all would—so we could continue with our lives, our *real* lives, not this imitation of life so many of us had settled for throughout our childhood. I wanted a real life, a peaceful real life, and I wanted to try to have that life with Kit. We just needed to get through this next part in one piece.

"Everyone ready?" I asked, unwilling to delay a moment longer.

I'd already spied the door where we were headed.

I went to it, my friends, Kit, my mother, Rain, trailing after me. We passed a door made of rainbows, diaphanous and glowing, another covered in spikes and signs that said *Keep Out*, doors of wood and doors of water and even doors that looked to be made of the earth itself, flowers and weeds and bright-green grass growing up out of them. Then I reached the door that had caught my eye.

Somehow I *knew*, I just knew to the center of my code, that this was the place. It was like a sixth sense, the kind of certainty you could download with the App of that same name, one that plagued you with a sense of déjà vu, a sense of dread, of disaster just before it hit. The Sixth Sense App was all make-believe, of course, but now, the suspicion that beyond this door would be the end of our worlds as we knew them, not to mention a series of virtual confrontations that made me dizzy and nauseous to think about, was all too real.

"This is it," I said. It was covered in sparkling Tiffany jewels, as ostentatious and over-the-top as the person who lived behind it. My mother kept twitching nervously, like her virtual self couldn't quite adjust to leaving its real body behind. Rain's eyes were worried, searching alongside Parvda, who was chewing the inside of her virtual mouth nervously. Inara and Trader stood off to the side, close, her hand in his. And Zeera and Sylvia were paired up too.

Only Kit spoke. "Where is it that we're going, exactly?"

I put my hand on the knob, which was comprised of a single gigantic, diamond, and answered Kit's question. "My father's house. He might be waiting for us. He always seems to know things before they happen."

We arrived just in time for the emergency broadcast.

This, none of us were expecting.

The moment the last one of us was through the door, the atmosphere crackled and popped and a hologram appeared. We were in a hallway of some sort. It led to a glowing room at the other end. At first I couldn't tell who it was that was speaking. The hologram lacked a sharpness, a definition, for a few long seconds, static sounding loudly, and I wondered if this might be because of the virus in the App World, that it was affecting everything now, even communications. But then the shape of the person grew clearer.

A collective gasp rippled across a number of us.

"Mother?" Rain breathed.

Lady Holt, regal and elegant, beautiful and captivating, stood there looking out onto the citizens of the City from wherever she stood. She seemed to home right in on her son. But there was no flicker in her gaze, no hint of recognition. Maybe it was just a trick of the atmosphere.

"Citizens of the App World," she began. "I know you are used to seeing my husband in this role, but today you will have to adjust to me in his place. I've appeared to inform you of the gravest news. As I've sure you've noticed, there have been many changes in the City these last months. Holes in the atmosphere that we've been unable to fix— holes that grow more numerous and bigger by the virtual day. There have even been disappearances among us that surely have affected many of you. Now, you all have a difficult decision ahead of you. We all do. The App World is dying," she said, without pause or hesitation, though after these words she stopped speaking, maybe to let such a statement sink in for her listeners. "And it's dying quickly. A virus has spread, and we have very little time left."

So it's all true, I thought.

We waited for her to continue, my eyes drifting beyond her image to what was behind her—no, *who* was behind her. I thought I saw Ree. And then beyond Ree, I thought I saw . . .

My father? And Jude?

My gaze shifted down the hall to that glowing light at the end of it. I pointed, silently, and the others followed my gaze.

There was an intake of breath. Lady Holt was about to continue.

"More details are forthcoming, but right now you must gather together with your loved ones and begin your good-byes. Difficult questions will have to be answered. Not everyone can be saved. You will each have to decide: Will you go back to the Real World? Or will you stay behind to go down with the ship?" Lady Holt paused, these two dark questions heavy in the atmosphere. When she spoke again, it was only to close her remarks. "I'll be back soon. But until then, I bid you good day," she finished, and the hologram blinked out.

37

Ree

reunions

LADY HOLT'S VOICE died out.

I started to clap.

But I was the only one. The echo of it danced off the cavernous walls of Emory Specter's throne room—not a place I ever thought I'd voluntarily return to, yet here I was. Lady Holt had been convinced that we needed the Defense Minister in on the plan.

Everyone else in the room had doom written all over their virtual faces.

So, the world was ending. Yes, this was a tragedy. But on another level, it was also incredibly exciting! When else was a girl around to witness the end of times? If this was the apocalypse, I'd been given a front-row seat! If only my mother were here. She would have loved to witness the spectacle of it. Char, too. She'd be so jealous if she knew what I was up to!

"What now?" Emory asked Lady Holt.

As though she was the authority in the room, not him. And not that crazy chick Jude, who'd wanted to sell our bodies to the highest bidder.

I *knew* Lady Holt was the right person to handle everything! I reached up and patted myself on my shoulder, still primly clad in a pink tweed suit jacket.

"We give everyone time for the news to sink in, since this is a lot to process." Lady Holt sent a nasty glare at him and I almost clapped again. "You never were good at, well, *people*, Emory. You're so puffed up all the time and so tone-deaf to emotion you never stop to consider what people actually *need*."

He puffed up now, as if to prove Lady Holt's point, clearly readying himself to offer some ridiculous emotionally tone-deaf response—as she might put it—when there came a clatter from down the hall. The three of us turned toward it.

People began to appear out of nowhere. Exciting people!

It was like something out of those old-timey movies, back when the Real World was all there was.

The drama!

First, Prince Rain Holt entered the room, in the virtual

flesh. He ran to his mother and she swept him into her arms, crying out, "My baby, I've missed you!" Then came a bunch of people I didn't know, who stood there looking a bit clueless. On their heels entered a woman who waltzed right up to Emory Specter and that Jude chick and crossed her arms, standing there before the two of them, glaring. And after her came Skylar Cruz.

Of course she was here.

She strode up to Emory Specter and the body-seller lady as well, unafraid, and planted herself next to the old woman. "We've come to help," was all she said.

Emory Specter seemed ready to explode with anger, but Skylar stood her ground. "You've come to help?" he raged. "Well, welcome then, daughter of mine," he went on, though he did not seem at all welcoming and, instead, very, very sarcastic. "It's so nice of you to offer, since it's your fault we're in this mess in the first place."

38

Skylar

brain powered

I TRIED TO unhear my father's words.

The App World is dying, and it's my fault.

Emory Specter stood there looking at my mother and me, his face reddening with rage, in a familiar bright-red suit—he'd worn something similar at the App World funeral for the seventeens left on the other side of the border. Maybe he had dozens of suits like this.

"Hello, Skylar. Hello, Mother," Jude said.

Virtual living seemed to suit her. She'd lost the angry glint in her eyes, there was color in her cheeks, and she looked relatively normal. She hadn't gone crazy with downloads or permanent enhancements. The dress she wore was simple. Black, long, with capped sleeves and a narrow red trim along the neck and hem.

Most interesting of all, she didn't seem angry at us like her father.

Our father, I meant.

We were in some sort of throne room. It was cavernous, as big as the space below Briarwood, but far glitzier. The throne itself was jeweled in much the same way as the door we'd entered. The pillars, walls, and floors were just as ornate, with dozens of patterns and decorations and fancy stones that met the eye all at once. Stranger still, Ree was standing there gaping at all of us, her outfit so prim and proper, clearly an attempt to match Lady Holt's style, though she hadn't *quite* figured it out. The ample cleavage she showed undermined the look. Seeing Ree made me glance at Parvda and wonder where in this world Adam was.

"How is it my fault?" I finally managed to ask Emory.

Emory crossed his arms to match my mother's. "By allowing a mass exodus from the App World, you weakened the entire fabric of it. You destabilized the App World. You might've saved some bodies from your sister's market"—he took a moment to glance in Jude's direction—"but in the process you jeopardized everyone here."

"That's a lie, Emory, and you know it," my mother said. "The Cure is at fault. I've been investigating this issue for months." My mother kept staring at Emory in his fiery red suit like she didn't know what to make of him. I wondered whether—hoped that—when my mother was with him, he had been different than he was today. I couldn't imagine them together, just as I still couldn't wrap my mind around Emory Specter as my father. I kept wishing she'd tell me that he wasn't.

My mother opened her mouth to say something else, but I put out a hand for her to wait.

"Is it a lie?" I asked.

Emory kept contorting his lips as he considered his answer. "Well. Maybe." Then he sighed. "Fine, it wasn't the Shifting App, but that Shifting App certainly did not help matters." He began to walk in a circle, stopping in front of Rain. "If this one over here had paid more attention to his grandfather's legacy, he might've stopped this situation before it began."

"Emory," Lady Holt warned.

"What does this have to do with my grandfather?" Rain asked.

Emory clasped his hands behind his back. "Your grandfather designed the City to be powered by the brain. The App World is quite literally *brain powered*—a combination of technology and the minds that connect to it. A mass, unplanned unplugging could be disastrous to the fabric of everything—which it *was*, in this case." His gaze flitted around the room, darting and landing on each one of us.

I took this in. Tried understand it. "So plugged-in

brains power the App World," I said. On one level that sounded crazy, but on another, it was logical. Smart, even. Marcus Holt had used the brain like a battery. I turned to Jude. "Did you know about this?"

She glanced at Emory. "Not in so many words."

Lady Holt stepped into the conversation. "What Emory *isn't* telling you is that none of us understood this aspect of Marcus Holt's design until *after* the Cure was won. And the Cure is what caused the virus. What created it."

Emory huffed. "I did *not* create a virus!" He looked around wildly, then his eyes landed on me. "This is *not* all my fault! It's *your* fault."

"No, it's not," my mother said, stepping into this back-and-forth. "It was when you started the research for the Cure that all the problems began. *You* are the reason we've gotten to this point, Emory. *You* are the cause of this virus."

Lady Holt nodded.

"So, the Cure was the beginning of everything," I said. "As bodies were removed, the App World was weakened, and it, it . . . caught a virus. Kind of like the body can catch a cold, right?" Lady Holt nodded again. "Then the Shifting App exacerbated the problem, because it further weakened things, and the virus spread faster."

Kit turned his attention on Jude. "But the Shifting App wouldn't exist if it wasn't for the Body Market."

Jude held up her hands. "I was as surprised as everyone

else about this virus. We were just trying to take advantage of the Cure."

Lady Holt was shaking her head. "It's true, the virus spreads and worsens when people unplug. It's as though each time a brain is removed, the virtual fabric of this City gets weaker."

Emory threw up his hands. "Does any of this really matter? Regardless of how everything started, our virtual world is in dire jeopardy! And time is running out!"

My mother stopped me from continuing. "Emory may be *very* misguided, but he is right about one thing: regardless of what started these problems—holes in the atmosphere, Death Apps, viruses, bodily death on the plugs—what I want to know is what we're going to do about it." Her eyes came to rest on Emory Specter. "Emory, you sound so fatalistic about the future. But is there really no turning back? No salvation from this?"

"Unfortunately, I'm sure that we're doomed," he said. "For the time being, at least." He returned my mother's stare. "If you actually want to save the remaining people on the plugs."

"Yes!" everyone in the room chorused at once.

"Well, then it's the end of the App World as we know it," Emory declared.

Kit was staring at the man in disgust. "Maybe that's for the best," he countered.

Jude turned to him. "That's easy for you to say, since

you have a body to go back to."

I winced at this reminder that my sister did not.

"So what now?" Trader asked. "What's our next step if we're to salvage what we can from this broken-down virtual place? Especially if it's soon to be a virtual graveyard?"

Emory dragged his throne into the center of everyone and sat down. He looked over at Lady Holt. "You tell them."

"There is one thing we can try, though it will only solve one of our problems," Lady Holt began. She turned to Rain. "Your grandfather was prepared, in case a day like this would ever come. The answer is both extremely simple and highly complicated." Her eyes moved around the room to each of us. "The simple part is that we can reboot the App World. Shut it down, then restart it and . . . see what happens."

A look of fascination crossed Trader's face. "That's even possible?"

"Anything can be done," Emory cut in, "if you know what you're doing."

Lady Holt inhaled deeply and took Rain's hand into her own. "Marcus would always say, 'If we created the App World, then we can uncreate it, if the need should ever arise.' Sometimes I wondered if your grandfather ever meant for the City to last as long as it has. Or for so many people to abandon reality the way we did. Maybe he knew this day was ahead of us."

Trader was nodding. "So, assuming what you're saying is true and we can reboot the App World, what would make it highly complicated?" Trader finished.

Emory looked at him. "Well, there's the issue of having to unplug every single citizen who still has a body before we shut it down. That is, unless you want them to die."

"Obviously not," my mother said.

"I figured as much," Emory said. "So, the complicated part, then, is figuring out how to manage a complete and total exodus, when a total exodus will also hasten the virus and literally destroy this world in the process." He sat back into his throne. Crossed his legs. Made himself more comfortable. "The issue is, we need to buy ourselves more time, and there isn't any way to do it. Plus there's the matter of a mass unplugging to manage."

"We're going to use the Shifting App," I said.

Half the room erupted at this suggestion.

"—too much for my daughter to handle—"

"—Skylar would have to power it again—"

"—no way—" Kit was saying.

"Hey, hey!" I shouted.

Everyone quieted.

"There's another way," I explained. "One that doesn't rely on me. I promise!"

Kit, Sylvia, Zeera, Parvda, Rain, and my mother all looked at me skeptically.

Emory crossed his arms. "You're forgetting that the Shifting App is a Real World App. We'd need to first code it for use here, then mass-produce it, and there's very little time left for this City. Maybe not even twenty-four hours!"

I thought about Lacy's plan, crossed my fingers that she'd come through. Her idea was nearly prophetic. "Someone is already taking care of that. And if it worked, the Shifting App should be adapted, mass-produced, and ready to download. Like, now."

"Really?" Emory actually sounded impressed.

"How in both worlds did you manage that without my and Trader's help?" Zeera asked.

"*I* didn't." I held Rain's gaze. "It was Lacy. She thought, well, with all the talk of a virus and the App World dying, that maybe we'd need it. So . . ."

Rain sucked in a breath. "Lacy went to see her father," he finished.

Trader wore a look of admiration. "I've got to give that girl credit. She might be complicated, but she can be shrewd and smart when she wants to be."

"What does her father have to do with this?" Sylvia asked.

"Lacy's father can mass-produce just about anything," Zeera said darkly. "He has a team of the best App coders at his disposal, ready and waiting, around the clock."

"Do you have any idea if she was successful?" Parvda asked.

"Not yet," I admitted. "But let's hope."

Emory tsk-tsked. "Even so, *now* you're forgetting that if everyone tries to go at once, then everyone will likely die. You would have to go in quadrants, and with each quadrant that shifted, the virus would spread and get worse, making it more dangerous for the remaining groups."

"I volunteer to go last," I said. Before everyone around me could protest, I spoke. "I'll be fine. And besides, Lady Holt already informed the citizens here that some people will have to stay behind. Hopefully, it will be enough to sustain everything until the last groups unplug." I turned to her now. "Let's say we shift in quadrants, and everything goes smoothly. Someone else will *still* have to stay behind to handle the reboot, won't they?"

"That's easy," Jude said, with forced cheer. "Father and I will do it. We've nowhere else to go anyway!"

My throat grew tight. I nodded. "And how long will the App World take to reboot?"

Emory shrugged. "That's difficult to say."

"A couple of hours? An entire day?" I pressed.

Lady Holt was shaking her head. "Emory is correct, we simply don't know. It's never been done before."

Rain placed a hand on his mother's arm. "Can't anyone make an educated guess?"

"If you *forced* me to guess," Emory began, "I'd say . . . maybe a year? Maybe even two?"

Gasps sounded throughout the room.

"A *year*?" I repeated.

He nodded. "If we're lucky."

"But . . . but . . ."

"But that's very unfortunate?" he supplied, his voice light despite having lobbed this news into the room like a bomb.

I stood there, gaping. "Unfortunate is one word for it."

"Tragic?" he tried. "Horrific? Do those work better for you?" He stood from his throne, seemingly energized by the dark drama of everything. "You have to remember, we're not simply rebooting one of those pathetic little old-timey Real World devices people used to carry around. We're restarting *an entire civilization*. Then again, taking a year or two is better than *never* and *total oblivion*."

My mother kept us on track. "What will be here when this world *does* restart? Do we even know? Will the City still exist? The buildings, the park, the neighborhoods? What about all the residents who no longer have bodies? Will their codes each reboot along with the App World itself?" She reached out to Jude, who didn't reach back. "Will you reboot, too, my daughter?" She pursed her lips a moment, before adding, to Emory, "And will you?"

"All excellent questions," Emory said approvingly. "Yet without answers at the moment."

"But it is *possible*," Lady Holt began, encouragingly, "that after the reboot, everyone's virtual self will also reboot with the App World, albeit on a much smaller scale"—she glanced at Jude—"saving the virtual lives of those people who no longer have bodies to unplug. Saving the City. Everything. It will be just like the beginning, when Marcus Holt created this world to sustain itself before even he plugged in. Before it grew to be the way it is now."

"Father and I are okay with whatever happens," Jude said.

I nodded, impressed by Jude's calm and her altruism in the face of potential virtual death. "But maybe things will be okay. Eventually. At least there's hope."

Lady Holt walked into the center of our group, her elegant heels clicking against the tiled floor. "Yes, there is. But I also meant what I said in that emergency broadcast. Not everyone will be able to return to the Real World. The City *will* collapse on the last citizens who remain from loss of power—brainpower," she reminded us. "The more people who shift, the shakier things will get. Some people still might not make it."

A long silence followed.

Everyone looked at me.

I knew what they were thinking because I was thinking it too.

But I shrugged. "There's nothing else we can do. We can't all go at once."

"I'll explain what will happen in another emergency broadcast." Lady Holt called up a Mirror App and began primping in front of it. Ree emerged from the shadows and began darting around her, brushing off her shoulders and helping to straighten her jacket. "Everyone will have one last night to say good-bye to loved ones, our City, our favorite Apps, and then we'll all just have to hope for the best." With a wave of her hand the Mirror App disappeared. "So you'll hear from me tomorrow morning, first thing. I'll mind-chat you so we can divide up the City in ordered quadrants for the attempted unplugging. And I'll let you know who's going when, first, second, etc., all the way until you, Skylar dear."

The rest of us nodded.

"Don't forget to leave your brains open to communications!" Lady Holt gestured at me. "You'll figure out if this Shifting App is indeed available?"

"Yes," I agreed. "We'll make sure that it's taken care of."

"In the meantime," Lady Holt continued, "we'll say our good-byes and good lucks to those we need to, do our last Apping if we should feel the urge, and hopefully survive the night to come back here in the morning and begin a City-wide evacuation."

"You mean *apocalypse*," Emory corrected.

"Not for everyone," Lady Holt shot back. "Just for certain people. Either the brave and altruistic, like those who choose to stay behind, or the power-hungry and despotic, like you." She brushed her hands together. "All right. Have a good night! I'm going to allow all remaining citizens free and unlimited Apps until it's time for every-thing to end. Now let me get on with this broadcast so I can catch up with my son," she added, summarily dis-missing all of us.

Meeting adjourned.

While Lady Holt began her second emergency broad-cast of the hour, the rest of the group began to dissipate. Everyone talked about who they needed to find, what needed to happen between now and the morning. Sylvia, Zeera, Parvda, and Kit were huddled together whisper-ing, with Sylvia and Zeera eventually peeling off and heading out. Emory sat back down on his throne and was talking to my mother and Jude. The three of them seemed deep in conversation. I was about to go over to them when Rain appeared at my side.

He was shaking his head. "How could you let Lacy do that, Skylar? Her father was always hateful to her, hateful *of* her. And you simply sat by and let her cross the border alone!"

"There was no stopping her," I said. "She was deter-mined to go, regardless of my approval. She knew that she could do this one thing for all of us. I thought it would be better to help her than to let her do it alone. Don't you agree? Shouldn't we just be grateful to her for it?"

Rain seemed conflicted. His big green virtual eyes were worried. "Is she still with her father?"

"That I don't know," I admitted. "I assume so, but someone needs to go check so we can find out for sure if she was successful or not. Our plan tomorrow depends on it."

"I'll go now." Rain glanced at his mother, who was gesturing earnestly as she spoke to the citizens of the City. "Tell her I'll be back later," he added, and was off.

The only other person missing apart from Lacy was Adam. Parvda was standing there wringing her hands, eyes distant, her mind obviously elsewhere. I went to her now and grabbed her hand, tugged her over to Ree. "Where's Adam? Do you have any idea?"

"Nice to see you again, Skylar," she said wryly. "I didn't know if I would!" She shrugged then, a bit guiltily. "I don't know where he is. He said he had something to do." Ree gestured at Parvda. "That's the girlfriend?"

Parvda didn't look happy about this comment. "Yes, I'm the girlfriend," she snapped. "And what are you, exactly?"

Ree backed away. "Not the competition or anything, so no worries there."

I turned to Parvda. Red blotches were breaking out all over her virtual skin. "I have an idea where he might be." I beckoned to Trader. "Will you take Parvda to your house in Loner Town? I think she might find Adam hiding out there."

He glanced back at Inara. "All right. Inara is going to see her parents anyway."

Parvda immediately grabbed his hand and dragged him away.

I went to Kit. "I'm sure you want to try and find your parents one last time," I said, but he shook his head.

"I'm done trying. They're lost to me." He sighed. "Though maybe we'll see each other in the Real World again. Some day."

There was sadness in Kit's eyes, but acceptance as well. "You never know. They might come find you."

He shrugged his virtual shoulders. "I suppose they do know where I still live," he said, though he didn't sound like he believed this would happen either, that his parents would magically materialize at the cottage one day.

My eyes went to my mother and Emory. Jude was staring in my direction. "Speaking of family, I should . . ."

His gaze followed mine. "Go spend some time with them?"

I sighed. "Yes. Probably. But—"

"—Skylar," Kit interrupted, his eyes full of emotion. "I need you to make it through this."

He reached for my hand and took it into his.

The sensation was strange. The fear and anxiety I'd felt over Kit, over loving him despite all that had happened between us, dissipated in that single virtual moment. I knew, I *knew*, that I'd love him no matter what world we were in, the real one or this one or some other that hadn't been invented yet. That sometimes love could transcend divisions and differences, borders crossed and past betrayals, that whether I was a virtual girl or a real one or some other kind of girl I couldn't even dream of, the love I felt for Kit would always be with me.

I stared at our joined hands, our fingers intertwined. "I know. I will. And on that note, I have one thing to ask of you."

"Anything," Kit said.

"Later on, say around midnight? Would you meet me at the entrance to Main Park? There are some things I'd like to show you, places in this world that have meant something to me." I blinked. "I really want to share them with you. Before this world comes to an end."

"Of course I'll be there. I'd meet you anywhere," he said. Then, quickly, in barely a blink, he leaned forward and kissed my virtual lips and was gone, leaving me to be with my family.

39

Ree

last hurrah

WHEN WE LEFT Emory's compound, everyone went their different ways.

I went off by myself. If it was to be my last night in the City, my only plan for this evening was to enjoy myself.

Apparently, I was not alone in thinking this way!

The second I was breathing in the fresh, though potentially virus- and glitch-laden atmosphere, this much was obvious.

The App World was one gigantic party.

The world was one big free App Store.

I was glad so many other people were willing and able to spend their last moments like me, not paralyzed by grief or fear, but instead enjoying the true meaning of virtual living, our reason for being, by engaging in the activity that brought us all together:

Apping!

The entire City was out and about, Apping like their lives depended on it. Apping like there was no tomorrow.

Because there wouldn't be!

I wandered among the revelry. The frenzy. It really was rather manic. The streets were like carnivals, bursts of color, beauty, and strangeness. People flew, they danced, they gorged themselves on weird-looking food. Icons filled the atmosphere like festive tiny balloons.

Fireworks lit up the virtual sky, the great big booms from the explosions nearly constant.

The Moon 11.5 and the Sun 8.5 were out at the same time.

I wasn't sure if the jumble of day and night was intentional, or was a result of the App World breaking down, the virus spreading, a sign of the doom that was about to befall us.

I angled my vision just so for a moment, and then wished I hadn't. More and more holes had appeared in the atmosphere. A man who'd downloaded some sort of Sinatra App was crooning as he walked down the street, no one paying him any real attention since they were all so absorbed in themselves. I watched as he tumbled through one of the holes and disappeared like his virtual self never existed in the first place.

My hand went to my mouth.

Where did he go? Was he virtually dead?

I forced myself to move on, but when I rounded the corner, things only got worse.

The carnival atmosphere was no longer so carnival-like. The neighborhood I was passing into had more of a, well, maybe a serial-killer vibe of sorts? Or maybe a violent-criminal one? Plus, the buildings were deteriorating by the minute. You could practically see them crumbling from one second to the next. Maybe this was what inspired the unleashing of so many people's baser instincts. Maybe they felt like, since the world was ending anyway, they had nothing to lose. Quickly, I made a left so I could head back to the happier Appers. It seemed like the safer move. Plus, I didn't want my last hours as a virtual girl to be so . . . ugly. So unseemly!

I reached Main Park and sat down on a bench.

Images of Char and my mother popped out from my head and floated in front of my virtual eyes, unbidden. I waved them off like pesky icons. I suddenly didn't want to be in the City anymore, surrounded by these memories, not even for one last night.

Maybe the Real World wouldn't be so horrible.

Maybe I'd make new friends. Find a new family.

Maybe I wouldn't be so alone.

This thought perked me up a bit, gave me a sense of direction for the hours ahead. I searched the sky, the atmosphere, for an App that would download me some friends for the night, a party maybe, or even a harem of virtual boyfriends. I refused to spend my last remaining virtual moments by myself, and instead would live by Char's inspiring mantra, one that I knew by heart, since she was always repeating it to herself over and over and over.

If your real virtual friends abandon you for some reason, just download some more!

It was fitting that Char's wisdom should send me off into possible oblivion, since it was her actual virtual oblivion that got me here to this place, somehow pulled into this apocalyptic drama of our world.

There.

The very icon I needed!

The Homecoming Queen App. It was perfect. Not only would I look glorious and get to wear a glittering tiara as the clock wound down on the City, but it came with an entire homecoming court of ladies and their dates, plus my very own king! Hopefully, none of them would fall through any of the holes in the fabric of the App World as we danced the night away.

But at least there would be plenty of them if a few didn't make it.

I reached upward to catch the rhinestone-encrusted App. The second my finger touched it, my code was flooded with the kind of relief only a download could offer.

40

Lacy

finally

"YOU CAME FOR me!" I clapped my hands with surprise. Happiness. With pure and total joy, as bright and shiny as the green glitter makeup I'd downloaded. "We have so much to celebrate! My idea was not only totally brilliant, but it *worked*! The Shifting App is adapted and ready!"

Rain stood in the doorway of my apartment. "You shouldn't have shifted without telling me," was all he said.

Well, my parents' apartment, since technically I no longer lived here.

Daddy made that clear in our time together. So sweet, like always.

At least soon neither one of them would live here anymore. Served them right.

Except for the relief written all over his face, Rain looked every bit the prince and playboy I fell in love with, or lust with, or whatever you call what happens when elevens develop their first crush and it turns out to plague them for the rest of their virtual lives and eventually becomes a connection they cannot shake, even in the real body.

"And of course I came for you," he said more softly.

I was tempted to shimmy right up to him and plant a giant kiss on his face. It had been *sooooo* long since I'd gotten to virtually kiss Rain. Like ages. Like, years and years.

Also, after tonight, I might never have another chance.

"Are you all right?" he asked.

My virtual mouth seemed tongue-tied, words tangled in my code, unable to free themselves into the atmosphere. Instead I crossed the distance between us and decided to plant that big kiss on his endlessly kissable virtual lips. Afterward, as his eyes widened, my speech was restored. "Don't I look all right?" I answered him finally. "Don't I look absolutely *amazing*?" I went on, laughing. "I certainly *feel* amazing. You chose me!" I couldn't help saying this. My arms were still linked around the back of Rain's neck.

He didn't say anything.

"Over Skylar," I clarified, blinking prettily.

"I know what you meant, Lacy."

Insecurity rattled through my code, and I unclasped my hands, letting them slide away. "Are you upset? Do you regret your decision?"

"No, Lacy, no." He was shaking his head. "And that's great news that the App is ready. But you took a risk, and what's more, you came back *here*. I know how you hate seeing your parents, never mind asking your father for something. They were always so awful to you."

I shrugged and turned on my spiky green stilettos, grinding them into the ugly unfamiliar carpet my mother must have downloaded recently. "Well, seeing Daddy was horrible as usual. But he helped me get the job done, which is amazing, don't you think?" I didn't wait for his answer, because *obviously* it was amazing. "I had to promise him things, of course. That I'd ensure no one unplugged his body if he still had one and that I wouldn't let him die and all that, since I know people in the Real World," I rambled on. I swiveled again and looked at Rain. "Skylar *did* tell you everything, didn't she? I figured eventually she'd say *something*."

Rain nodded. "Skylar didn't say anything until about an hour ago."

Huh. Skylar actually kept her word. Impressive.

I teetered back over to where Rain stood, still in the open doorway. My fabulous green dress swished as I walked. I'd downloaded about a thousand different ones before I found this absolutely perfect one on a Roaring Twenties App. It had fringe and feathers and it was a total masterpiece of high vintage fashion that flattered my incredible virtual legs. "The App World may disappear into oblivion, but at least you and I have something to go back to in the Real World. We do, don't we?"

Rain bent his head toward mine. "Yes. We do."

Were there really bells ringing in the atmosphere right now, or was I imagining it, my joy was so complete?

I smiled up. "So why don't we enjoy one last night of debauchery, for old times' sake? What do you want to do on our last virtual night in this world? We can do anything you want! We can go to your favorite clubs! We can fly to the moon and bungee jump off it! We can—"

"Honestly," Rain cut in, "I just want to spend it alone with you."

Virtual tears sprung to my green eyes, hearing him say this. It was the kind of thing I'd longed to hear ever since my heart began beating out his name, *Rain Holt, Rain Holt*.

"I couldn't think of a better way to pass the hours," I told him, wondering if he could hear the way my virtual self sang his name from every fiber of my code. "Alone with the only virtual boy I've ever loved. And the only real boy too," I added, because it was true. And when I put a hand on his chest, and rose on my tiptoes to plant another kiss on his virtual lips, I was nearly certain that I could hear Rain's own heart beating *Lac-ee, Lac-ee*, too, in response to mine.

41

Skylar

transcendence

KIT WAS WAITING there for me at midnight.

A series of rainbows arched to the ground all around Main Park. Glittering droplets of water hung in the atmosphere. Children with their parents marveled at this wondrous vision.

I saw him before he saw me.

I took this moment to study the virtual Kit. I knew this Kit was an imitation of the real boy with the tattoos, the motorcycle, the dark and sad past, that I was seeing a copy of Kit just as he was seeing a copy of me. But the virtual Kit still made my pulse leap, reached into me in a way that I could not ignore, and made the virtual me feel realer, fuller, more alive.

I loved him.

"You're here," he said when he saw me.

"You always sound so surprised," I said.

A group of boys flew past us on snowboards and skateboards. My hair went everywhere with the force of them. "I'm always worried you'll change your mind about seeing me."

Fireworks exploded overhead, the atmosphere crackling with loud booms. "I won't."

We started to walk amid the noise. The frenzy.

"Did you say your good-byes to Jude?" Kit asked.

I nodded. "It was strange, after everything she's done, everything we've done to each other." I stepped sideways to avoid a tiny hole in the atmosphere. "But she seems all right. She's made her peace."

Kit looked around at the celebratory scene unfolding everywhere we looked. "I wouldn't be surprised if a lot of these people felt that way. They seem to live for their Apps."

I kicked at an icon that kept diving at my feet. "I'm sure some of them do. A lot of them."

"It's going to be difficult when the unplugged wake again in the Real World," Kit said.

The thought of what lay ahead, the end of the worlds as we knew them at least for the time being, sapped my energy. "Let's stop thinking about that for now. For the rest of tonight, I think we should just worry about *us*." I glanced around at the giant party that lit up the park, the buildings, listened to the shouts, the cries, the laughter. "There are places I want to show you before all this goes away." I looked into Kit's eyes. "I thought I'd hate seeing the virtual you, but instead, I'm grateful. You know the real me, but I want you to know the virtual me, too, what that Skylar used to be like."

"Okay," he said. "So show me."

I took him to see my school, to the building where Inara lived and where I'd spent so much of my time in this world. We went to see the Water Tower, the virtual version of it, and I remembered what a virtual landmark it had been for me. We admired the famous skyscrapers from all over the world that were replicated here in the City. I took him on a whirlwind tour through my favorite landscapes in Odyssey, after which we drank virtual whiskey at a bar Kit wanted to try. As the night wore on and we were on our way to our final destination for the evening, Kit's eyes darted everywhere, at the chaos all around us. The App World had never been like this, not even after Jonathan Holt made the announcement about the borders closing. People were Apping like I'd never seen, one download after the other, their basic selves transforming once, twice, three times in succession over the span of only a minute or even less. Icons buzzed around us like festive gnats, promising glorious possibilities for our minds, our virtual bodies, our abilities, our personalities.

But I couldn't care less about downloading a thing right now.

Kit and I stopped in front of a single tower, modest next to all the others, with portholes for windows, no longer lit up against the virtual night. It looked abandoned.

"This is Singles Hall," I told him. "Or at least, it was. I thought I would show you the place where I grew up. My old room. Whatever is left of it, at least."

The two of us looked upward.

Tomorrow, this world will be gone. So many memories with it. An entire City, the virtual dream of entire generations, vanished like it was never there.

What mattered most would survive, though.

Kit and I. What we had. That would go on. Because that much was real.

"I was thinking," I started, before we went in. "It's just," I began again, then stopped. I wasn't sure exactly what I wanted to say. Everything about my virtual self felt strange. The sensations I was feeling in my code, the pulsing of my virtual heart, the way blood seemed to rush through me even though here I had no veins. All of these were tricks of technology, programmed into the code of each citizen of the City to remind us of the reactions of the real body, to make us feel as though we were just as real as before we entered this virtual world. But now, maybe because I knew what it was like to experience these sensations naturally, they somehow felt just as real to my virtual self. It was as if the real and the virtual had meshed together.

"You were thinking what, Skylar?" he prompted.

How could I explain?

Kit was standing so close.

We had our own virtual world, just the two of us, even as the entirety of the City jostled and celebrated and wept all around us.

"Well," I tried, once more, hoping that this time I could find the right words. "I think maybe love has the power to change our makeup, our chemistry, our flesh and blood and bone and our codes. I think love transcends worlds."

Kit took one of my hands, his gaze steady. "I know what you mean," he said.

And I knew, I trusted, to the very center of my being, that he really did.

42

Skylar

apocalypse now

IT STARTED BEFORE it was supposed to.

The entire App World was shaking.

People all around were screaming.

IT'S HAPPENING!

THE END!

EVACUATE NOW!

I could hear them roaring outside Singles Hall.

Alarm crossed Kit's face, his coloring turning as white and stormy as a blizzard's. "It's too soon."

We were in the empty lounge. The chairs, the tables, the once bustling front desk were blurry from all the movement.

I grabbed onto an armrest, trying to steady myself. "Our mind-chats!"

I'd forgotten to turn mine on.

I opened myself to all incoming communication and waited for instructions, but there was only static, interrupted by the occasional clip of a word or syllable. *Get . . . . hel . . . . shut . . . ord . . .* Then nothing. Kit grabbed my arm and held on, pulled me away as a piece of the ceiling crashed two feet away from us, the rubble disintegrating and leaving behind another hole in the atmosphere.

"What are we going to do?" Kit shouted.

The two of us jumped to the side as another piece of the ceiling fell, nearly taking my left arm with it. "I think we should try to get back to the meeting place from last night," I yelled over the din.

A hologram, jagged, crackling, appeared suddenly above one of the couches, so blurry it was impossible to see who was speaking.

We ran closer.

And for one lucky minute, the City stopped quaking and steadied itself.

The hologram grew clear.

It was Emory Specter. Alongside him were my mother, Lacy, and Rain.

"We had to begin the reboot of the App World prematurely," Emory said. "A result of the virus coursing through the fabric of our City. There's not much time, so listen carefully." A rumble shook the floor beneath us, the hologram disappearing for two long seconds before calm returned along with the image of Emory and everyone else. "Everyone needs to get into their assigned quadrants immediately—check your mind-chats for the location and the order of shifting—and find their group leaders." Kit was to go in the third group, on the side of Main Park closest to Loner Town. I would to be stationed not far from Singles Hall. I breathed deep. I'd be going last, of course. "At the appointed time the Shifting App will appear before everyone," Emory was explaining. He sounded almost excited. "When you touch it, the process of unplugging will begin, and hopefully this City will last long enough to get you to the other side. Hurry! Good luck, everyone. Hope you make it to the other side! And for the rest of us going down with the ship, good-bye from all of us! For now, at least!"

The hologram blinked out.

For one blissful second, the entire App World was still.

The City was without sound, without screams, without signs of imminent destruction.

Then the moment passed.

"Kit," I yelled, yanking his arm as hard as I could toward the front desk as half the ceiling caved in, nearly blocking the exit.

The two of us ran outside, just as the glass doors

shattered, leaving a wide black hole where the entrance to Singles Hall used to be. Then the rest of the building crashed to the ground and was gone, swallowed by blackness.

A collective scream broke through the roar of the shaking.

The streets were brimming with citizens of the City. Women, children, couples embracing, families huddled together in fear. Their downloads drained away until all that was left were basic selves, pale as sheets, frozen in shock.

"Skylar," Kit said, holding me close, whispering in my ear. "I'll see you in the Real World. Promise again that you'll be okay."

I gripped him tight, the world falling down around us. "I promise. Promise me back."

He didn't speak, but just before we pulled apart, he said, "I love you," and was off, racing through the thick crowd and down the street.

I pushed through the people, trying to make my way to the spot where I was to meet my group. Kit's words rang through me, giving me heart. When I arrived I climbed the gates of the park and stood there, looking out, trying to keep steady amid the shaking. There must be hundreds, thousands of people, and I was responsible for all of them.

Thunder ripped across the sky, the atmosphere growing dark and heavy with clouds.

Rain poured down on us.

"We're all going to virtually die," a young woman cried.

Others nearby shouted their agreement.

Were we?

"Try to stay calm," I called out to everyone.

Just as I said this, a man in the group pointed upward, and everyone's gaze followed, peering through the massive drops that fell. Gasps ripped through the atmosphere.

The tops of the trees in Main Park.

They were disappearing.

Fading away, until they were just gaping holes in the atmosphere.

"It won't be long now," I promised, doing my best to sound calm, to sound reassuring that everything would be okay.

But would it?

43

Lacy

rose-colored glasses

DESPITE EVERYTHING, DESPITE the fear and terror everywhere I turned, I felt oddly calm.

Maybe this was what it was like to be happy.

Maybe happiness created a protective shell around you.

I certainly felt invincible after my night with Rain. I guess love could do that to you. Make you hopeful even when the world was tumbling to the ground around you.

I looked around. Things sure were tumbling to the ground all right.

My group was waiting for me at the base of the Water Tower.

Even with the world ending, there were shouts of delight.

At least, that's what I thought at first.

I'd just reached the place where I could address everyone, reassure them that all would be well, when a truly terrifying sight met my eyes. If I didn't know any better, I'd say that a tidal wave was rippling across the City, but a tidal wave of buildings. They swelled, rising high into the atmosphere, before dropping carelessly to the hard ground, where they shattered, sending thick clouds of dust into the atmosphere.

Everyone was screaming now.

It was headed straight for us.

I looked above me.

The Water Tower swayed and shimmied, the fish on its surface darting away.

"It's going to fall," a man to my right was shouting.

People ran in all directions.

A pressure was growing inside me—it was hard to describe—like my entire virtual self and mind were squeezed into a vise. Like a faulty App was running through my code that was meant to make me taller and thinner but was somehow flattening me out instead. Even speaking grew difficult, like the code in my virtual body was becoming viscous and slow, too thick to function. I wasn't sure how much longer I could hold out.

I couldn't move. None of us could.

Was this—

No—

With every last ounce of energy in my code, I opened my mind to Rain.

I love you. You and only you. Forever and for always.

There came a second, a blissful second, when Rain's voice resonated throughout my being.

Lacy, he began. *I—*

I was floating. I was warm. I was happy as I waited for him to finish his thought.

And then—

44

Skylar

decreation

FINALLY, THE SIGNAL came.

The Shifting App appeared before each one of us. It was nearly identical to that icon that had started this long and difficult journey for me, what felt like forever ago now, the one Trader had offered each one of us—Lacy, Adam, Sylvia, and me, when we were to cross the border to the Real World, all of us with hopes for our time there. History was about to repeat itself, but on such a grand scale I couldn't fathom what would happen on the other side of this.

If there was to be another side.

I poised a finger in the air, barely an inch from the dark, foreboding icon hanging before us. A rumbling started beneath our feet, but I kept my eyes steady on the App, refusing to take in the doom above and below, to the left and right. I knew the City was nearly gone, the park likely to go with it any second, plunging us into a black hole of nothingness and oblivion. "On the count of three everyone reach out and touch the App," I shouted. The roar grew louder and louder. I worried no one could hear me. "One," I screamed. "Two!" My virtual lungs were burning.

Then, with all my might, one last syllable.

"Three!"

PART FOUR

45

Skylar

whole again

I SAT UP.

Stretched my fingers. Wiggled my toes.

Breathed.

Blinked.

Looked around.

I was in Kit's bedroom. In Kit's bed.

Alone.

But alive.

Alive.

I pulled the covers away. Stared at my knees. Began to bend and stretch my legs, my arms. Put a hand to my head. Slowly, I swung my legs around and placed my feet on the floor. Stood. Waited.

I waited for the dizziness, the nausea, that terribly sick feeling I always got after unplugging to come over me, to nearly knock me down with pain and agony. And yet, I felt . . . fine. I took another step and waited.

Still . . . nothing.

A tremendous sense of relief flooded my every cell.

A strange peace came over me, over every inch of skin, every bit of my body, my heart, my soul. I felt nothing but rested. Nothing but . . . whole.

I felt *whole*. Whole in a way that I hadn't felt in ages.

Whole in a way that I'd never felt in my entire life.

Not virtually, and not as a real person either.

It was as though for months, for years, even, I'd been split somehow, like there were two of me living in a single brain, a single body. A single person, but one always pulled in two directions, the center of a perpetual tug-of-war between two disparate places. A person at once real but also virtual, always both, but never quite one or the other.

The strangest part was that I hadn't realized any of this until now, only after this tug of division had vanished. The split sense I'd carried within me had been so embedded, so normally a part of who I was, that I didn't notice it there, didn't notice it dragging on me until it was gone.

I was lighter. Unburdened. Everything about me seemed . . . new. Brighter. Shinier.

The feeling made me want to run, to laugh, to swim across the ocean.

To celebrate.

But I should be in mourning.

A whole world was gone, maybe gone for good, and many of its people with it. My sister. My father. Others I didn't even know about yet. So why did I feel so . . . so *good*? So alive? More alive than ever before? Why did my body feel so . . . relieved? Had the App World and the Real World been pulling me apart, not allowing me to ever truly be whole?

Could it be that other people felt this relief, this *peace*, as well?

Maybe for the first time ever, I could truly be myself. I could figure out who Skylar Cruz was without a division between worlds settling a dark cloud over everything. Over me.

There were clothes folded on a chair next to the door. I pulled on the pants and the sweater to ward off the cold. Beneath everything was a scarf—Kit's scarf, the one I'd always loved, that I'd stolen from him, then buried away somewhere in Briarwood so I didn't have to look at it. I wondered how it had gotten here. Only Parvda knew about it.

She must have given it to Kit.

I wrapped the scarf around my neck. This meant she was all right.

But who else was all right?

And how long had I been out this time?

Last time I'd shifted on behalf of others I'd been out for days.

I threw open the door to Kit's room and stuck my head out, hoping to see him there, sitting next to the stove drinking his homemade whiskey or sitting on the old couch reading a book. But he wasn't anywhere in the room.

"Skylar," Maggie said, turning to me. "You're awake!"

Her voice was enthusiastic. But she didn't smile.

My heart thudded. "Where's Kit? Where is he? Is he . . . did he . . ." I couldn't even finish the sentence.

Maggie rushed over. "No, no! Skylar, no. He's fine. Kit's perfectly fine." She took my arm and led me to a chair. Pushed me down until I was sitting. She bent forward and peered into my eyes. "He's all in one piece, I promise. One hundred percent all right."

I nodded slowly. Began to breathe again. "Then where is he?"

Maggie stood straight again. She hesitated. "Out."

The way she said this, it sounded like she was hiding something. "Doing what?"

"You're meant to rest," she said.

"I'm not tired."

"Kit brought you here to recover."

I stood up from the chair. Looked Maggie in the eyes. "I'm recovered."

"Skylar," Maggie sighed. "Please, just be patient. Kit will tell you everything when he gets back."

"But what is there to tell?" I asked, exasperated.

"Let me make you some tea," she tried.

"I don't want tea! Who's all right and who . . . who isn't?"

"That's not for me to say. And besides, I don't know all the details." Maggie turned her back on me and went into the kitchen. She grabbed a kettle, filled it with water, and put it on the stove to heat.

"I don't even drink tea."

"Then I'll make you coffee," she said. Then she sighed. "Fine, I'll tell you one thing, because it feels cruel not to, but the rest you'll have to get from Kit."

I joined her in the kitchen. Leaned against the counter, watching as she scooped coffee, waiting for her to go on.

"Your friends are fine, Skylar. They're all fine."

I swallowed. Happiness seeped back into me like a download spreading its cool relief throughout my code one last time. "Thank you for telling me that," I said.

Maggie didn't look at me. Her gaze was on the kettle, but she nodded.

"I need you to do me a favor," I told Maggie, after I'd sipped coffee for a while. "To help me pass the time while you're avoiding telling me what I need to know."

Her eyebrows arched. "Oh?"

I took a deep breath. "How long will your brother be gone?"

"Maybe until this evening, if I had to guess," she said.

I explained to Maggie what I was thinking. "Is that enough time to get it done?" I asked.

She looked thoughtful. "Well, it's enough for the first pass. There would have to be others. Maybe three or four. Are you really up for that?"

"I am," I told her, feeling more sure about my decision as every moment passed.

"All right then. Have a seat."

Maggie went into Kit's room, and when she came back she held a great wooden box in her arms. She opened the top of it and began to take out a series of strange pens. She laid them neatly across the table. Then, when she was ready, she spoke. "Roll up your sleeve, Skylar," she said. "So I can get to work."

By the time Kit walked in the door, Maggie had finished. The two of us were seated at the table in the kitchen, drinking small sips of Kit's whiskey. Maggie had planted a half-full glass of it in front of me and said, "For the pain," after she'd put her pens away. But then she'd poured some for herself and joined me as I drank the strong liquid.

"Kit," I said, getting up.

He smiled when he saw me there, a smile of relief,

I thought, but also a smile of sheer happiness. "You're awake."

"She has been for hours now," Maggie said, getting up herself. She went into the kitchen and busied herself with the dishes. "You two should talk," she called over her shoulder. "You have a lot to catch up on."

Kit arched his eyebrows and gestured toward his bedroom.

The two of us went inside and closed the door behind us.

The second it clicked shut, Kit put his arms around me and pulled me close. "How are you feeling?" he asked, when we finally let go.

"Strangely, better than ever," I said.

Kit hadn't stopped smiling. "I know what you mean."

I smiled back. "Do you?"

He nodded.

I sat on the bed. Then I pulled the sweater I wore over my head and set it aside, so only the tank top I'd slept in remained. Kit's eyes grew wondrous.

"Skylar," he breathed. He came over and sat down next to me.

I held out my arms to him.

He bent closer to study the scene Maggie had inked onto my skin. It started at the base of my left wrist, then continued over onto my right shoulder, starting at the top and making its way down to my forearm.

"Maggie did this," Kit said, as his eyes made their way across everything. "It's beautiful."

I nodded. "She's talented. I knew I was in good hands." I joined Kit in looking at her artwork. At my left wrist, the beginning of an ocean wave rose up and crested across my elbow, sending droplets of spray upward, droplets that—when they reached the top of my right shoulder—transformed into sparkling snowflakes that fell onto a solitary tree, descending down my other arm. The tree in the yard outside Kit's cottage. "I wanted to mix the sea, which feels like it's mine, with the tree in winter. Which feels like it's ours," I added.

"I love it," he said, his gaze returning to mine. "Thank you."

I folded my hands in my lap. "It barely hurts."

"I wondered. It's a lot for one day." Kit got up and moved toward the door.

"Where are you going?" I'd waited and longed for us to have a moment's peace. "Come back. We have a lot to catch up on."

"I know. But your mother made me promise to let you rest," he said.

This perked me up. "You've spoken to her?"

"Yes, she's fine. Busy with everything. Everyone." I opened my mouth to ask, *What, exactly, is she busying herself with?* Kit got there first. "Busy with everything you're not supposed to worry about at the moment."

"But—"

Kit was shaking his head. "No, Skylar, don't even think about it. I wasn't even supposed to wake you until tomorrow at the earliest."

I let out a breath. "All Maggie would say is that my friends are fine."

"The world will still be here tomorrow. You can worry about it and everyone else in it then."

I looked up at him, allowing myself to accept this. To let myself be taken care of for once. "So I'm not expected anywhere?"

"No."

I patted the bed next to me, gesturing for Kit to join me again. "Okay. I won't worry about anything else until tomorrow."

He sat. "Good. Tomorrow we'll talk about everything."

"Then tonight"—I leaned closer, my eyes on Kit's, my eyes only for him—"is just for us."

46

Skylar

reunions and good-byes

WHEN I WOKE the next day, I had visitors.

My Keeper. My mother. Adam and Parvda.

Kit had gone early to Briarwood to tell them I was up and about.

"Mom," I exclaimed when I saw her there, standing awkwardly by the couch, and I hugged her. "We have a lot to catch up on."

"We do, sweetheart," she replied. "But there's time. We have all the time in the world now."

"Adam," I squealed. "Parvda!" They were holding hands and smiling.

I laughed. I hugged each one of them, long and tight,

relieved that for my friends, for my mother, things had ended up all right, that they were with me now in Kit's cottage as though we gathered here all the time. Maggie made everyone coffee, and my Keeper filled me in about the state of New Port City, how her fellow Keepers had risen to the occasion of tending to such an enormous influx of refugees, how the Real World was spreading out again to rural towns and other once abandoned places—out of necessity, out of the desire to return to the homes that people had occupied before they left for a virtual future. It had been hard, she explained, and it would be hard for a long time to come. Many families sustained great losses during the evacuation. But people were doing their best to cope, to move forward, to try and live in honor of those who did not make it back.

"Where's Rain?" I asked eventually, realizing that no one had said a single word about him since they'd arrived.

That was the moment that everyone's faces fell.

The memorial was small. Intimate.

Just friends and loved ones.

We gathered on the beach, the little group of us.

We held champagne flutes in our hands.

Rain was the last person who spoke. His words were brief, but heartfelt, punctuated only by the soft *shhhhh* of the waves coming in to shore.

Maggie had said that my *friends* were all fine. What she didn't say was that someone who she thought was *not* my friend wasn't.

"Lacy would never want us to lie and say something simple like, *she was loved by all*," Rain began, and was met with sad laughter. "But I think it would be true to say that we all grew to *like* her, and at least one of us grew to love her." A tear ran down his cheek. He brushed it away. "And I think she would want us to remember her not so much as loved by everyone, but as a sparkling, glittering girl who could never be forgotten. Certainly not the virtual version of Lacy, but not the real version either." There were murmurs of agreement. "She died as she lived, with drama and flair and without fear, wearing the best dress she'd ever downloaded in her life—her words to me." Everyone chuckled again. Rain raised his glass.

We followed him in raising ours.

"To Lacy Mills," he said, the tears flowing freely now.

"To Lacy," we chorused, and clinked glasses.

As our words and the ringing of glass died away, I was surprised to find that my cheeks, too, were wet with tears.

The whole world was starting over.

The sun rose above the ocean, a bright-yellow coin hovering over the waves. The birds sang and darted through the branches of the big beautiful weeping beeches of New Port City. The children of Keepers stepped out into the streets and the parks and on sidewalks to play. The refugees who'd filled up once abandoned mansions and apartment buildings and houses opened their eyes to a Real World on yet another day. And everywhere there had been plugs, in the caverns of Briarwood and in the various underground locations where everyone was taken after the failure of the Body Market, there were people beginning to walk again on their real legs, to see again with their real eyes, to speak again with their real mouths after decades of a virtual existence. Fingers and toes twitching, knees and elbows bending, lips murmuring speech still unintelligible, eyes opening and closing, lashes fluttering, vision blurry and confused but growing clearer, surer, by the day.

Keepers everywhere were at work helping with the unplugged, with the care everyone needed, shifting people from the glass coffins where they'd lain, day in and day out for years, to any and every available space they could find to care for them. Refugees teemed on every green, every park, in every available house and warehouse, mansion, and apartment, spilling well beyond the borders of New Port City into the surrounding area. My Keeper had spent all the time we were in the App World recruiting every available and willing hand to help, managing to convince some of those who'd voted against taking in more citizens from the App World to chip in. She'd even recruited the Body Market refugees to the effort, since anyone with at least some time spent in their real body was in a good enough place to assist the recently unplugged to begin to adjust to life in New Port City.

As I traveled from one site to another, I was amazed by the work ethic I encountered everywhere I went. The Keepers worked with purpose, as though driven by something far greater than just the basic need to get things done and settled. The refugees did the same, bustling about, led by Andleeb and Rasha, shuttling food to the camps and help centers, being willing to simply be present, by the bedsides of those who were older, more in need of rest and time to emerge from their body's long slumber.

Even Ree, with her long red hair, was tireless.

The real her reminded me of Lacy.

Well, the virtual her had as well.

Despite the losses, despite the reality that not everyone made it, people did the best they could.

Funerals were planned for the dead, memorials and cremations.

But weddings were planned, too.

Zeera and Sylvia.

Adam and Parvda.

There was a lot to look forward to for many of us.

For now, at least, New Port City was at peace.

With Rain, though, I wasn't so sure.

Rain and I had made up, though we both knew that things would never be the same, that he might never be the same after Lacy. But then, one afternoon, I saw him talking to Andleeb, caught the spark in his beautiful eyes as he spoke to her and she looked back at him, and I thought, well, maybe they would. Or at least, they wouldn't be the same, but I thought they might be okay. Even happy, eventually.

One could hope.

We all could.

Those of us who'd lived to see the end of the App World and had come through on the other side.

Every morning now, so many questions flowed into my mind.

Would today be the day when the App World would finish its reboot? Would it suddenly exist once again, out of nowhere, restoring itself to its former glory? Would it restart in the place where it once was, a great and populous virtual City? Or would it be a mere shell, diminished, broken, waiting for people to abandon their real lives once again and give it life?

And what about my father, my sister? Did they still somehow exist in the ether, tiny ones and zeroes circulating, reordering, waiting to be arranged in the impossibly unique order that was an individual, virtual person, waiting to feel the breath enter their virtual lungs once more?

Or was it all over, forever? The App World an experiment gone wrong, a failure, soon to be a mere history lesson in the lives of future generations? A warning about technology and hubris?

It would be months, maybe years, before we'd know the answers.

But I could live with these questions.

I was alive.

I was real.

A real girl with a real body and a Real World to live and breathe in.

To love in.

It wasn't perfect. Nothing real was ever perfect or sure.

I turned my head on the pillow.

Kit was still fast asleep.

But sometimes, it was close.

EPILOGUE

Skylar

the world as it is

THEY LEFT BY boat.

They left on foot.

By car, too, though cars were still scarce.

Kit and I were down by the water, watching a ferry pulling out of the harbor. People spilled in from the windows, all over the decks, despite the cold, wintry air. We still looked for his parents amid the refugees. Maybe one day we would find them. Maybe we never would.

I leaned over and kissed him on the lips.

He smiled, but then his smile fell away. "This is how it all started," he said, his eyes on the ferry, then shifting to the long line of people walking over one of the bridges, on their way to new towns, old cities, to find more permanent places to settle. "You know, before the App World came into existence. This was what led to the split between the real and the virtual. It's happening again. . . ." His voice trailed off in a whisper.

I let my gaze follow his. "We don't know that."

I said this because I wanted to be hopeful.

But it was the same way everywhere we turned.

A woman. A man. A child. Each one of them with a tiny tablet in their hands. Each one of them staring down at the smooth, colorful screen. Some held them so close their noses nearly touched the device. Others held them high, like they were looking into a mirror. But one thing was uniform—that they stared, they looked, they couldn't tear their eyes away.

They were, uniformly, transfixed.

"Zeera's idea seemed like a good one," I said, defending her as we stood there, taking in this now-common scene unfolding around us. "She thought it would be the humane thing to do, and it is, isn't it? Providing the refugees access to old-world technology helps them manage the transition to the Real World."

"Or makes it so they never manage it at all," Kit countered. "Makes it so they live for another virtual place even as they move and breathe in their real bodies amid real people."

Right then, a child on the upper deck of the ferry looked up and waved toward the shore. I waved back, a smile finding its way onto my face again. "I'm choosing to be more optimistic than that."

Kit turned his attention to me now. Even as I watched the child, took in the joy that lit up his beautiful young face, I could feel Kit's eyes on me. "Well, Skylar," he said.

"Well, Skylar, what?" I asked, when he left it at that.

Kit stepped into my line of vision, so he was all that I saw. Not the ferry or the line of people walking over the bridge, all of them looking down. "Well, Skylar, your optimism is one of the things I love about you," he said, and finally smiled again. "That, and the fact that you never remember to bring your own tablet anywhere no matter how many times your friends scold you about it."

"Not *everyone* is obsessed," I reminded him. "Plenty of people are like me. Besides"—I gestured toward the harbor, the boats, the bridges—"they'll get bored of those things eventually. The Real World is pretty great once you get used to it."

"I guess we'll have to wait and see," Kit said.

I nodded. Then we turned our backs on the sea, on the harbor and the boats and the bridges, on all the people looking down at their screens. We made our way toward the very real cottage that sat perched up on the hill and overlooking the ocean, with the single beautiful tree that stood next to it, just as the first snow of winter began to fall from the very real sky.

DONNA FREITAS

is the author of the Unplugged series as well as other young adult and middle grade novels, including *The Possibilities of Sainthood*, *The Survival Kit*, and *Gold Medal Summer*. Donna is also a professor in Fairleigh Dickinson's MFA program and at Hofstra's Honors College. Her nonfiction book *The Happiness Effect* is based on research about young adults and social media. Donna lives in Brooklyn, New York, where she likes to spend most of her time unplugged. You can visit her online at www.donnafreitas.com.

READ THEM ALL!

JOIN THE

Epic Reads
COMMUNITY

THE ULTIMATE YA DESTINATION

◄ DISCOVER ►
your next favorite read

◄ MEET ►
new authors to love

◄ WIN ►
free books

◄ SHARE ►
infographics, playlists, quizzes, and more

◄ WATCH ►
the latest videos